DARK

DSD Trilogy

A.M. Bain

DARK

DSD Trilogy

A.M. Bain

ACKNOWLEDGEMENTS

To my family for putting up with me through
the writing, editing, and printing process.

PROLOGUE

The key slid into the lock, and the tumblers rolled to the open position. Onyx turned the knob and opened the door. He put his keys and cell phone on the table and reached for the light switch in the entryway. He quickly changed his mind about the light and pulled his hand away from the light switch. He turned and shut the door gently, without a sound. There was no need to turn on a light; he knew where each piece of furniture was located even though he had not lived here long. He was used to seeing in the dark, and his eyes adjusted quickly. Lights had never been a necessity for him. In fact, light often bothered his eyes, so he preferred the dark. He strode across the darkened room, making his way to his favorite chair. It was a high back, dark green leather chair. It had been his favorite piece of furniture for too many years to remember. The old chair was relaxing to him. The leather was soft as silk to the touch from the decades of use. He would sink into the depths of the cushions and let himself be enveloped and protected from the world outside. This was the place he wanted to be right now. Away from the world and protected.

He sat in the chair briefly before he pulled off his boots. He had returned to the apartment, or rather penthouse, much later than expected, and he was exhausted. The cool, soft leather felt good against his body as it conformed to his structure. He sat in the chair thinking over the night, what he had to work on the next day, and trying to relax from the stress of the evening. He was jolted out of his meditative state by the brashness of a telephone ringing. He did not feel like getting up to grab the phone off the table, but he knew it could be important information about his Beloved. Damn it, he was comfortable and wanted the protection of his chair for this call. He reached out into the darkness in the ringing's direction and caught the phone in his hand as it flew toward him.

"Hello?" His voice sounded exhausted, even to himself.

"Hello there, my friend. It has been too long since last I spoke with you." The voice on the other end paused for just a moment. "I do believe that I have some information that may be of great interest and importance to you." The voice was perverse and sarcastic, the pattern of speech a mixture of old and modern; he knew it held truth, which made the fear in him rise. The only reason Xavier would call was if he had information that was not common knowledge, and his damn cousin would use it against him.

"What do you want, Xavier? I don't feel like playing your games today," he said harshly with a hint of exhaustion still evident.

"Well, if you are not interested in knowing about your Beloved, then I will just keep it to myself." Xavier said and proceeded to end the call, "Good…"

He interrupted Xavier, "Wait! What do you know? Where is she? Don't hurt her. What have you done…"

"Hold up there, Cousin. I thought you weren't in the mood to play games tonight?" Xavier laughed as he began toying with Onyx.

Onyx bowed his head and took a deep breath. "I am sorry, truly sorry. I was wrong to be curt with you. You are family, and I should respect that fact. You mentioned my Beloved…Have you found her, or are you just teasing me?" Even though he asked, he knew Xavier had the information he wanted about his Beloved. That much was clear, which made him regret the rude outburst because he knew Xavier would make him pay for it in some way.

"Apology accepted. And yes, I have found her. I know her name, her location and have even purchased a house in her neighborhood so that WE may be close to her."

When Xavier emphasized the word "WE," Onyx knew exactly what that meant, but he tried not to sound worried as he replied, "That's wonderful! Thank you for calling me! What's her name?

Where does she live? Please tell me." Onyx refused to let his hopes rise Xavier would actually give him the information, but he had to ask.

"You know, if you wouldn't have been so rude, I might have told you, but I don't think I will now. I think I will just keep this information to myself. Elizabeth and I will have so much fun with your Beloved if you are not around to protect her. You know how Elizabeth likes her toys and likes to share them with me. She could just make your Beloved our toy. What do you think?" The words oozed from Xavier's mouth as he laughed and waited for Onyx's response.

Onyx sat in his chair, listening to Xavier's laughing, completely mortified. He knew he should have played nice with Xavier. He knew he would pay for his actions as soon as he answered the phone and began their conversation in such a rude manner. Xavier may be his cousin, but they were not friends. Now he had to do something to try to get Xavier to tell him what he knew. Allowing them to get to her first was not an option. He had to get the information from Xavier somehow so that he could save her even if he wasn't able to be with her this time around. He had been foolish for being so rude, but more than likely, even if he would not have been rude, Xavier would not have told him. He would have found another reason to not give up the information. This was just a game to him and causing Onyx pain, even if it was only emotional rather than physical, was good enough for him.

"I will give you anything for the information Xavier, and you know it. What would you like?" Onyx answered after pausing for a moment.

"Your death, dear cousin." Xavier said in a whisper. "That is all I have ever wanted from you. YOU are a monstrosity that needs to die. YOU are not human and you are not one of us. YOU belong nowhere and taint our bloodline." The meaning coming through loud and clear.

"That I cannot do, nor will I, and you know it. You know I have waited an eternity to be with her again. Please, I beg of you, please give me the information. What would you have done if this happened with you and Elizabeth? You know I would have helped you."

Xavier snarled into the phone. "First, I wouldn't have lost my Elizabeth like you lost your 'Beloved'" he sneered the words. "No, I will not tell you ever. I do hope you find her before Elizabeth takes her as a toy. You know she is as good as dead if Elizabeth gets her. Humans don't last long in her care. Good luck." Xavier's depraved laugh echoed through the phone just before he hung up.

Onyx threw the phone across the room, hearing it smash into pieces as it hit the stone fireplace. He would have to find her fast and could no longer waste any time, not that he had been, but he was being pushed to act rashly, which he had been trying to avoid. He hated being pushed to do it this way, but there was no longer a choice. He had to save his Beloved from Xavier and Elizabeth. He had to get to her before they did. Even if this protection meant he couldn't introduce himself into her life and be with her, he would still be there in the background to ensure she lived out her natural life.

He pulled his boots back on and got up from his chair. He had eaten recently, but if he was going to find her tonight, he would have to be completely sated; no more half feedings to keep his hunger in check. His sleep could not be disturbed by anything. He left the penthouse and took the elevator to the lobby of the building. It was already very late, or extremely early, depending on the point of view, but he knew he could still find something to eat.

He lucked out almost as soon as he walked out of the building- saw them, two college students walking down the street. Falling in step behind them, he proceeded carefully because this was a part of town that didn't have many missing people or dead bodies. He would have to transport them, but he needed them away from his home first. He followed them for a while, taking his time to catch up to them. They had finally walked into an area that was not bad but was not good either; here was where he would have to do it. Time was growing short, and he needed it done.

As they neared a long, dark alleyway between two downtown storefronts, he knew it was time to strike. He grabbed them both from behind before they knew what was happening and threw them into the alley. The woman started to scream, but Onyx was on her immediately. He covered her mouth with his hand and attacked her neck. He didn't care if it hurt her or not. As he fed, he looked at the man who was with her and watched him pass out.

"What a protector! She deserved better," Onyx thought as he took the last of her blood. Then he drained the man quickly. He hoisted their bodies on his shoulders and ran to the edge of this section of town that bordered the crime-ridden section, throwing them in an alley by a dumpster before he sought out a drug dealer. He found one immediately and bought some heroin. Onyx asked the dealer to shoot up with him as was only polite, and once that was done and the dealer was passed out, he took the paraphernalia and dealer back the bodies. He shot enough into his victims to show up on a tox screen and left. He laughed quietly to himself, thinking, "Thank the gods for crime shows to help him cover his tracks."

He returned to his penthouse when he was finished, just as the sun was peeking over the horizon. He took off his boots and left them by his chair. The chair that had always been a comfort did not provide any relief now. He stood and stripped the clothes from his body as he walked through the living room, feeling the heat of the sun on his skin. In his bedroom, he immediately pulled the sheets back and slid into bed. He was completely sated with the blood of those two people. He was sorry for their deaths, but knew that it was the lesser of the two evils, at least to him. His Beloved would not be as lucky as those two if Xavier and Elizabeth got ahold of her. He could feel sleep overtaking him even with all the anxiety he felt from the phone call. He thought as if he were praying to the god of sleep, "Sweet sleep, please bring me the information about my Beloved that you have hidden from me for so long. I need to save my Beloved. Please help me and do not shroud her in the air of mystery you do so like to use. Hear my pleas and take me to her." As he finished the last sentence, sleep overwhelmed him.

CHAPTER 1

Onyx laid sleeping in his bed and dreamed of his Beloved, the woman who had eluded him since their first lifetime together over 500 years ago. He could see her clearly in his dream as he began the assent to wakefulness. She was short as she was in their original lifetime together, but now her hair was blonde and not as long. Her eyes were the same hazel as his but were more on the blue-gray side. She had some meat on her and like it. After two kids, he didn't expect her to be model thin, not to mention skinny women in his time were considered unhealthy and sickly. He enjoyed looking at her, just as she was right now.

His long eyelashes fluttered as his eyes opened to see the layers of reds, oranges, deepening blues, and purples filling the sky as the sun set outside his bedroom window. He laid there for a long while, thinking only of her, but his dream had still not shown him where she was located. He had known every important moment in this lifetime, such as the birth of her first child, when she married her now ex-husband, the birth of her second child, and her divorce before the age of 30. For the past 33 years, he had felt her happiness, sadness, elation, and incompleteness. He knew he was the one to complete her and make her truly happy for eternity. If only he could find her before she found another companion, or worse, Xavier and Elizabeth found her. In his dream, she had been preparing to go out with a man this evening. She was not very excited about this date, he could feel that, but she went anyway. The dream had ended there, as the need to feed woke him. He promised himself that after he had fed, he would try to locate her again. He had to find her and show her he could alleviate all her sadness before he lost her again.

"No, I won't lose this time. She will be mine again," he promised himself, just as he did every evening upon waking.

Onyx threw back the sheets of his bed and he felt the chill of the night touching his bare skin, making a shiver ripple through his body. He went into the master bathroom and turned on the water in the shower. As the steam began billowing around him, he climbed into the shower and let the hot water run over his broad shoulders, down his firm, ripped abdomen, finding its way to the drain after falling from his defined thighs and calves. He just stood there watching the pink tinged water run down his body and realized he must have been messier than he thought the night before. He closed his eyes and enjoyed the relaxing moment, but the urge to feed was becoming stronger.

That was the problem with being so sated. It made the body want it all the time, which is why he avoided doing it. The episode last night and probably for the next few nights would take weeks, if not months, to recover from and get back to a smaller nightly portion, and he would be in pain most of it. For now though, he would have to hurry. He did not want to be careless and become obvious, like some others. He had time tonight, so multiple donors would reduce the need for anyone to die again tonight.

He climbed out of the shower, dried off, and placed his towel on the rack to dry as he walked into his closet. His closet was more like a room than a closet. He had five centuries' worth of clothes to take care of and this closet had been created just for that purpose. Three walls held a different style of clothing and the far wall was shelving from floor to ceiling. In the middle of the room was a column-like creation that held shoes, jewelry and other accessories he had collected over time, as well as a full-length mirror to ensure he had the right look for whatever the evening was offering.

Tonight, he dressed for a night of clubbing at a local Goth club. He preferred Goth clubs because he blended easily, kept an air of mystery, fed even easier, and was still known by those he chose to befriend. He grabbed a pair of tight leather pants that accentuated his firm, tight ass, matched a frilled long sleeve white shirt from the 17th century, and a long, fitted leather overcoat. He chose a pair of black leather boots, and of course, a cane and top hat to give the total effect he wanted. He had barely dried his shoulder length dark blond hair and let it hang to finish drying naturally under the top hat. Adding his favorite rings and a piece of finger armor in the shape of a dragon his father had given it to him from his personal collection was the finishing touch. It allowed the wearer to make a single small puncture wound from which to feed rather than the telltale two punctures. At the Goth club, it was not a necessity, but he loved wearing it. Actually, Onyx treasured it more than any of his other possessions. It was the only gift he had accepted from his father in all these years.

He left his penthouse and ventured out into the cool Seattle evening. First thing on his agenda was to dine, but he had to decide what would delight his palate tonight. He walked as he thought about it, "Innocent is always tasty, but tonight I would like something a little rough around the edges. Plus, there will be plenty of innocents at the club."

He walked down the street and saw the perfect donors, the name he preferred for his victims, especially if he planned on leaving them alive. Last night were victims; these would just be donors if all went well. Whether or not they were willing was of no concern to him. They donated themselves for his sustenance, but he had had no one in this current time deny him.

He finally decided on the pair — a pimp and a low-class hooker. These two could be easily discarded if things got out of hand. His hunger was gnawing at him and making him feel like an addict, which could end badly for them if he let it go much longer. He knew no one would notice their disappearance, and if the bodies were found, they would simply be considered more victims of the street.

He wouldn't even have to plant anything on them. They were perfect.

He closed in on them. The male was shorter than Onyx at about 5'10," slim, and looked about 40 years old. He had thick gold chains around his neck and on his wrists that looked like they should be much too heavy for his slight frame. He also had bulky gold rings on most of his fingers. The female was short, plump and could not have been more than 18 years old. Onyx wondered if she was a runaway or turning tricks for her father's drug habit. She looked as if she had not eaten or bathed in days. She wore cheap costume jewelry that could have been bought in a dollar store. Watching them made him thirst and was causing him to have a hard time controlling himself, as the need to feed took over his senses.

As he walked by the couple, the male offered the whore to Onyx, as he knew the guy would. "Hey there! Buddy! I bet you would like the company of this lovely lady here for the evening, wouldn't you? Her name is Lavender and she will do whatever you want."

Onyx grinned slyly and ogled the girl while her pimp spoke. He slowly turned his eyes from the girl and asked the pimp, "Really? Anything? Even give me her life?" There were times he couldn't resist scaring people especially when the hunger was this close to the surface. Playing with his meal before feeding would only make it sweeter, even though under normal circumstances he would not have been so cruel. But these were not normal circumstances.

The girl started to back away nervously from Onyx; her instinct kicking in that he was a danger to her. She was tugging on the pimp's shirtsleeve, whispering and pleading to forget this 'John.' The pimp pushed her off without even looking at her, "Now, why would you want her for life? She is nothing but a cheap whore, but I'll let you borrow her for the night for fifty bucks."

God, this guy was giving her away for next to nothing. Onyx decided he had wasted enough time. He wanted to play a bit more, but it was time to dine. "OK. Let's go and complete the deal in the alley. Then I will take her."

The pimp grabbed the girl and dragged her as they followed Onyx into the alley. As soon as they were out of the sight of the people on the street, Onyx grabbed the girl by the throat and held her against the wall. He grabbed the pimp by his throat and pulled him closer to his own body. He could smell their blood mixed with the sweat of the warm evening. He was having an extremely hard time keeping himself in check. He had to move fast, or he'd grow reckless. He looked at the frightened girl and growled, "Say one word, or make one sound, and I will kill you. Be quiet and you might live."

He turned away from the girl and drew the male to him. To make his point to her, he bit the pimp's neck ferociously. He felt the thick, warm blood slowly draining from the pimp and fill him. Oh, it was good — hot, metallic, and thick. He felt the ecstasy of sweet blood. It was definitely the best; he could never get enough of it. He could feel his shaft getting hard as the pimp went limp in his arm. He tossed the man aside as death overtook him. Young blood was next. He looked at the girl and thought, "Maybe I should get some pleasure before I finish her," but the image of his Beloved entered his mind and the thought left, "No. She had listened. I will not violate her and I will let her live."

He finally moved the girl closer to his mouth and whispered. "You listened, that is very good. Because you have listened, I will let you live. I will feed from you almost to the point of death. When you wake up in the hospital, your bill will have been paid, and Mr. Gold will be there. He will arrange for you to return home or go somewhere safe. He will help you register for school. He will take care of your bills for housing, food, clothes and necessities, and he will monitor your educational progress. If you do not do what I say, and if you do not follow the instructions of Mr. Gold and stay in school, I will find you, and I will kill you. Do you understand?"

The young girl nodded her head yes as tears streaked her dirty cheeks.

"Good. I will always take care of you if you listen to me and follow all my instructions from this point forward. Now we shall proceed. It will pinch and hurt a little, but I will be as gentle as possible. If you tell anyone about this, I will find you and kill you. Do you understand?"

Again, she nodded her head yes, and mouthed "thank you" to him.

Onyx stroked her hair and gently pulled her to him. He delicately kissed her forehead, her eyes to close them, and her lips to relax her as he proceeded down to her neck. Then he pierced her neck; she moaned quietly, still afraid he would kill her. He fed from her slowly, taking her precariously close to the point of death, and then laid her gently on the ground in the alley. Her sweet blood had finished bringing him to a full erection but had not completely satisfied him as it would have if he had been able to kill her. But killing hadn't been the plan tonight, and yet he had a corpse to take care of anyway. He sat down on the ground beside her to calm down. He had to release before he could continue for the evening; otherwise, he would be dangerous to himself and others. He opened his pants and stroked himself until he reached his release. Masturbation was never as good as a person and definitely not as good as blood, but it allowed him to go on his way and enjoy the evening. He knew he would have to feed again before morning. For now, he was ready for a night of feeding to satiation and a day of finding his Beloved.

He left her there in the alley next to the dead pimp, and proceeded down the street, pulling out his cell phone and to call his attorney, Brian Gold.

"Hello Brian, it's Onyx. Have the girl, Lavender, in the alleyway behind the 7-11 Store on Highland Street picked up and taken to the hospital. Take care of her hospital bill and be there when she wakes up. You are to return her to her home or locate somewhere safe for her to stay. Set up a fund for her to use while she is attending school. Keep an eye on her, and if she returns to the streets or doesn't finish school, tell me. I will handle it from there."

Brian let out a sigh, "Not a problem, Onyx. I know what has to be done. We've been through this before, but you really should stop doing things like this; eventually, one of them will talk."

"Maybe, but I don't think so. I've been doing this for centuries and no one has ever talked. Good luck with her. Bye." Onyx knew he should be more careful, but what could he do? He had felt genuinely sorry for her.

He continued to walk to the club; it was only a few blocks from his location. As he reached the door, the attendants cleared a path for him to enter the club. He had come to receive certain privileges because of how often he came to the club and because of how much he spent while at the club. He entered the dark cavernous club and could immediately feel the beat of the Industrial Goth music as he slid into a dark corner to watch and enjoy his prey.

There was a young blonde on the dance floor flowing with the music. He looked at her, "Mmm, she would be a good dessert. Maybe I can take her and enjoy the mortal side that still survives while I finish my immortal side's desires and needs." He suddenly sat up straighter and shook his head. Where had that thought come from? He rarely gave in to mortal sexual pleasures because the thought of his Beloved was normally too close. Plus, his focus should be on his Beloved, not getting laid. He shook his head once more and then the blonde woman caught his eye again, and he was lost.

While he watched the blonde, another young woman came up to him. He did not recognize her and was definitely not interested.

She was a bit overly plump and of medium build; she would have been considered healthy in his youth, but there was something about her or rather there was nothing special about her, not even the color or style of her flaming red hair. Everything about her was flat compared to the blonde on the dance floor. She stopped beside him, "Are you here alone?"

He was going to ignore her, but changed his mind. "Yes. Why? Are you?" He had to get his mind off the blonde woman. He couldn't understand why she intrigued him so much, so he decided he would focus on this red-head.

"Actually, I am here with some girlfriends, but I can leave without them. My name is Alexandria." She answered almost too quickly. He followed her finger to a group of girls that he recognized from other evenings there, but she had never been here before; he was sure of it. Her friends had told her about him, the elusive man that was sexy and always left alone, and probably put her up to coming over to talk to him. He thought nothing of the talk. He didn't think of himself as sexy, and he did leave alone, most of the time, but not always. So most of the talk was fact.

"Onyx." He knew she knew his name but wanted a way to start a conversation rather than the silence and her staring at him. This was almost pathetic. He also knew what she wanted. That was one of the great parts about his life. He could sense sex almost as if it were a smell, like a mortal would smell a bouquet of flowers. When he wanted, he could hear the thoughts of those around him, when he chose to listen. Yes, sex was on her mind.

"Onyx. I like that. So do you want to leave and go make a party of our own?" She felt the heat of the offer rush to her face because she obviously had never been so brazened before. Just as her friends said, he was hot. When she saw him, she wanted him, and knew she had to be the first one to talk to him. She was sure it was her turn to have some fun for a change. She had stayed locked up and away for far too long, and she would prefer to break her celibacy with him.

He stole a glance at the dance floor and found her. A rush of need for the blonde woman and he answered coldly, "Sorry, not interested." He gave her a look with his intense hazel eyes that scared her and melted her at the same time. In his mind, he still was unsure why that blonde was distracting him so much.

She handed him a piece of paper, "Well, here's my number if you ever decide you want to have some fun, just give me a call."

He took the piece of paper. "Don't expect me to call. You are not my type." He said and handed the paper to the first male to walk by the table. "Call this number for a good time." He needed her to go away so he could watch the blonde.

"Thanks. I really appreciate it." The male said as he eyed Alexandria up and down, thinking she was a whore.

"How can you be so cruel? Everyone says you are so cool, so perfect. Why do you treat people like this?" she sobbed.

Onyx, in his desperation and frustration and the giving in to his immortal needs, found this a fun diversion and kept up with the charade, while he watched the other woman. "Because I can. And I don't treat all people like this, only the ones who bother me."

Alexandria followed his gaze to the dance floor before turning and running off. As she left, he thought, "I haven't done that for so long; it was fun. I should do that more often. Then again, maybe I was crueler than I should have been...Nah." He laughed cruelly to himself as his vampire side pushed out more. He continued to watch her with her friends. She told them how cruel he had been, but they could not believe what she was saying; they would not believe it either, and he would make sure of it.

He continued to watch the blonde and kept trying to shake himself from her. This fascination with the blonde was wasting precious time. By not taking advantage of Alexandria's offer or finding any other willing donor, he could not feed well if he did not change his thought process soon, but he couldn't see, think, or do anything but watch the blonde. In the back of his mind, he knew he was being distracted on purpose to keep him from feeding, but he was mesmerized and could only free himself from the hold for mere moments. He knew this was Xavier's doing. She was a plant to keep him occupied and away from his Beloved, but then the thought left and the blonde was all he could think of and all he wanted.

She stayed in his view all evening. She never left it, not even for a moment. Around 3:00 am, he sauntered over to her on the dance floor. "Are you hungry? I thought you might like to go to breakfast with me?"

She turned around, acting like she was getting ready to tell whatever loser that was bothering her to "get lost." However, she looked at him and realized immediately who it was asking her to breakfast, "Oh my god, it's him! It's Onyx, and he is asking me to breakfast!" She answered quickly, "Yes, I am hungry. I would love to."

Reading her thoughts, he wondered if she knew she was brought here to distract him. Her thoughts were so real and pure. She was really surprised that he asked her to breakfast. He just stared at her as he introduced himself, "My name is Onyx."

"Yes, I know." She still couldn't believe that he was asking her to breakfast. Her girlfriends would be so jealous. Everyone wanted the attention of Onyx, male and female alike. He was so incredibly sexy that everyone was intrigued and turned on by him. Many fought for his eye and his smile. He was the perfect specimen of a lover even though no one seems to have actually been his lover.

Smiling slightly, to ensure he showed just the tips of his fangs, he knew that she didn't know she was a distraction, but that she was definitely been used - unwittingly. Because even now, he couldn't think straight. He was pulled back into the web and asked, "What's your name?"

A look of sheer horror crossed over her face. She reprimanded herself silently. "Sophia. My name is Sophia."

The mental slap was hard, and Onyx's mind cleared immediately. He knew why she had been chosen to be a distraction. He was not expecting her name to be Sophia. It threw him off guard, and he had to recover quickly, thinking, "What are the chances she would have my Beloved's name?" He was usually careful, wanting to ensure the name was different, but this woman had intrigued him so much that he had forgotten to find out her name. In fact, she had intrigued him almost too much, which meant that someone was definitely clouding his mind, but again the thought fled as soon as it arrive. His Beloved's name was different in this lifetime, as it had it been in every other lifetime. Sophia was her name, or at least a version of it; it had been Sofija, when it all began.

Quickly, he regained his composure, "Come on, let's get out of here." As they were leaving the club, they passed Alexandria standing alone. Onyx stopped and turned to her while holding on to Sophia. He leaned in and whispered, "This is my type." Tears started to fill Alexandria's eyes. Onyx smiled and led Sophia out of the club. He came to again and wondered what was making him so cruel. Even his immortal side had never been this bad before. It had to be…and it was gone.

He hailed a cab and told the driver to take them to the closest all-night restaurant that served breakfast. He looked at Sophia, who agreed with a nod of her head.

At the restaurant, they were seated almost immediately, and he ordered food for them. Sophia ate and talked, and quickly finished her meal, while Onyx had barely touched his. When she questioned him about it, he explained he had eaten a very large dinner right before he arrived at the club and was still not very hungry. He was hungry but not for this kind of food; he couldn't tell her that. Maybe he needed her, Sophia, to find his Sofija once he closed his eyes.

They eventually made their way to Sophia's apartment. He had one rule; no one was to know where he lived. Many times, he had caught people trying to follow him, but none had succeeded and lived.

They immediately undressed and climbed onto the bed. Onyx caressed her, but only had thoughts of his Beloved. His mind was finally clear, but at this point he needed to feed and this woman would have to do. He wished it was Sofija instead of this imposter. He fulfilled his blood needs only while he fulfilled the dreams of this young girl throughout the early morning hours. When she was finished, they were hot and sweaty. He had pierced her in three spots to ensure he would be sated as possible upon his return to his penthouse. As he laid beside her, she repeated over and over she had never had anyone make love to her like that until she finally fell asleep. He had the urge to tell her she was just a fuck, but stopped himself. He knew he would never be with her again; in fact, the next time she saw him at the club and tried to talk to him, he would ignore her. He did not make love to anyone but his Beloved. This girl was just for blood and a little sex, and now that he knew she was used against him and by him, it was as simple as that. Once he was sure she was asleep, he gently laid her head on the pillow, crawled out of bed, got dressed, and went home alone.

The sun was just coming up as he got to his bedroom and he watched it rise over the horizon. All the beautiful shades of blue giving way to the purples and reds until the sun was full in the early morning sky. He knew he had made Sophia's night. She could say she slept with him, but whether he confirmed it, she would know. He no longer allowed himself to get close to anyone. No person could ever replace his Beloved. They would have to walk in her shadow, and that would not be fair to any of them. He only loved one woman and all the rest would just have to suffer the same way they had for centuries.

He undressed and put his clothes on a chair in the closet and his boots away. He gently placed his jewelry in the velvet lined drawer. Looking at himself in the mirror, completely naked, he found a man with blond hair that was too thin and stringy. His nose was too large and overall he was too skinny and a little worse for wear with old scars, many from Xavier himself. He saw a man who would look "around 30" forever unless he stopped drinking blood completely, and then he would age at a normal rate. Standing there looking at himself, he could not understand why people found him attractive, but there was obviously something.

He took a quick shower to remove the night before he walked to his bed and climbed between the cool sheets. As he laid there waiting for beautiful sleep to overtake him, he could think of nothing but the night when he had given in and created this future. It seemed like only yesterday that his Beloved, his Sofija, lay in his arms dying while trying to give birth to the son they had so desperately wanted. Neither Sofija nor the infant had lived through the night. The memory of the moment came rushing back, Onyx closed his eyes. He saw the smoky blue of a dawn's twilight, feeling her warm neck on his lips, piercing her flesh with his teeth, and the sensation of ecstasy with the first taste of human blood coming from his own Beloved, an ecstasy that was comparable only to making love to his Beloved.

Yes, he had taken Sofija's blood. He had given into the part of his nature that he had been denying for so long. He did not drink for long; it was just enough to keep a part of her with him while he waited for her return. The part of her he had taken would bind her to him, allowing him to know each time she was born. It would be his beacon to finding her, to being with her again. It was for this reason he had taken her blood as she lay dying.

If it had not been for that first taste of blood, he would not know that his Beloved had returned to him in each successive lifetime. He always tracked her through his dreams until she reached maturity when he could contact her. He had spoken with her every lifetime, but she always had reasons she could not be with him. And never did the circumstances of her life allow him to tell her the truth. Now, in this lifetime, he would locate her and make her his again. He had to. Living this nightmare had to stop.

As sleep overtook him, he saw her waking up. He wanted to find out how her night had been with this new man. His watch over his Beloved had begun for the day. Hopefully, he was sated enough to sleep deeply and tomorrow wake knowing her location.

CHAPTER 2

Reyne unlocked the front door of her townhouse and slowly walked inside. After turning on the light in the foyer, she locked the front door behind her and made her way to the kitchen to make some coffee to help her recuperate from the evening. As she prepared the coffee, she thought, "This is the last one. No more. I give up on men. No more dates." The reverberating sound of the telephone ringing interrupted her thoughts.

"Who would call this late?" She asked aloud as she looked at the clock in the kitchen. "Why wouldn't someone call" she said, realizing it wasn't even 10:00 pm. She groaned, thinking "Damn I must be a fun date," as she walked to her purse and grabbed her phone.

It was Leigh, and now she would get a lecture. She answered, "Hello?"

"Hey Sweetie! I was hoping you would have still been out on your date. In fact, I was expecting it. Shit Reyne, it's not even 10pm." Leigh said, exasperated.

Leigh was her best friend, the only person Reyne confided in anymore. "Oh god Leigh, it was horrible. After this one, I've decided that I will never go on another date again." Reyne emphatically stated.

"You know that's bullshit. The next gorgeous hunk of a man to ask you out will get an answer of yes from you." Leigh chided her.

"No, he won't! Hear me now, Leigh Ann Stein. The only way I will ever fall for anyone again is if the guy is chivalrous and strong, sweeps me off my feet while saving me from some supernatural perilous event. He will take me into his life and our future together on a white stallion. And I mean this literally. What are the chances?" Reyne knew deep down her mind wouldn't waver. She may end up dating again, but she would never fall for any guy. This scenario, which was impossible in the middle of congested, overbuilt Montgomery county, was the only way she would date anyone ever again. She continued with the conditions of her next date. "He has to be dark and mysterious. He has to have eyes that meld to mine instantly and bring me to almost the point of an orgasm without even a touch. This is the only way I will give my heart away again."

"But you will still date." Leigh laughed as she said this, but she also knew that right now Reyne was serious, but it would pass. She would make sure of it. But for now, Leigh automatically changed the subject. "So, am I still invited to our weekly Sunday dinner tomorrow?"

Reyne sighed with Leigh's change of subject. She had been too curt with Leigh and thought, "What would I ever do without her? I have no one else." She finally answered Leigh, "Of course, same as always. And…I am sorry. I'm just tired and depressed. I haven't been very lucky in love since my divorce. You know that."

"Yeah, I know. But, hey, things will get better. I promise. Tomorrow, we will drink wine and talk after the kids are asleep." Leigh was desperately trying to comfort Reyne as much as possible.

"Ok. Well, my coffee is ready, so I'm going to go." She hesitated a moment. "Hey Leigh. Why don't you come on over now? I really need a friend." Reyne almost pleaded.

"Give me 20 and I'll be right over." Leigh promised.

"Thanks. See you shortly." Reyne hung up the phone. Already she felt better knowing she would have someone to cry to tonight. She wouldn't have to be alone after the horrible date.

Reyne sat down at her kitchen table, sipped at her coffee, and waited for Leigh to get there. Stirring her cup of coffee, she began to think about her home, trying to get her mind off the evening. She had moved into this townhouse with Benjamin, her ex-husband, Tyler, her daughter, and Taylor, her son. She and Benjamin had separated and divorced shortly after they moved in.

After he left, she decided to fix up the house just a little to put more of herself into it. She felt there was a lot she could do with this place. On the first floor was the kitchen and breakfast nook, which she had redecorated almost as soon as they moved into the house. She had removed the wallpaper, then painted. She had replaced the one large blind in the front window with window treatments that felt more airy and earthy than blinds. The powder room was fine for the moment, but eventually would have a complete overhaul. Then there was the living/dining room combination, that was the next area to be redecorated.

The second floor had three bedrooms. The only bedroom she had redecorated was Taylor's room. Her six-year-old son had wanted racecars and speedways. Reyne's room was almost bare. She had done nothing to it but get rid of all the furniture and start over, and that was fine with her. She was just glad that she didn't have to share it with anyone anymore. The third bedroom would eventually become Reyne's office, but for now, it remained a storage area. The last room upstairs was the only full bath in the house. It was ugly but fine. It would be one of the last things she renovated because the only people who saw it were in her family. She had decided that they would redecorate the second floor after everything else in the house was done.

The family room in the basement had been recently overhauled. The ceiling was showing signs of falling, so Reyne had a new ceiling put in and painted the walls a stark white. Thank goodness she had. The sheetrock had been put up running the length of the joists instead of across them. It was just an accident waiting to happen. With the new ceiling and paint, it already felt more spacious.

The television, video games, and toys were in the family room. It was more than just a playroom; it was the family entertainment area and much of their time was spent in that room. Tyler's bedroom was in the basement as well. Reyne had told her to decide how she wanted to decorate the room, and that she would be glad to help in any way. There was also a small storage room, laundry room, and the skeleton of another full bath she would eventually have finished, but for now, it at least had a toilet and sink Tyler could use in the middle of the night.

Reyne enjoyed sitting at her tiny kitchen table, thinking about her house and how she was going to decorate it. Designing her house always gave her hope that things were going to be all right. Initially, the thought gave her pride and excitement. She knew she had a good job and could take care of her two children and herself, all by herself. Then the phrase hit hard- "all by myself"-she said it aloud with pride as a way to make the thought less lonely, but it wasn't working this time.

As tears filled her eyes, the front door opened. Leigh had let herself in with the key Reyne had given to her months ago. Leigh was tall with long, light brown hair and green eyes. She was willowy and gorgeous, with long legs and delicate features. Leigh found Reyne in the kitchen, crying quietly. She refilled Reyne's coffee, made herself a cup, and joined Reyne in the small breakfast nook. As soon as she sat down, Reyne broke into uncontrollable sobs.

"Leigh, I am so lonely. I have had to do everything on my own for so long. Even when I was married, it didn't feel like we were together much over the last few years. I know it was neither of our faults, but now I'm lonely and scared. What am I going to do?"

Leigh hugged Reyne and stroked her blond hair. She let Reyne cry for a while just to get it out of her system. Then she lifted Reyne's chin and looked in Reyne's eyes, "You will never be alone, I promise. Anytime you are scared or lonely, I will be here for you. Even when we are old and decrepit, I'm here for you. No matter what, I've got your back. As to what you are going to do…You are going to do whatever it takes to survive with me at your side." She hugged Reyne again and just held her, comforting her, and letting her get the soul-cleansing cry over.

"Leigh, you are so wonderful. How would I ever get through any of this without you?" Reyne whispered between rasping sobs.

"You would because you have to for the kids. But we both should feel privileged to have one another as friends. You are there for me as much as I am there for you," Leigh replied gently, knowing it was the truth on so many levels.

"Thank you for coming over. After this last date, I really need a friend, and you are pretty much the only one I have. I needed to vent and you are definitely the only person who would understand."

"Not a problem, Sweetie. What time are Tyler and Lazarus due back?" Leigh wanted to make sure she would have plenty of time to get Reyne calmed down completely before Reyne's daughter and her boyfriend returned to the house.

"They are staying at Lazarus' parent's house tonight. That is one reason I wanted you to come over. They aren't due home until tomorrow afternoon." Reyne breathed easier as she sipped her coffee.

Leigh knew now that they had plenty of time, so she asked Reyne, "What happened tonight? Tell me all about it and don't leave anything out."

Reyne told her about the date. She was reluctant to relive it, but knew she had to tell someone. "Well, let's see. I told you about this hot guy from the building down the street from where I work. We kept bumping into each other at different meetings, and restaurants and such. Remember? I told you about Steve. He is a blond, blue-eyed hunk at 6' tall and 180ish pounds, completely muscular and masculine." Reyne said with a glint in her eye as she remembered how she thought the date would go. "Well, out of the office and out of the business lunch time run-ins, he is a bit different. Let's just say he pretty much reeked of testosterone. It was like a totally different person." Reyne added sarcastically, "You know how much I like that type. Just dripping in testosterone."

Leigh made a face that looked like she was going to get physically ill.

"Yeah, that kind." Reyne giggled and continued as she got up to refill their coffee mugs. "He was obnoxious, over-bearing, couldn't hold an intelligent conversation, and only spoke about himself. Best part is that he spoke of himself in third-person, so it was 'Steve this' and 'Steve that.' He seriously never did that before. I couldn't stand it. I told him I wasn't feeling well and asked if he would bring me home. He said, and I quote," she said as she made little air quotations, "'Steve will not take you home, but Steve will call a cab for you.' Which he did. I took the cab home and paid my fare. Steve was already working on some blonde with big tits at the bar before I walked out the door of the club. He was such a hemorrhoid."

Leigh laughed at this statement. Reyne had explained to her years ago that men were not assholes, as most women thought. Assholes served a purpose. Men were hemorrhoids, just pains in the asses of women. They served no other true purpose. Since that time, it had been their secret way of judging men. Not too many made the honored "asshole" status. "Well, it's over now. You have another learning experience under your belt… No more dating services."

They both laughed and continued their man bashing session for a while longer. Eventually, they went upstairs to Reyne's room. The evening had been exhausting for Reyne and she was ready for bed. She and Leigh both changed into their boxers and T-shirts, and crawled into bed. They laid there for a while facing each other and talking, when Reyne asked, "Leigh, this is weird, I know, but would you spoon me tonight? I want to feel the arms of someone who loves me around me for a change."

Leigh, unfaltering, answered, "Of course I will."

Reyne turned over and squiggled her butt into Leigh's stomach. Leigh giggled, "No wonder no one sleeps with you. You wiggle too much."

Reyne looked over her shoulder, giggling, "Shut up and sleep."

Leigh held Reyne and listened for her breathing to become deep and regular. Then she prayed, "If there is a God in heaven or wherever, you need to send this woman, Reyne, a man that will treat her the way she deserves to be treated. She needs to be pampered and adored. Please help them find one another. Amen." Then she too fell asleep.

CHAPTER 3

Dreams came quickly to Onyx's satisfied body. He needed to use this time to learn as much as possible. He needed this feeding induced sleep to watch his Beloved for her life depended on it. If Xavier and Elizabeth were already near her, then he may be too late already. He had tried to avoid using this power to its fullest extent because he really did not like taking lives, but now he had no choice. The bits and pieces of information that usually came to him were no longer adequate. He had to focus in on her. As he slept, he watched her day unfold.

Reyne woke and felt the other side of bed. Leigh had been there last night, but she wasn't there now. Suddenly, the smell of bacon, eggs, and coffee filled the air around Reyne. She hurriedly got up and ran to the bathroom before heading down the stairs. She slowed her step as she worried about the previous night and what Leigh's reaction would be this morning. She proceeded cautiously, trying to figure out what she was going to say when she got to the kitchen.

She turned the corner to the kitchen and saw Leigh standing at the stove making breakfast. Leigh looked beautiful and the sight of her made Reyne relax.

Leigh turned around, "Hey Sweetie, how'd ya sleep? Once you stopped wiggling around, I slept wonderfully. I'm starving; aren't you? And no, things have not changed. Spooning you is just another way to say you are my bestie and I'm here for you. We are best friends and nothing will change that. I figured you would feel weird about that, and I didn't want you to, so I decided to just go ahead and open the conversation this morning so that we weren't all awkward and stupid until we finally said something about it."

Reyne started laughing, "Thanks, you are the best friend any-one could have."

"Well, what did you expect of me? Did you think I'd be all awk-ward and weirded out or expect me to leave and never talk to you again just because you wanted me to hold you? Get real." Leigh said like it wasn't a big deal.

Shyly Reyne said, "I wasn't sure. Yeah, you've spent the night, but always on the other side of the bed. I was afraid I was asking for too much. Thank you for not making this more than what it is."

Leigh gave Reyne a hug, "No problem. It's what best friends do. Now get some coffee and sit down. Oh, by the way…Benjamin called and said he'd be bringing Taylor home early, so my guess is about 2 hours."

Reyne did as she was told, getting coffee and sitting down. She took a long drink of the coffee, "Good, that gives us time to clean up a little before they get here. The house is a mess."

"Seriously Reyne? Your house is never a mess. I don't know what you mean, but I'll help out cleaning too." Leigh said as she made up a plate for Reyne and herself before heading to the little table.

The eggs and bacon were wonderful, the coffee perfect. Reyne took Leigh's hand in her own and squeezed. "Thanks again for let-ting me vent and cry and just get it out of my system."

Leigh squeezed back, "I know. Now shut up and eat while I tell you about Andy."

"What do you mean 'tell me about Andy?'" Reyne shot Leigh a hard stare that, if looks could kill, Leigh wouldn't have survived.

"I want to introduce you to him and think you two would make a great couple. I trust Andy; he's a good friend of mine. I've been telling him about you and I wanted you to meet him before your date last night, but you threw it on me so fast, there wasn't time." Leigh blurted out, keeping her eyes focused on her own plate so she wouldn't have to look at Reyne. She knew this was a sore subject, especially after the fiasco last night with whatever his name was, but she knew Andy would be good for Reyne.

Reyne gently put her fork down and stared at Leigh, "My turn– Seriously Leigh? I just bawled like a baby last night and told you what would have to happen for me to date again, let alone fall in love. I don't know Leigh. I don't think I am ready to do that again."

"It will be perfect." Leigh promised. "He is a gentleman, kind, and you're kind of handsome. And he's not all about himself or the testosterone. Just say yes to one date and see what happens."

"I don't know. Let me think about it while we clean. I'll do the upstairs; you do this floor. That's your punishment for laying this on me today." Reyne chided, but smiled afterward.

"You got it, then we can both hit the basement." Leigh agreed because she knew that her "Andy" announcement was definitely bad timing.

Reyne cleaned the full bathroom completely and changed out linens. She stripped the beds and threw all the laundry and laundry baskets in the hallway. Then she changed the sheets, dusted, and waited for Leigh to finish vacuuming. When Leigh was done, she brought the vacuum up and went back down to continue cleaning. Reyne vacuumed for the rooms to be ready for this evening and the bedtime routine. She could hear Leigh getting the mop and bucket out as she finished up.

Reyne walked downstairs as Leigh finished the mopping the floor. Leigh looked up at her "Well you've had time to think about it. Can I give you his number so you can set up a date?"

Reyne scowled at Leigh and was about to say no when the doorbell rang. She realized at that moment that it was already early afternoon and had taken way too much time upstairs and obviously slept in too late for everything she had to do on Sundays. She had not even thought about what to make for dinner.

Reyne hopped down the last two steps, "That must be Benjamin with Taylor."

Reyne opened the door for them, and Taylor ran into the house and jumped into Reyne's arms, "I missed you, Momma."

"I missed you too, baby." She told her son with a smile and a big hug.

"Can I go out and play?" Taylor asked.

"Before you go play, say bye to your dad. Stay right out front, OK? Dinner will be ready soon." Reyne let go of Taylor.

"OK. Bye Daddy." Taylor ran off to play with the other kids on the street.

Benjamin turned to Reyne after watching Taylor run off, "I see you have new neighbors moving in?"

"Yeah, they bought the house last week. It seems they wanted to move in immediately. It is a man and woman, no kids. They will probably complain about the noise, but they will just have to get used to it." Reyne said as if the new neighbors bothered her already.

"That is one reason I have always loved you; you don't take shit from anyone." Benjamin said with a smile.

Reyne laughed, "Yeah, right. Thanks."

"Well, I gotta go. Paintball tonight. See you next weekend. Be careful." Benjamin hugged her good-bye and walked away.

"You too. See you then." Reyne closed the door and walked into the kitchen.

Leigh was already looking through cupboards and the refrigerator, "What are we making for dinner?"

"Mom, I'm home!" screamed Tyler as she barreled into the house.

"Hi baby girl, where's your other half?" Reyne worried about Tyler, but Lazarus was really good for Tyler and helped keep her out of trouble.

"He's getting the stuff out of the car. We're going to the basement. I'll clean it, so I'm taking the vacuum with me. Then Lazarus and I will be watching TV until dinner's ready. Oh, hi Leigh." Tyler smiled at Leigh while hugging her mom, then went to the basement door and down the steps as Lazarus came in. He nodded hello to Reyne and Leigh and followed Tyler to the basement.

"Well, it appears that the only thing you have all the ingredients for is spaghetti with a salad. I guess that is what we're fixing." Leigh stated as she stood up out of the fridge.

Reyne laughed. "I guess it is, and I guess I'll go grocery shopping tomorrow after work. I would rather shop today, but it is what it is."

Leigh and Reyne made spaghetti with a salad and garlic bread. As the noodles boiled, Leigh decided she and Reyne needed some wine and ran out and picked up a bottle of Mondavi Sauvignon to go with the dinner while the noodles were cooking. Once everything was finished and the table set, they all sat at the dining room table and ate until they were full. Leigh, Tyler, and Lazarus cleaned up the dinner dishes, while Reyne made sure Taylor's school project was completed and got him ready for bed. Tomorrow was Monday and the day would start early for them all. Reyne put Taylor to bed, read him a story, and tucked him in. She turned on his night light, told him good night, and went back to the kitchen.

"I feel like I got nothing accomplished today. I didn't finish laundry; hell, I barely started it. I didn't get to the grocery store. I'm a day behind and the week hasn't even started," Reyne said unhappily.

Leigh grabbed the bottle of wine and some wine glasses and headed to the living room. "Come on Reyne, I have to tell you more about Andy."

Reyne was exhausted, unhappy, and she had to be up early the next morning, so she just gave in, "Set it up Leigh, I will go out with him. Tell him I will meet him at Chevy's Tex-Mex Restaurant on Friday at 8pm in the Cantina. I am too tired to fight about this anymore and too depressed about being behind already that I just want to go to bed."

Leigh picked up the wine and her glass and walked to the kitchen, "Good! It's settled. I will let you know tomorrow what he says. But now I am going to let you get to bed. What time do you have to be at work tomorrow, or have they started allowing you to work from home yet?"

"I have to be in D.C. by 7am. That means I have to leave here by 5:30am. This is killing me. Pretty soon, I won't have any life left in me. I have to find a new job. I can't take this commute anymore."

"Starting this week, I will not only set you up with this incredible man, but I will help you find a job in this area. OK? And I'll help you get caught up on the home life stuff tomorrow."

"Sounds great. Thanks," Reyne replied unenthusiastically.

"Go to bed, Sweetie. I am going home and doing the same." Leigh hugged Reyne gently and gave her a kiss on her cheek before she left.

Reyne was still sitting on the sofa drinking her glass of wine when Lazarus appeared. He stood over six and a half feet tall, would scare most people on sight, and would scare the rest of the people when he spoke in the deep timber of his voice that almost sounded unreal and more demonic than human. Reyne laughed at this though since she trusted this man more than most other people in her life. Something about him let her know that she and her family were safe with him.

"Hi, Lazarus." She said as he came into the living room.

"Hey, Mom. I want you to know that you are being watched. It is nothing to worry about, but someone is watching you. Just be careful. If this man can watch you through his dreams, it is unpredictable what else he can do. Just be careful. And if you need me for anything, just let me know." Lazarus didn't sit but just stood in front of her.

Reyne smiled, "Thanks, Lazarus. Now please sit and tell me more. You standing is hurting my neck." Lazarus sat and Reyne continued, "How do you know? Is there anything else you can tell me about this watcher?"

Lazarus shook his head, "I could sense the presence when I entered the house this evening. It was as if someone was sitting off to the side watching your every move. Almost like I could reach out and touch him. I wish I could tell you more. All I know is that it is a man."

"Thanks, I will keep this in mind." Lazarus moved to stand, "Goodnight Lazarus." Reyne let him return to the basement before she took her glass to the kitchen and went to bed. She laid there for a few minutes, wondering who would want to watch her and why. It made little sense, but she knew better than not to believe Lazarus. She drifted into an uneasy sleep, wondering what the male watching her was capable of.

CHAPTER 4

Onyx's eyes flew opened, and he sat up as if he had never been asleep. There was no drowsiness, only excitement and terror. His Beloved had told him where she was and he knew he had to get there immediately. His mind was going a mile a minute over her day, her talk with her friend, Leigh, cleaning the house, seeing the kids, then another date. He also realized there was some talk about a new neighbor moving into her neighborhood. It had to be Xavier and Elizabeth. He had to hurry; he had to leave now!

He called Brian on his way into the shower. "Brian, it's Onyx. Sorry for calling so late, but this is urgent."

"As if night fall is late. You forget who you are talking to, but go ahead. I take it you finally did what you should have done long ago and have found her." Brian could not resist the little stab at Onyx with his last statement and snickered. He had been pushing Onyx for years to do it.

"I don't need the 'I told you so's right now. I need a plane ticket to Washington, D.C. I need a car and a hotel room that will cater to my eccentricity and not question my activities. I also need to have arrangements made to send some of my things to the area within 48 hours of my arrival. You have the list I gave you still, don't you?"

"Of course. Call me back once you have prepared for your day and have fed. You need to have your strength for this. Remember that. No matter what, you must continue to feed. When you call me back, I will have everything prepared for you." Brian instructed, as if he were the one in charge.

"Thanks Brian. I'm glad you are on my side. Where would I be without you to help guide me?"

"You know it's always good to have a literal blood sucker for an attorney. That's what makes me so good. Talk to you shortly." Brian hung up.

Onyx knew Brian would have the preparations completed as soon as possible, but he felt a nervousness that made him rush. Onyx did not like this feeling, but there was nothing he could do about it. He had to get to his Beloved. He got into the shower and finished quickly. His normal routine of carefully picking out his attire for the evening did not even enter his mind as he grabbed a pair of black jeans and a plain black shirt. As he pulled the T-shirt over his head, he could not remember from where he had gotten it, which was unusual for him. He quickly reminded himself that remembering the origin of the T-shirt was unimportant; only his Beloved was important. His nervousness returned as he quickly pulled on his boots and grabbed a small bag for some of his clothes and grooming items. While working on his packing, he called Brian, "Well, what are the arrangements, Brian?"

"Your limousine has been placed on call and is at the front door of your building, waiting to take you to the airport. Your flight leaves the airport in 25 minutes. Go! You have to hurry. The hotel information is in your phone; I sent it there myself. If you have any questions, I am here for you. I will be accompanying your belongings to D.C. myself. I will see you in a few days. Good Luck." Brian hung up the phone before Onyx could say thank you again.

"Thanks," he said to an empty line as he grabbed his leather jacket and ran out the door, forgetting his bag and forgetting to feed.

Onyx arrived in Washington D.C. at Reagan National Airport as streaks of purple and rose-colored the eastern sky with the approaching dawn. He prepared to disembark from the airplane when he realized he had left his bag on the bed in his penthouse. "Damn!" he said out loud, and continued his thought, "This is going to throw my plans off somewhat, but that is ok. I will be with my Beloved soon. I have waited this long and hopefully I won't have to wait much longer." He left the airplane and found the driver that was to take him to the hotel.

As the limousine left Reagan National Airport, Onyx looked around and saw all the things he would love to experience with his Beloved. He saw the exit for Arlington Cemetery, where many of the veterans and presidents of this country are buried, the Washington Monument and the Mall, as well as many of the museums. He would see them all with her before long, he promised himself.

He arrived at the hotel and was greeted by the hotel shift manager, who registered him and told him a little about his suite. Onyx was told that Mr. Gold had graciously discussed the situation to the hotel's General Manager, and left the visitor's care to the hotel's shift managers. He guaranteed the staff would not bother him and would work around his schedule. Onyx thanked the hotel manager as he followed him to his suite. It was not as nice as his penthouse, but it would do for the time he would be in the nation's capital searching for his Beloved.

Onyx found the phone in the living room of his suite and called Brian. "Hey Brian, here's the direct number to my room in D.C. Thanks for all this, but what is 'the situation' that you explained to the General Manager?"

Brian started laughing, "Oh you will love this one. I explained you are a reclusive and passionate schizophrenic artist given to extremely violent outbursts if interrupted or not catered to when the inspirations come. You needed a suite with a view of the gardens and the Potomac River for inspiration but didn't want to hear anything that may sound like a city. Then I told him I would be there in a day or two to control you, but until then he would have to keep you comfortable. So, how's your room?"

"The room is exactly what you requested." Onyx laughing, continued, "One side is the river, the other is the gardens. But now I know why I was given the looks of fear and dread from the staff as the hotel manager was showing me to my suite. I guess I also helped your story a bit, because I came with no luggage, not even a small bag."

"What do you mean, you have no luggage? We agreed I had two days to get your stuff to you."

"I left it on my bed when you told me that my plane left in 25 minutes. I think I left everything on in the penthouse too. When you go over, just turn it all off. I'll see you as soon as possible but two days at the latest."

"I guess I'll be there before the rest of your stuff, but I can definitely do it in two days, see ya."

Onyx laughed again as he thought of Brian's story. It was probably one of the best stories Onyx had ever heard. He settled down onto the sofa, knowing he had to make one more call before he could sleep. He dialed the number and waited for an answer.

"Hello?" The voice of an older woman with an Eastern European accent answered the phone.

"Hello Motina."

"Onyx! You must have found her, or you would not be calling me at this time. It is still very early."

"I'm sorry. I didn't think of the time difference. But you are right. I am in Washington D.C. and will have contact with my Beloved before the end of the week. Unfortunately, Xavier and Elizabeth are here too. They bought a house in her neighborhood. I believe it is actually just a few doors down from her house," Onyx explained.

"It will be all right, my Oniksas. You just find her and bring her to us. WE will protect her. You don't have to do it alone, you know." His mother instructed.

"But I do have to do it alone, otherwise Xavier and I will never be over this feud."

"You do what you think is best," she sighed before continuing, "I will let your father know and we will await your return. Be careful. Xavier is dangerous."

"I will Mom. I love you. Bye." Onyx hung up the phone and looked out the window. This was unfamiliar territory, and it was daylight. He was starved. He decided to feed by using his artistic situation to help him.

Onyx called the hotel shift manager and told him he wanted companionship. He explained gender was of no concern, but he must have two to three options sent to his room within 30 minutes or the inspiration would be gone. Within 20 minutes, two females and a male showed up at his suite. They were obviously hotel staff used to accommodate the crazy artist within the short time frame given by Onyx. He felt guilt start to rise but decided he did not have time to care. He proceeded to have them all undress. Although he was starved, he wanted to play the role so that if he let any go, they would report back about his eccentricities.

Without prompting, the girls started to kiss and touch one another briefly before the red-head reached out for the male. The young man knelt on the floor in front of the red-head.

"Do you want to join us?" The young, blonde woman asked with a flirtatious smile while the red-head was kissing the other man in the room.

"No, thank you. I prefer to watch for right now. However, each one of you will eventually experience me." Onyx answered as he pretended to watch them for a short time more; had anyone asked him what had gone on, he could not have told them. He was only thinking about his Beloved and the display in front of him meant nothing but food.

Onyx realized the male was lying on the floor, catching his breath. He looked at the young man and said, "Come, sit with me and watch the beautiful women." Onyx patted the sofa cushion beside him because the time for fun was over. It was time to feed. The male started to dress. "No, remain as you are, please. I need the inspiration. Now, please join me."

The male did as he was told. When he sat down, Onyx immediately placed his hand on the young man's inner thigh to keep up the charade. The male startled initially at the touch, but relaxed as Onyx massaged his thigh, making sure his finger grazed against his intimate areas every few strokes. He knew Onyx was no longer watching the girls. This aroused him even more and his shaft was again becoming erect.

"Go play with the brunette and have the blonde come sit with me to watch you fuck her friend." Onyx instructed.

The young man walked over to the brunette, who immediately took his cock into her mouth and began massaging the base and sucking the top.

"I did not say suck. I said fuck." Onyx roared.

The two startled and quickly changed position, ending with the brunette woman on her hands and knees as the male came up behind her. The blonde quickly moved to sit beside Onyx. She looked at Onyx only briefly, because he gripped her chin in his fingers and turned to watch the two others fuck one another. She tried to touch Onyx, but he pushed her hand away. He stood abruptly and grabbed her by her hair, pulling her from the sofa.

"You two, please continue. It is my turn with this beautiful woman." Onyx said as he dragged the blonde behind him and into the other room of the suite brutally. She had excitement and fear in her eyes but waved to her co-workers before the door to the other room shut them out.

Onyx returned to the living room area a few minutes later, without the blonde to watch the brunette finish the young man. As soon as the man was done, Onyx walked over to the brunette and grabbed her by a nipple with his fingernails piercing the skin. She grimaced at the pain. Onyx turned to her and smiled, but told them male, "Lie down on the sofa and take a nap, but do not dress. You are next. It is my turn to pleasure this wonderfully sexual woman.

She performed well today." She smiled at the thought of having Onyx as he pulled her into the other room.

When he returned to the living area of the suite a short time later, the young man was asleep on the sofa. Onyx decided to let him sleep while he discarded his feminine meal. The two girls had given him the release he needed and satisfied his hunger for the moment. The male could be saved for later.

Onyx discovered he had full access to all areas of the hotel. Discarding the bodies was an easily completed task. He found the incinerator with no problem. He opened the door of the big funeral pyre and kissed each corpse before throwing the body into the fire. When he returned to the room, the young man was still sleeping. He carried him to the bedroom and laid him on the bed. He took off his own clothes and climbed into the bed beside the male. As he drew closer to the young man, he kissed him on his neck and gently penetrated a small vein. He drew just enough blood to ensure this man would sleep until the evening. He covered the wound marks and quickly fell asleep and found his Beloved already starting her day.

The male awoke late in the day to find himself in bed with Onyx. He quietly got out of the bed so he did not disturb the artist. He walked to the window and opened the curtains, staring out the window as the sun set on the Potomac River, deep purple, red and blue colors dancing and mingling with the black of night that was quickly coming to overtake the day. His mind wandered when a voice startled him from behind.

"This is a beautiful view." Onyx whispered in his ear.

The male jumped and moved away quickly.

"I'm sorry. I didn't mean to scare you." Onyx said.

"I didn't hear you get up. Where are the other two?" The male asked as he looked around.

"They left hours ago. You were spent, so I put you to bed. I hope you don't mind that I crawled into the bed with you." Onyx smiled at the beautiful young man.

"No, just kinda surprised." He answered.

"Why?" Onyx asked.

"Most men are not like me. Most don't like both or at least won't openly admit it." The man looked down as if he was ashamed that he was sexually active with both men and women.

"I don't see gender. I see beauty and to me you are beautiful. I want to get to know you. Tell me about yourself, like what is your name?" Onyx moved back to the bed, and the male followed.

"My name is Stuart. What else would you like to know?" He answered softly.

"How old are you? What are your interests, your likes? Tell me about yourself," Onyx asked in a calming tone, to help Stuart relax.

"Why would you want to know about me? I am no one of importance, especially not in this city," Stuart asked as he stared into Onyx's eyes. "What about you? Tell me about you. You're an artist and must lead an exciting life."

"My name is Onyx," Onyx answered. "Tell you what. We will tell each other about ourselves. Everyone is important in some way, and I am intrigued as much with your voice as I am with your body. That is why I want to know you."

"Ok, I will agree to that," Stuart smiled.

"In fact, my dear one, I will start. I will tell you about me." Onyx smiled and got more comfortable on the bed.

Stuart wriggled up higher on the bed and got comfortable as well. He sat cross-legged across from Onyx, which allowed a full view of his shaft, hoping this would turn Onyx on.

"I came here in search of an old friend I have not seen in a long time. I am a self-made millionaire, as is my father. No, I have received none of my father's help in creating my own fortune. I was not that privileged. In fact, I did not even know my father until after

I had started to accumulate my own personal wealth. Now you. How old are you? Tell me about you." Onyx laid his hand on Stuart's knee and squeezed gently.

"I am 23 years old and studying art on my own. My father disowned me when he found out I like men as much as I like women, but he had already stopped helping me financially or in any way several years before when I refused to go to law school and follow in his footsteps. I've been on my own since I was 18, and I'm currently surviving. All my extra money goes to my painting supplies, lectures by artists and exhibits. It's what I want to do with my life. When I heard an artist was staying here, I knew I had to meet you. I am a waiter here in the restaurant downstairs. When the hotel manager came around asking for models, I offered immediately. I had to meet you, and I knew that modeling for you would probably be my only chance." His eyes had grown wide with excitement and his voice sounded happier and sexier as he spoke of art.

Onyx knew he had learned too much about Stuart, but he also knew that from the moment he stepped into the hotel room, he never really wanted to kill this young man. "Maybe this young man, Stuart, would let Brian be his sire and let me help him become a world-renowned artist. If not, he will die when Brian's from him," Onyx thought, and decided he would have to think about this more. "Stuart, will you be my guide while I am in this beautiful city?"

"Sure, but I really don't know that much about D.C. I just work down here. I live in Maryland, Gaithersburg, Maryland, to be exact. It is about 30 minutes from here, with a lot less traffic. Some friends and I have an apartment we share," Stuart answered.

"Let's go see your friends. Go get a shower…" Onyx hesitated for a moment. "Are they your lovers?" Onyx had to know if he would be stealing this man from another. He could not do that.

"I have no lover. I am too focused on becoming an artist. The girls were the first sexual encounters I have had in about two years.

I am not that experienced. I'd rather be painting or drawing than having sex." He looked away with embarrassment.

Onyx took his hand and gently lifted him to stand. "Experience is not everything. Are these friends good friends? I mean, are they people you truly care about or are they just roommates?"

"I care about them. They are friends I have had since I was little. I guess I have known them most of my life," he answered.

"Then I will see to it they are taken care of if only you will stay with me while I am here." Onyx offered as he led Stuart to the bathroom. "Let's shower and go see your friends."

When he entered the bathroom, everything he needed was already there. "The staff must have brought these items to the room before I arrived to make sure I didn't need to call them for anything." Onyx decided as he quietly laughed.

He and Stuart took turns in the shower and got ready to leave. As they prepared to walk out of the suite, Onyx realized he had been very presumptuous. He never had to worry about that at home. People would drop anything to spend time with him. But here he was unknown and his requests may seem outrageous, "Do you have other plans or need to be at work? I didn't think to ask earlier."

"No. I have no other plans, and I don't have to work. I was told that I should stay with you until your inspiration was complete. The hotel promised to pay me for my shifts no matter what. I told them that wasn't necessary, but I don't know if they believed me." He turned off the light and headed to the door of the suite, where Onyx stood waiting for him.

They took the elevator to the lobby. When the woman at front desk saw Onyx, she immediately picked up the phone. By the time they were passing her, she said, "The limousine is outside waiting for you."

Onyx just nodded and headed out the doors with Stuart. The driver was opening the door and the two men got into the back. "Are there places to shop by where you live? I need some new clothes. I grew tired of the clothes I had and left them when I came here." Onyx asked.

"Of course there are," Stuart answered.

"Tell the driver your address. We will stop by your apartment and then go shopping," Onyx announced.

"I think the mall will be closed by the time we get there," Stuart said.

"What is the name of the mall?" Onyx dialed the phone while waiting for Stuart's reply.

Hesitantly Stuart answered, "Lake Forest Mall in Gaithersburg. It's the closest. There is the Montgomery Mall, which is better, but not as close to my apartment." He continued to stare at Onyx.

"Hello Brian. How is the move coming? Good. I need a favor. Call the Lake Forest Mall in Gaithersburg, Maryland. Some friends and I want to go shopping." Onyx looked at Stuart and smiled. "How many roommates do you have?"

"Two," Stuart said, looking at Onyx in disbelief.

"There will be four of us, Brian. Yes. At least two restaurants and all the stores should stay open. Yes. Text me and let me know when it is done. Bye." Onyx looked at Stuart, knowing this young man did not believe what just took place. "What?"

"You want them to keep the mall open for the four of us? That is crazy. They will never do it." Stuart started laughing.

"We'll see." Onyx smiled.

The rest of the ride was silent. Stuart did not know what to think, but he was getting just a little afraid of this man and the power that he apparently had.

"Stuart, do not be afraid of me. All will become clear to you soon." Onyx told him without looking at him as they reached his apartment building.

Stuart took Onyx to his apartment and introduced him to his roommates. Stuart showed Onyx around the tiny apartment, including his bedroom. As they were returning to the living room, Onyx's cell phone rang. "Is there a problem, Brian? Why call?" he waited for an answer then said, "Really all of them?" Onyx scowled and looked toward Stuart.

"See, I told you." Stuart said trying not to laugh.

Onyx held up his hand, asking Stuart to hold on. "Ok, which entrance? Hold on… Stuart, can you tell the driver where the Ruby Tuesday Entrance to the mall is?"

Stuart's eyes grew wide as he answered in a whisper, "yes."

"We will be over there shortly. Thanks Brian. See you tomorrow night." Onyx hung up. "Ok you guys, let's go."

"What do you mean let's go?" Stuart's roommates asked.

"Didn't Stuart tell you?" He smiled at the roommates. "I guess not. He did just finish showing me around. We all are going shopping. Come on, they are waiting for us." Onyx said with a smile.

Stuart spoke up first. "Onyx, we have no money. We barely get by. Plus, where are we going shopping at?"

"You told me Lake Forest Mall. They are waiting for us. You do not need money. Now, come on." Onyx smiled and headed for the door.

Stuart shrugged at his roommates, and the three followed Onyx out the door and into the limousine.

Onyx took Stuart and his friends to the mall. He had them pick out presents for each other, their families, and themselves. He purchased everything they wanted and treated them to a late-night dinner. After dinner, everyone piled back into the limousine. Onyx had the driver stop at Stuart's apartment to drop off the young men.

As the two roommates got out of the limousine, Onyx touched Stuart's hand. "Will you stay with me a while longer?"

Stuart stopped getting out of the car and settled back into the seat. "I was both terrified and hoping you would ask me again." Then he yelled out the door, "See you guys later."

Onyx and Stuart watched them carry their bags into the apartment building and begin the ascent up the stairs. As they rode back to the hotel, Onyx knew Stuart would never see his friends again, for one reason or another. This made him sit back and think hard about what he was contemplating. Stuart noticed Onyx was troubled about something; he took Onyx's hand into his and stroked it softly. Onyx smiled at the young man.

They sat beside one another for a few more minutes, before Onyx softly whispered, "You are such a beautiful person and a beautiful soul."

"I am not. I'm just who I am," Stuart said, blushing.

The rest of the ride to the hotel was silent. Once they arrived back at the hotel, they went straight up to Onyx's room. Onyx noticed there was a message on the phone. He knew the message was from Brian, telling him he would be there tonight when Onyx awoke. It was the same message he texted to Onyx's phone earlier.

He turned to Stuart, "Are you ready for some sleep?"

"If that is all you want, then yes, I am ready for sleep." Stuart tried to keep the disappointment out of his voice, but he couldn't.

"Do not worry, my precious one. When you wake, you will be in for another surprise. Possibly everything you desire. Possibly not." Onyx said softly. He wanted to make this young man's dreams of becoming an artist come true, and that could only happen if he was willing to let Brian sire him to a new life. Onyx had never done this, but this young man deserved it, and if things did not come to fruition with his Beloved in this life, he would have someone to be his companion until she returned again.

He grasped Stuart's hand and took him to the bedroom. The sun would be rising soon and tonight would be Stuart's rebirth or his destruction. Onyx had not completely figured which way it would go. It really depended on Stuart. He needed to sleep and think. He needed someone to stay with him in case he was too late. He would know when he awoke.

CHAPTER 5

Onyx woke to find boxes had been delivered to the front room his suite during the day. He found Brian asleep in an adjacent bedroom and woke him up.

"Wake up sleepyhead. I have something for us to play with."

Brian sat up groggily and scowled at Onyx, "What do you mean?"

"I mean that we have a gentleman to play with. I want to help him, but I need you to do it." Onyx smiled widely and innocently, knowing Brian would not be pleased.

Brian's eyes opened wide in astonishment, "Onyx! What are you saying? You want me to make him one of us?"

"No. I want you to make him like you. I'm not like you. Remember? He deserves a chance, and I can help him if he stays with me." Onyx turned away from Brian's lethal stare.

"Onyx, you're more like me than you want to admit. If I like him, I'll do it. But if there is anything I don't like about him, I'll refuse and he will be my food." Brian smiled at Onyx to soften the blow of his last statement. "I think we should show him or explain to him first…" He started.

"I think you should just do it. He will have to feed so then he can learn what he has become." Onyx interrupted with a devious smile. "Then we will know if he can handle it."

"I don't like to do it that way. You know that. I would like to know if he could handle it before he is changed. Once I have done it, he'll be dangerous. Please reconsider," Brian said with a hesitation Onyx had heard before.

"You may be able to know before anything comes to pass." Onyx answered as he left Brian and went to wake up Stuart for the evening's festivities.

Onyx entered the bedroom and sat on the bed next to Stuart. He leaned over, "Wake up my beautiful one." he whispered in Stuart's ear.

Stuart opened his eyes slowly and smiled at Onyx.

"I am going to give you something you have probably never had before, but will crave from today until eternity." Onyx smiled an evil smile knowing he was making Stuart nervous.

"Wha…" Stuart began groggily, but Onyx grabbed him and took his mouth with his own, cutting off the question Stuart was about to ask. Onyx thrust his tongue into Stuart's mouth deeply. Stuart leaned into Onyx and tightened with excitement.

Onyx ended the kiss and asked him, "Now, what were you going to say?"

"I don't remember." Stuart answered groggily as he leaned against Onyx and tried to kiss him again.

"No. First I have someone for you to meet." Onyx stood naked before him and offered Stuart his hand.

Stuart took Onyx's hand and followed him to the other bedroom. Onyx opened the door and the two men looked at one another. "Brian, this is Stuart. Stuart, this is Brian."

Stuart whispered to Onyx, "I've been with two men at once before. This is nothing new."

"You have never been with two men like us before." Onyx said with no emotion in his voice as he grabbed Stuart's right arm so hard it made Stuart jump. Brian rushed and grabbed his left arm at the same time. Stuart started to struggle, but their hands grasped him harder and tighter, causing so much pain in both of his arms he feared his arms would break.

Brian looked at Stuart in the eyes and felt the fear run through him. He hated siring this way, but Stuart would be easily controlled once changed. However, he still wasn't convinced Stuart would work out. He would know more when he tasted the young man's blood. At that point, it wouldn't matter what either said. Brian would have his answer and would know if Stuart would be his son or his breakfast.

"Now listen to me, Stuart. Stop struggling. Just give in and you will live to see another..." Onyx stopped his sentence as he watched Brian sink his teeth into Stuart's arm. Onyx kissed Stuart's face gently.

"Onyx, what is going on? What are you doing to me?" Stuart whispered.

"Keeping you forever and making all your dreams of being a famous artist come true," Onyx said as he continued to kiss Stuart's face and neck.

When Brian fed from Stuart to the brink of death, Onyx laid the young man on the bed. He turned toward Brian and asked, "Is it time?"

"Yes." Brian said before biting his wrist and pressing it to Stuart's mouth. Stuart's hands clasped onto Brian's wrist, trying to push him away. A low grumble began deep in Stuart's throat. His eyelids fluttered open showing the blood red eyes filled with hunger.

"Take me. Brian will make sure you do not take too much." Onyx said as he offered himself to Stuart as Brian pulled his wrist away.

Stuart hesitated and looked questioningly at Onyx for a moment. He couldn't understand what Onyx meant until the pulsating vein within Onyx's neck called to him.

"Brian, show him what to do or he will die." Onyx pleaded.

Brian shook his head no. "You know he has to do it on his own or he will not survive. The choice has to be his. You chose this way, not I." He turned and looked Stuart in the eyes, "Stuart you must either drink from Onyx or myself, or you will die. Enough of my blood made it into your throat before you pushed me away, enough to turn you, but you must feed."

In a voice barely audible Stuart asked, "What do you mean 'drink from Onyx'? I don't understand. Why am I starving? Why am I so hungry suddenly?"

Brian sighed, "Onyx will make a cut on his chest or arm for you, and you must drink some of his blood." Brian knew this was not going well and was afraid of how Onyx was going to take it. He knew from the moment he started feeding Stuart would be his food and he felt immense pity for Onyx. He was sure that Onyx knew it too and probably knew it even before today but was not willing to give up hope just yet.

"What have you two done to me? What have you done?" Stuart tried to sit up as he screamed hoarsely at Onyx and Brian.

"Onyx, you realize this is not going well. I will finish him." Brian said.

Stuart started weeping, "Onyx, please explain."

"My beautiful one. You are now on the verge of becoming a vampire. You must feed, or you will die a very painful death in just a few hours. You will literally starve to death. Alternatively, Brian will feed from you and finish killing you and will give you a hint of pleasure. Now, please drink from me and stay with us forever." Onyx explained and pleaded.

"You bastard, you made me a killer! How dare you! Why would you do that? You're a killer. You're not even human. Get away from me. I will never drink from you or anyone." Stuart screamed as best as he could.

Onyx looked at Brian in acceptance. Brian leaned over and bit hard and deep on Stuart's chest above his heart. He drained him quickly, then both he and Onyx left the room.

"You were right. He was not ready, nor would he ever be. I guess I already knew it, but after all these years, I am lonely and desperate. I wanted to make his dream of being an artist come true. He was a tortured soul. Plus, I think he would have made a great companion." The emotion in Onyx's voice was thick. But then he shook his head, and with a complete lack of emotion, looked at Brian and said, "Now, let's get rid of the body and go enjoy ourselves this evening."

Onyx quickly showed Brian where the incinerator was located, then returned to the room and dressed for the evening. They started making their way through Northeast D.C. for a night of fun on the town. They worked their way up to U Street, to the 9:30 Club. It was a place Brian had heard about during one of his earlier trips to the area, and he had wanted to check it out. The club featured live bands, and tonight two local bands were opening for Lords of Acid. Staff at the hotel had told Brian that the local groups were extraordinary and lots of people came out to see them whenever and wherever they played. From this information, they knew they could feed easily and within the part of town the club was located, and if things got out of hand, well, no one would be missed.

The two men enjoyed admiring the feast. They listened to music, danced with the crowd, and fed until they were sated without the need to kill anyone else. They returned to the hotel just before sunrise and began preparations for the initial meeting with Onyx's Beloved the next evening. Onyx grew nervous; he still did not know her name, but he could pick her out of a crowded room. He would be with her tomorrow night.

CHAPTER 6

Friday afternoon, Reyne left work early so that she would have time to prepare for this unwanted date with Andy. She tried to come up with a way out of it but was unable to devise anything believable. Now she would have to go through with the torture of another date.

Lazarus opened the door for her as she and Taylor got to the house. "Mom, I've got to talk to you. It is really important. It is about tonight."

"OK, let me get my cigarettes and a drink and we will go talk on the deck. Taylor, Daddy will be here soon. Why don't you go get packed and start your homework?"

"Yes, Momma. I love you." Taylor said before he ran upstairs to pack.

"I love you too, baby." She called after him.

Reyne got a cup of coffee, she knew Lazarus had made, and her cigarettes. Lazarus was on the deck when she got there. "OK Lazarus, what is it?"

"The watcher I told you about before, he is here in the area. He will be watching you closely tonight. You may even meet him. I know it isn't your date, Andy, but I don't know the person's exact identity either. I am not telling you this to worry you because the watcher will not hurt you. He is here to protect you and you should let him into your life. You will need him soon and if you block him, it could end badly. I don't know that the four of us could take care of the evil that has decided to hunt you, but your protector can take care of it with no problem. You must be open to people tonight. Promise me, Mom." Lazarus implored and just the look in his eyes told Reyne this was really important information.

"You're telling me some possible stranger I may meet tonight is my protector? Without this person, I will be in real danger." Reyne repeated back to him to ensure she had heard him correctly.

"Yes." Lazarus stated curtly.

"If this came from anyone else, I'd be on the deck rolling around laughing. I will believe you because you have never been wrong about these things before. I promise to be open to all. Now I wish you were coming with me. You would know him upon sight. I can't do that. Plus, if I'm in danger, I definitely want you there." Reyne said.

"Don't be afraid of your own gifts. Open up and you can know him on sight. He is more protection than I can ever give you, and Mom, thanks. I have to pick up Tyler from work. Maybe we will stop by the restaurant tonight," he offered, and Reyne nodded. "Bye," Lazarus said as he left Reyne sitting on the deck.

Reyne finished her coffee, had another cigarette, and relaxed for a while, thinking about what Lazarus had just told her. She finally got up and walked into the house. She began the ascent up the stairs to her bedroom when there was a knock on the door. She stopped on the stairs and yelled, "Come on in, Benjamin. I'll get Taylor."

Reyne finished walking upstairs to Taylor's room. "Daddy's here to pick you up. Are you ready?"

"Yeah Momma. Can you help me finish this project real fast?" Taylor asked.

"Sure baby." Reyne helped him finish his math project and put it away, then he finished packing. She carried his suitcase down the stairs. When she arrived at the bottom of the stairs, Taylor was hugging Benjamin. She would have to talk to him about starting to take Taylor every weekend. She wanted weekends with Taylor too, but now wasn't the time.

She gave Taylor a kiss and hug before he left with his Dad. She told him to call her the next day, and they left. She shut the door and went back upstairs. She really did not want to go out now. She was sitting on her bed naked, procrastinating about getting a shower, when she heard the front door open.

"Anybody home?" yelled Leigh.

"Up here." Reyne knew there was no backing out now. The date must go on.

Reyne heard Leigh running up the stairs. She grabbed her towel and put it around her body. "Hey Leigh. I am glad you came to help me get ready. I have to be honest, though. I am really not up for this tonight," she admitted.

"Look, Andy will be at Chevy's tonight. You should at least go and tell him you're really not interested. It's too late to back out now, so you have to go," Leigh responded.

"I know," Reyne snipped, "but I really don't want to. You should go out with him, not me."

Leigh laughed. "Shut up and get in the shower." Leigh dragged Reyne into the bathroom and pushed her into the shower.

Reyne got her shower, brushed her teeth, and dried her hair before returning to the bedroom.

"Took you long enough, so I picked out what you are going to wear tonight. Hope you don't mind." Leigh glanced at Reyne and smiled coyly.

Reyne took one look at the clothes, "These aren't even my clothes. They're yours. I can't wear this stuff."

"Sure you can." Leigh grabbed the towel that was covering Reyne and pulled it away.

Reyne grabbed for the towel and missed. Standing there chilled and naked, she gave in, knowing she couldn't change Leigh's mind. She picked up the clothes and began dressing. She put on the black lace thongs and the matching bra. "I feel sleazy already. Are you trying to get me laid or something?"

"No. I bought these for you because you deserve to feel sexy and feminine. I think you are beautiful, and you should show it more," Leigh answered.

"But I'm a mother. I can't dress this way," Reyne retorted.

"Where is there a law that says 'mothers have to look dowdy? Mothers cannot be, look, or act sexy.' There isn't, so do it. You are sexy and you need to show it a little. You'll love it. I promise." Leigh said as she handed Reyne the leather pants.

"Fine." Reyne growled her response. She slid into Leigh's deep gray leather pants. They formed to her body and showed more than Reyne liked. However, she had to admit a feeling was coming over her. It was a feeling she had not experienced since before Tyler was born. She felt sexy. She smiled and grabbed the lace shirt and pulled it over her head. "Well, how is your artwork progressing?"

Leigh smiled, "Perfectly! Now for face and hair."

"What is wrong with my face and hair?" Reyne couldn't believe this. She was wearing the clothes. What more did Leigh want her to do?

Leigh grabbed her hand and pulled her into the bathroom. She sat Reyne on the toilet and began putting on her make-up. When the make-up was complete, she worked on the hair. Leigh backed up and smiled. "Done. Have a look."

Reyne stood up and dropped her eyes to the floor. She was a little afraid to see what she looked like as she headed to the full-length mirror in the hall. She slowly started to look at herself, beginning at her bare feet and working her way up. She was impressed with the shapely woman standing in front of her, hips not too large and the breasts not too small. The reflection looked almost perfect. Then she raised her head and looked at her face and hair. It did not even look like her. Who was this person staring back at her? "Leigh…."

"Yes Sweetie, it is you. I knew you had it in you. I just helped bring it out."

"Thank you," Reyne whispered still awestruck at her reflection.

Leigh looked at the clock. "It's 7:15 pm, and it is time for you to go. Are you ready?"

Reyne answered shyly, "As ready as I'll ever be." Reyne picked up her purse and slid on the heels Leigh had set by the door. She looked at Leigh once more.

"Knock 'em dead Sweetie. Tonight you are the hottie. Go work it."

Reyne's head turned suddenly with realization, "Wait a minute! You don't care if Andy likes me. You want me to go out like this and find a man, don't you?"

All Leigh could do was smile, "I will be here when you get back, so you can tell me all about it. See ya later." She turned her back on Reyne and walked into the living room.

Reyne walked out of the house and to her car. This new feeling coming over her was crazy. The new look, be open to people and meet my protector. Reyne wondered if Leigh and Lazarus were working together on this. She drove to the restaurant and to her unknown destiny.

CHAPTER 7

At 7pm, Onyx arrived at the restaurant in a limousine, which caused a great commotion. The restaurant manager ran out to the limousine and walked Onyx into the restaurant. It took Onyx several minutes before the manager understood he wanted to sit in the Cantina area and not receive any special treatment. The manager finally gave in and sat Onyx at the bar and told the bartender to give him anything he wanted.

He was used to the special treatment but wanted none of it tonight. He regretted using the limousine. He wanted to be normal, to be approachable to his Beloved. He hoped none of the people in the bar had seen him come in the limousine. He did not want them to talk to him or be staring at him when his Beloved arrived. After a few minutes, he began to worry he had the wrong restaurant, or she had backed out of the date. Then Onyx feared her date would arrive first, but his mind became distracted when a beautiful woman arrived. He did not recognize her. She took his mind off his Beloved, and this scared him. No woman had ever been able to do that, but this woman was incredible. It took him a moment until he regained his composure and reminded himself why he was here tonight, his Beloved, she was coming. He looked at his watch 7:30 pm, she would be here soon. While he drank his Tito's on the rocks, his eyes returned to the mystery woman, who was now sitting at a table not far away. He figured he had time to go and talk to her for a moment. If things did not work out with his Beloved tonight, he would at least have a meal to drown his sorrows.

He walked over to the table where she was sitting. She looked up from her wine spritzer and straight into his eyes. He stopped dead in his tracks. Those eyes, he knew those eyes, but he did not remember this woman. *"Who is she?"* He wondered as he continued walking to the table.

"May I sit with you?" Onyx asked as he stood by the table.

The feeling Leigh promised her took over, as did the message from Lazarus, and she answered with a smile, "Yes, you may."

Onyx realized as soon as she answered him that this beautiful stranger was his Beloved. He thought, "Is she really into this guy she is meeting? She has not fixed herself up like this in years." He sat down beside her as a hush fell over the Cantina. All eyes were on them, Onyx knew it but hoped Reyne did not notice.

"I saw you walk in and had to meet you. You are exquisite." He blurted feeling like a school boy.

"Thank you, but to be honest, I don't really dress like this, at least not in the last few years. A friend said it would bring me luck tonight and another believes it would be good for me."

Onyx knew she was talking about Leigh, but who was this other friend, "Damn not being able to sleep and focus." Onyx was just glad to have time with her before her date arrived. "Are you meeting someone, or may I treat you to dinner?" He finally said even though he knew the answer.

"I'm terribly sorry, but I'm meeting someone here." She answered, almost embarrassedly.

"I understand completely. However, if you are interested, I would like to take you to dinner at some time. I am only in town for a short while and I expect nothing but a beautiful view and nice conversation," He offered.

"I don't know. I'm not like this normally. My best friend thinks I need to get out more, and my daughter's boyfriend thinks I should be more open to people. I don't know that I'm really into all this." To emphasize the 'this,' Reyne gestured at her hair, face and clothes. "I'm not really comfortable dressed up like this. How you would see me the next time would probably be a disappointment."

"I truly doubt that, but why don't you think about it..." Onyx stopped mid-sentence.

"Hi Reyne? I am Andy," he said and gave Onyx a look saying go away.

"Well, M'lady, your date has arrived. I hope you two have a wonderful evening. Thank you for the conversation. Good-bye." Onyx left the table, went back to the bar, and ordered another drink. He watched Andy and Reyne from the corner of his eye.

"I hope I didn't keep you waiting long. I surely didn't mean to have other people bothering you." Andy glared in Onyx's direction.

"Oh, it was no bother. He is from out of town and just wanted to talk to someone." She answered her date.

Andy took Reyne by the elbow and moved her out of the Cantina. He would have preferred to stay in the Cantina to eat because of the comfortable atmosphere, but not while that man was in there. Andy made sure they sat as far from the Cantina as physically possible. Within a few minutes of being seated, the waiter was there to take their orders. The mysterious man was forgotten, at least by Andy. However, he stayed in the back of Reyne's mind. She wondered if this stranger was her protector. Then she remembered he said he was only in town for a few days. "A protector wouldn't be leaving so soon, would he?" she thought to herself and quickly pushed the man from her mind and focused on Andy.

Reyne and Andy talked about work and their personal lives until their food arrived. Little was said during the actual meal. The food was too incredible to worry about talking and getting to know one another. Reyne was glad they didn't talk during dinner; she was uncomfortable and didn't really want to be here. She hoped Andy didn't feel her discomfort.

The waiter returned and took away their empty plates. Andy looked at Reyne, "Reyne, I would truly like to see you again. I find you intriguing and would love to get better acquainted with you."

Reyne smiled, realizing that Andy had not noticed that she was uncomfortable. "I would like to see you again, too. You have my number but here is my work number. You can call me there if you can't reach me at home. We can make plans when you call." She figured she would give him a chance. He seemed sincere and did not act that it was all just about sex or being fake. He was real and acted as if he truly wanted to get to know her better.

"Great. I'll call you soon so that we can make plans." He stood and pulled her chair out for her. She grabbed her purse, and they walked together to the door. At the hostess stand, Reyne stopped and picked a mint out of the basket. Her eyes were drawn to the table where she had met the stranger. She wondered where he was and then she saw him still sitting at the bar. He turned toward her and smiled. He raised his glass to say goodnight. She returned his smile and left the restaurant.

Andy walked her to her car and offered a platonic goodnight handshake. Reyne got in her car and drove home exhausted and exhilarated all at once. The date had actually exhausted her, but the stranger had made her feel things she had never felt before and she did not even know his name. She kept thinking about him until she parked the car by her house. She had arrived home and couldn't wait to tell Leigh everything.

As she put the key in the lock, Leigh opened the door. "Reyne, my god, tell me what happened. You are glowing, but you weren't gone long enough to have dinner and sex. You didn't? You and Andy had sex instead of dinner, didn't you? No, that isn't like you. Not even dressed like that. Fine, you gonna tell me or not?"

Reyne was laughing hysterically from Leigh's outburst. "If you would let me in the house, I will tell you. I couldn't wait to get home and tell you. It was a very strange night."

"How? You don't like him? You do like him? You got sick? You didn't like the food" Leigh started throwing questions at Reyne faster than Reyne could answer.

"Shut up and let me in the house," Reyne laughed and pushed through Leigh. "You know I left early to have a drink before Andy got there, right? Well, I am sitting there in the Cantina area of the restaurant and this man walks up to me. He is tall, and handsome, like out of some dream of mine. He was totally sexy. All he was missing was the white stallion of my Mr. Right. We talked for a few minutes and then Andy arrived."

"What is the stranger's name?" She asked sarcastically.

"I don't know. He asked me to dinner one night, but I never gave a definite yes or no answer." Reyne answered.

"Good! The way I dressed you, what was I thinking? You couldn't know how to act with men that you would have attracted." Leigh said before she realized how it sounded.

"Thanks for the vote of confidence." Reyne said sarcastically before finishing her description. "He had a way about him that made me very comfortable and like my dress and make up had nothing to do with his coming over to talk to me. It was really weird, but in a neat sort of way. Then Andy arrived, we ate dinner, and he asked if he could see me again and I said yes. He is going to call me so we can set a time."

"Oh, I am so happy." Leigh hugged Reyne. She was glad that Reyne was finally finding a man that wasn't going to treat her badly. Reyne deserved so much better than just any man.

Reyne and Leigh had made their way up the stairs and into Reyne's bedroom, while talking more about the evening and what Reyne would want to do the next time she went out with Andy. Reyne wanted to talk more about the mystery man, but Leigh kept nixing that subject completely and redirecting the conversation back to Andy. They took a bottle of wine up to the bedroom and quickly changed into their pajamas. Reyne turned on the radio and started dancing around the room from the excitement of meeting Andy and the stranger. Leigh, happy to see Reyne finally enjoying herself, joined in the dancing with her.

"You know with the lights on the neighbors will be getting a show of us dancing," Leigh giggled.

"Who cares. Let's just have fun. This has been a great night for me and I want to keep it going a while longer," Reyne said as she swayed to the music.

Onyx sat outside on the roof of his limousine watching the two women silhouetted against the blinds. He made sure that Reyne had not seen him following her. He had to know where she lived to find Xavier and Elizabeth and protect his Beloved. His Reyne. He watched the women and listened to them for information until the lights finally went out. They really were just best friends and while Leigh would need some convincing, he knew she would be his biggest ally when it came down to it. Once they were asleep, he resolved himself to feed. He had to focus during sleep the next few days so that he would be able to get all the necessary information to set up their next meeting.

CHAPTER 8

The rest of Reyne's weekend was uneventful. She and Leigh went shopping, watched movies and spent time working on redecorating Reyne's house. Leigh left on Sunday to take care of some things before Monday, but promised to be back for dinner, as usual.

On Sunday evening, Benjamin brought Taylor home. Benjamin seemed distracted when he arrived. Reyne knew something was bothering him. When she asked, he said it was nothing. Reyne decided to leave it alone, she would find out eventually. Then Benjamin promised to call Taylor later and left.

Reyne gathered up Taylor's bag and headed for the stairs, "Come on big boy, let's get you unpacked."

"Ok, Momma."

Taylor was acting distant too. He did not seem like he was sick, but Reyne knew something was wrong. Something must have happened between the Taylor and Benjamin for both to be acting strange. "What's wrong, baby? Is something bothering you?"

"No…not really." Taylor hesitated as he answered. He seemed to ponder whether he should elaborate.

His hesitation re-enforced Reyne's belief that something was bothering her little boy. The look on his face showed he was deep in thought. Reyne knew whatever was on his mind was more than any little boy should have to deal with, but she wouldn't intrude on his private thoughts. "Well, you know, if you ever have anything you want to talk about or if something is bothering you, I am here to listen and help you through it."

Taylor smiled and hugged Reyne, "I know Momma. Thank you. Let's go get me unpacked. I like being back where I belong."

Reyne knew through this last statement that someone had said or done something to Taylor. He would tell her, but it would have to be at his own pace. He wouldn't tell her anything and would withdraw more if she pushed him. He was probably afraid he wouldn't be able to see Benjamin, but Reyne would never keep Taylor from his father. She knew she would just have to wait. They unpacked and straightened Taylor's bedroom. Once the task was completed, she helped him pick out his clothes for the upcoming week.

"Momma, why do I have to decide today what I am wearing on Friday?" Taylor asked.

"You know the answer. We have plenty of time today; we don't have time in the mornings." She answered him with a smile.

"Fine." Taylor grunted as he picked out five outfits from which he would choose in the mornings. "Can I go out and play before dinner?"

"Sure, just don't go into anyone's house and stay right out in front, OK?"

"OK Momma." Taylor ran down the stairs and out the front door, letting it slam behind him.

Reyne followed him down the stairs but turned and went into the kitchen. As long as she was in the kitchen, she could keep an eye on Taylor outside. Lazarus and Tyler would be returning from Lazarus' parent's house soon and would be ready for dinner. Leigh was due back soon too. She had decided to make vegetable stir-fry and sticky rice. As she began chopping the vegetables, Lazarus and Tyler came in the front door.

"Hey Mom." Tyler said as she entered the kitchen with Lazarus right behind her. "Where's Leigh? I would have figured she would be here by now."

"Hey you guys. Nope. Not back yet, but I suspect she'll be here right after Taylor goes to bed, if not for dinner. You know she runs late when she isn't already here by the time I start making dinner." Reyne picked up the cutting board and scraped the vegetables into the wok. She placed the cutting board in the sink and turned around to talk to the kids.

"Mom, we have to talk. Well, it's not really me that needs to talk to you. It's Lazarus." Tyler stood staring at Reyne.

Reyne hated it when Tyler talked to her like a child, but she pulled out a chair and sat down. Lazarus joined her at the table. Reyne turned to Tyler, "Since dinner is almost ready, can you please finish dinner and set the table? Call your brother when it's ready and eat with him if this talk takes too long." She turned to Lazarus, "Again?" She shook her head, "OK Lazarus, let's talk."

Lazarus looked at Reyne and began slowly. "You are going to have to make a choice soon. The options all lead to happiness; however, depending on your decision, the road to happiness can be very easy or very hard." He broke off to gather his thoughts about how to proceed with this conversation. He really hated this gift, but when he saw something, he had to tell the person.

"So, which option should I choose for ultimate happiness? You know what my dreams are, help me here." She heard Tyler call Taylor in for dinner. Taylor came in and the two of them sat down at the dining room table to eat.

"Both roads lead to your ultimate happiness. The ideals of happiness are different for each road, but the end is what your idea of happiness is no matter which path you pick, so there will be no regrets." Lazarus started to continue, but stopped before any sound came out of his mouth.

"Lazarus, please, don't talk in such vague terms. I need to know. What are you talking about?" Reyne pleaded with him.

"Ok, Fine. You currently have two men in your life. The two men want to be with you forever. One knows you better than you know yourself, the other wants to get to know you better. You must choose between them. Either man you choose will bring you the happiness you desire, but each will do it in a different fashion." Lazarus frowned. "Just remember, it may not be as easy to figure this out now that you know because sometimes not speaking in vague terms can mislead you."

"Two men. The one knows me better than I know myself would be Benjamin. The one who wants to know me better would be Andy. Is this right?" Reyne knew he wouldn't tell her because he usually did not get that clear of a picture.

"Mom, don't jump to conclusions. It may not be as easy as it seems. I don't think it is Benjamin. It doesn't feel like Benjamin. Please be careful." Lazarus answered. "I am not sure of names. I just know there are two men. You would know better than I would; however, they may not be whom you expect. Even though it doesn't feel like Benjamin, the two you named, would probably be a good guess…" Lazarus sat for a minute, then continued, "but honestly, it doesn't feel like Benjamin. I know him and it doesn't feel like him."

Lazarus had a way of driving Reyne crazy sometimes. She knew that he did not like to get her hopes up, but he also tried to help her find and ground herself. "Ok. If it is the two men I named, then my choice was made when I signed the divorce papers. But if it isn't Benjamin, then I don't have another man in my life."

"Remember, nothing is ever final. You may have someone but not realize it. Everything can change at a moment's notice. Finality is a human creation, not a universal or spiritual reality." Lazarus emphasized these beliefs.

"Lazarus, eventually we will have to find your biological parents because you are definitely not a product of the people you call your parents. How did your parents deal with you?" Reyne joked with Lazarus.

"The best they could and don't change the subject, I need you to understand. I have seen a lot of problems and danger coming your way. You need to be serious about this." Lazarus retorted solemnly.

"Sorry. Lazarus, I always listen to what you say, and this seems too clear cut. However, I will think about it. If there is anything else you can think of, please let me know. It may better help me to understand." She sat for a moment and looked at Lazarus, "Do you think it could be the protector?"

"I honestly couldn't tell you. I don't know. I tell you what has been revealed to me," Lazarus sat back and stared at Reyne. "You have met your protector. You must keep him close; you will need him very soon." Again, Lazarus seemed to drift to another realm, but quickly returned without a word.

"What? Oh, the protector you told me about. Are you sure it isn't Andy?" Reyne hoped Lazarus' answer would change.

"Of that I am sure. I believe the other man you have just met is your protector," Lazarus answered.

"How do you know…oh nevermind. OK, but I don't know his name or anything, and he said he was only in town for a few days." She told Lazarus.

"Not everything is as it seems. And not everything is cut and dry as you think or expect it to be. Remember that," Lazarus said.

Tyler came into the kitchen with the dinner dishes. "He's fed and ready for a bath, Mom. Do you want me to give him a bath?"

"No, I can do it. You go spend time with Lazarus. Thanks for helping out." Reyne stood and took the dinner dishes from Reyne.

"No problem. I'll clean up the kitchen while you bathe him. I have to wait for Lazarus to eat anyway," Tyler said, taking the dinner dishes back from Reyne. She then walked to the sink and began rinsing the dishes and putting them into the dishwasher.

"Thanks again," Reyne said as she went to get Taylor. "Time for your bath, baby."

"But Momma, I don't wanna take a bath yet. I wanna play my video game," Taylor whined and rubbed his eyes.

"Nope. Bath time. We have to be up early tomorrow." She reminded him.

Taylor started stomping up the stairs, "I hate school, and I hate you having to work."

"I know I hate to work, too," Reyne replied honestly.

Taylor got his bath, while Reyne pulled out his pajamas and pulled down his blanket. He ran into his room, dripping and shivering. Reyne dried him quickly and helped him get dressed. She read him a story and tucked him into bed.

As she left his room, she realized that Leigh had not come to dinner and still had not arrived. Even late, she never missed chilling on Sunday evenings in all the years they had been friends. Reyne thought, *"I wonder where she is? I hope she is ok. Maybe I should call her."*

Reyne walked into her bedroom and sat on her bed. She turned to her nightstand and went to pick up the receiver of the phone when it rang. Startled, Reyne answered the phone. "Hello?"

"Hey Sweetie." Leigh's voice came through the receiver.

"Leigh! Where are you? I was getting worried about you." Reyne laid down on her bed while she waited to hear Leigh's story.

"I'm sorry. I should have called earlier. When I got home, I wasn't feeling so well. I thought I would lie down, take a nap and try to feel better. Well, I fell asleep and woke up 20 minutes ago. I figured you were busy with your nightly ritual with the Taylordude, so I waited to call. I think I'm catching a cold or something. I just wanted to let you know, so you didn't worry and to let you know I am going to bed again. I'll call you tomorrow, Ok?" Leigh sounded exhausted as she explained, but Reyne had been with Leigh most of the weekend. This obviously came on suddenly.

She shook her head and realized she was overthinking. "Ok. Take it easy and if you need anything, don't hesitate to call. I'll talk to you tomorrow. Bye." Reyne placed the receiver back on the cradle. As soon as she removed her hand, the phone rang again, startling Reyne again.

"Hello?" Reyne said to the caller irritably.

"Hello Reyne? Did I wake you up?"

"Oh. Hi Andy. No I was still up, but thanks for asking." Reyne tried to sound like she wanted to talk, but she was exhausted too.

"Well, I just called to see if we could meet for lunch this week? We could meet outside TGI Friday's on 22nd Street in Northeast." He asked.

Andy sounded so sweet on the phone. How could she resist? "I would love to. How about Tuesday at 1:30?"

"Perfect. I will see you then. Oh, do you like the theater?" he added this new question to the conversation.

"I love the theater, why?" Reyne asked wondering what he had planned.

"Just wondering. Gotta run. Bye." Andy hung up the phone abruptly.

Reyne lay on her bed, dumbfounded. He had hung up on her. Well not exactly. He did say he had to go, so she couldn't get mad at him. She wondered what he was planning. He was definitely going to be fun getting to know.

Reyne prepared for bed and crawled between the blankets. She heard the front door open and close as Lazarus left for the evening. Hearing him leave reminded her that he had told her about the two men that wanted to be part of her life. She laid in bed, thinking about Benjamin and Andy. She knew her history with Benjamin and didn't think she was up for that again. However, Andy showed potential. She would just have to wait and see where it led her. She would make her decision soon from what Lazarus said, but not tonight. Not like there was really any decision to make. She thought about Andy's phone call, then she thought about him. His tall, lean body, golden brown hair, and bright hazel eyes. As she thought about his image, it changed ever so slightly and the stranger from Chevy's replaced his. The man Lazarus claimed was her protector. *"How strange. I did not notice it before, they were so similar they could be siblings. I had not noticed before…how strange…"* Reyne thought to herself as drifted to sleep.

CHAPTER 9

Reyne's week started out the same as every other week, but on Tuesday, she walked the seven blocks to meet Andy at TGI Fridays.

Andy was waiting in front of the restaurant as she walked up the sidewalk. As soon as she saw him, she remembered her thoughts of Sunday night. She looked at Andy, and yes, he did look like the stranger, but there was a slight difference. Nothing physical and nothing she could put into words, but there is definitely a difference.

Andy grabbed her hand and pulled her close to him. He hugged and kissed her on her cheek. "Hello Beautiful."

"Hello Andy. Pushing the 'Beautiful' thing, aren't you?" Reyne hated being called 'pretty,' 'beautiful,' or anything like that. She had never mentioned it to Andy, so she let it slide with the snide remark, hoping he would get the hint.

"Maybe, but I knew your face would radiate a heavenly aura when I showed you what I got..." He stopped to tell the hostess, "Table for two."

They followed the young hostess to their table. Reyne did not know whether to be upset with Andy or not. She couldn't decide if he had insulted her. She let it go as they arrived at the table.

As soon as they sat down at the table, the waiter took their order and went to get their drinks. Service at this restaurant was quick and efficient and the food was always good. Reyne believed it was because of the location, surrounded by federal agencies, and law offices, all within walking distance. You could get in, eat, and be back at work on time.

Andy took Reyne's hands into his, "OK. Here is your surprise. I would like to take you out to dinner and the theater on Saturday night. I know it is short notice, but I figured you would like it. Well?" The waiter arrived at that moment and placed their drinks on the table.

Andy sat across from her, smiling, waiting for her answer. She hesitated a moment and decided she had better say something. "I want to know where we are going to eat, what we are going to see, and where we are going to see it. I could say great, sure and end up with McDonald's and a movie." Reyne smiled to soften her questions.

"Intelligence to go with the beauty...." The waiter arrived with their lunches and interrupted Andy long enough to refill their drinks and make sure they had everything. Once the waiter left Andy continue, "Your transportation will pick you up at 5:30pm and take you straight to Maximus. You will be promptly seated and served your requested dinner at 6:30pm. After dinner, the limousine will drive us to the Kennedy Center to see Phantom of the Opera. The Broadway cast is doing a US tour. After the theater, the choice is yours: drinks, home, or whatever you choose. How is that for an evening?" Andy's eyes twinkled as he smiled, waiting for her response.

"It sounds wonderful. I would love to accompany you to the theater. Let me get a sitter set and I will let you know..." Reyne started to say.

Andy cut her off, "Done. Leigh has been paid by me to watch your Taylor if he is home, your house, and even your fish if you want, just so you can have a wonderful time with no worries."

"You've thought of everything. I guess all that is left for me to do is say yes, I would love to accompany you to the theater." Reyne was thoroughly surprised. Here was a man that barely knew her and yet was going out of his way to please her. She must be dreaming. Leigh was right; he was wonderful.

"I will call you on Thursday to get directions to your house. Unfortunately, I have a 3pm meeting and have to run," Andy said as he motioned for the waiter to bring the check.

The waiter immediately brought the check over to the table and Andy paid for it. Reyne got up with Andy and prepared to leave. "No, please stay and finish your lunch. I will call you later. Thanks for saying yes" and he left smiling.

Reyne sat there, totally awestruck. No man had ever thanked her before for going out with him. No man had ever wanted to please her in the way Andy seemed to want to please her. She picked at her lunch in a daze for another few minutes before deciding she had better get back to work, too. She stood up and started toward the door. As she passed the bar, she had an urge to stop. She turned to look in the bar area, not knowing what she was looking for. Her eyes moved straight to a man, her stranger, her protector. He turned to look at her, smiled, and raised his glass to acknowledge her and turned away.

Reyne came out of the daze she was in, and started for the door again. She walked back to work, but had a hard time accomplishing anything for the rest of the afternoon. She thought about Andy and his surprise, but then the stranger would creep into her thoughts. She spent the rest of the day thinking about the two of them instead of working.

As she rode the redline Metro to the Shady Grove Metro Station, she had a strange realization. This whole time she had been thinking about two men, but the wrong two men. Now she realized the stranger was one of the men. She had known it before, but didn't believe it could be true. Now she was trying to decide how they fit Lazarus' prediction. Both seem interested in her. The only part that did not work was that neither one knew her better than she knew herself because only Benjamin fit that part. The stranger couldn't know more about her than anyone else, could he? Maybe he did since he was her protector. She decided she should talk to Lazarus and Leigh about this, preferably together. They should be able to help her figure this out, but not tonight. Tonight was Taylor movie night, and she couldn't allow herself to be distracted.

Reyne arrived home and found dinner had been made by Lazarus and Tyler. They had already picked up Taylor, too. Everyone sat down to eat before watching the movie that Taylor had picked for the evening. Reyne only half watched the movie. She did not even remember which movie they watched after she put Taylor to bed. It did not matter; Taylor would remind her in the morning. Once Taylor was in bed, Reyne put herself to bed, too. Her mind still wondering, thinking, and being as confused as it was earlier in the afternoon. Her mind was again on the mysterious stranger when she finally fell asleep.

CHAPTER 10

Reyne was a bundle of nerves by Friday evening. Benjamin called as Reyne walked in the door to say he wouldn't be able to take Taylor this weekend, hoping it wouldn't interfere with any plans she had made for the weekend. She told him it wasn't a problem because she loved spending time with Taylor and had wanted a weekend or two with him, anyway. Reyne looked around her while she spoke with Benjamin and realized that Tyler had made dinner again and was setting the table. She mouthed 'Hello' to Reyne as she came back into the kitchen for another dish. When she and Benjamin hung up, Reyne put her purse down and went to the door as Taylor ran in. "What are you doing home already?"

"Tyler and Lazarus picked me up early again today. Was that all right Momma?" Taylor asked, afraid he was getting his sister in trouble.

"Yes, it's all right." Reyne hesitated for a moment. She had to tell him his Dad called. She was afraid of how he was going to take it when she told him. "Sweetie, there is something I have to tell you. Your Daddy just called…"

"I know Momma. He can't pick me up this weekend. It's OK. I didn't really want to go over there anyway. It's boring. Is it Ok that I stay with you this weekend?" Taylor asked so innocently it made Reyne want to cry.

"I love you being here, big boy. You are always welcome to stay with me. However, I had made plans for Saturday night, but if you want, I will stay with you."

"Who's watching me? Where are you going? Who is taking you?" He asked like a little adult.

"Leigh will watch you if that's okay. I'm going to dinner at a fancy restaurant, and to the Kennedy Center to see a play. The man who is taking me is named Andy. I want you to meet him before we leave, and if you don't like him, I won't go," Reyne explained.

Taylor thought for a moment. He hesitated and began to answer slowly, thinking of the exact words and phrases he wanted to use. "Leigh will be fine as a sitter. You deserve to go to the fancy restaurant and get to play at the Kennedy Center. One day I would like to play there too. But you can go without me this time. I would like to meet Andy, and you can go whether I like him or not, but only this time if I don't like him. I will give you my final report when you get home."

Reyne stood there trying not to laugh in the face of her little man. "Of course, my dear. Since you are here tonight, let's have another movie night. What movie would you like to watch?"

"None," he stated. "I would like to play outside until dark and then play my video game since I don't have school tomorrow, if that is okay," He continued. He looked just like a little man. It was scary to think that he was still so young. Reyne agreed to his request, and he ran out the door.

Leigh was walking up the sidewalk to the house as Taylor went running out the door. "Hey Sweetie." Leigh gave Reyne a hug, "What's wrong?"

"Oh, Leigh. I am stressing out, that's all. I don't have anything to wear, I have to actually have you babysit tomorrow night, and I am scared out of my mind that I will embarrass myself at the restaurant or the theater. It's been way too long since I had to do fancy," Reyne rambled as she walked into the kitchen.

"Mom, why did you let Taylor go back outside? He has to eat. Dinner is ready." Tyler was going to make a strict mother one of these days, and Reyne was very glad that she wasn't one of Tyler's children.

"He's not going anywhere, so he can eat in a little while. Let him have fun with his friends right now," Reyne said with a giggle.

"Benjamin isn't taking him this weekend? When did you find this out?" Leigh sounded surprised and irritated.

"Just today, about 5 minutes ago. I had a feeling, but wasn't sure until then. I just got off the phone and had just finished telling Taylor when you arrived. I guess I will call Andy and tell him this weekend is off." Reyne did not want to impose on Leigh, even though Andy had been the one to hire her.

"Get real. The guy is treating you like you deserve. I told him I would babysit, and I will. Taylor and I will have a blast," Leigh stated emphatically. "I'm just irritated that Benjamin would wait until now to tell you. What an ass."

"Are you sure? I mean, about the babysitting?" Reyne asked.

"Positive. About Benjamin being an ass and babysitting. Plus, you seem to be a nervous wreck. We need to do something about that. Any wine in the house, or do I need to make run?" Leigh smiled and hoped Reyne would relax.

"No wine currently. I have to run out for a few minutes, I'll grab some," Lazarus said as he was heading for the door.

"Why in the hell do I bother?" Tyler started in a tirade. "I finally cook and take some responsibility and you all just blow me off. You don't sit down to eat; you just stand around talking or letting people leave. I give up." Tyler sulked off to the living room.

"Tyler, how long until everything is ready and on the table?" Reyne asked her sympathetically, understanding exactly how Tyler felt. She had been in that same position many times. It always hurt, no matter how many times people left her waiting.

"Twenty minutes, if that," Tyler pouted.

"Lazarus, you've got fifteen minutes; be back on time," Reyne snapped. "Oh yeah, grab Taylor to come back inside when you get back. Thanks."

Lazarus left and a few minutes later Taylor came in. He went straight into the bathroom and began to wash up for dinner, acting as if Lazarus warned him. Reyne looked at Leigh and they both started giggling. Obviously, Lazarus had the foresight to let Taylor know what was going on and what was expected. When Taylor left bathroom, he went to the living room to watch television until dinner was on the table.

"Your kids are crazy. I love being here. It's like a real family." Leigh giggled as she and Reyne walked into the dining room table and sat at the table awaiting dinner and Lazarus.

Lazarus arrived back right on time. Taylor placed the last bowl on the table and Tyler brought out the drinks that had been made. Lazarus went to the kitchen, opened the bottle of wine and then handed it to Reyne when he entered the dining room. They all gathered around the dining room table and thanked Tyler for cooking a great meal. Taylor gave the blessing to the Lord and Lady and they ate. After dinner, Taylor went to play his video game, and Tyler and Lazarus went out to see a movie. Leigh and Reyne cleaned up the dinner dishes and the kitchen.

Reyne remained nervous and fidgety until Leigh finally made her take a soak bath. Reyne protested at first, but after Leigh gave Taylor his bath and got him to bed, she cleaned the bathtub and refilled it for Reyne. She placed candles all over the bathroom and brought in the speaker for some soothing music. She pulled Reyne to the bathroom, undressed her, and helped her into the bathtub.

"Why are you so nervous? You've been out on plenty of dates" Leigh was beginning to worry about Reyne. This was so unlike her.

"I don't know. There are several reasons. First of all, Lazarus told me the other night that two men are interested in me. They both want to be with me. One knows me better than I know myself and the other wants to get to know me better. I figured it was Benjamin and Andy, but I'm not sure. Remember, I told you about the stranger I met at Chevy's that first time I went out with Andy? Well, every time I go out or meet up with Andy, the stranger is there. I'm kinda worried that he will show up at the Kennedy Center. If he does, I'm just really gonna freak. Of course, he doesn't fit Lazarus' premonition because the only male person that probably knows me better than I know myself is Benjamin. So the two have to be Benjamin and Andy. Then there is the fact that maybe it is Benjamin and the stranger. I don't know. Then I realized that the stranger and Andy are almost identical in every physical way. They are the same height, similar build, hair and eye color, everything. And yet, there is something different about them, so you don't notice the similarities right away. I don't know. Then Lazarus seems to think that the stranger is my protector. He told me that I would be meeting someone who would be my protector and I was to keep that person near me. I don't know what to think about anyone. I really want to talk to you and Lazarus together about this. Plus, I don't have anything to wear and I don't want to embarrass myself. I am scared to death that I will do something wrong and Andy will never speak to me again." Reyne stopped long enough to catch her breath and was on the verge to begin rambling again when Leigh broke in.

"Sweetie... Stop. You are driving yourself crazy. First things first. Lazarus' premonition about the two men has to mean Benjamin and Andy. You know that and you will know what choice to make when the time comes. Second, the stranger may be your protector, let him be wherever you are. I doubt he is a stalker. Lazarus would have told you about a stalker. Don't be so uptight and there is nothing really to talk about in terms of men now. Last. This date isn't going to make or break any relationship you could have with Andy. He is almost as scared as you are. He really likes you. Just relax. We will dress you and make sure you look beautiful before he gets here, and I have faith you won't embarrass yourself. OK?" Leigh said reassuringly.

The bath was having the perfect effect on Reyne. She seemed to have relaxed. "I know. I am just getting myself worked up, because I really like Andy, and I hope things work out for a change. I know you like Andy too."

"I hope you two work out if that is what you want. In fact, consider finally getting laid. Please! Maybe it will relieve some stress. Dating for you two will be much less formal and nerve-racking if you do."

Leigh made sense. Since Reyne was given the discretion of making all decisions tomorrow night, maybe she would make a move with Andy and see what happened. It had been a long time since she had been with a man, and he was gorgeous.

Reyne got out of the bath and went to her room. Leigh followed her after snuffing out the candles and straightening up the bathroom. Leigh found Reyne in bed and asleep when she entered the room. She got changed and curled up next to Reyne. Reyne moved into her to be closer, and Leigh let her, knowing that Reyne needed comfort tonight. Their legs automatically entwined and Leigh's arm went around Reyne's waist. It wasn't long before Leigh and Reyne were both in a deep sleep.

The next morning, they awoke to Tyler and Taylor arguing in the kitchen. Reyne got up and went downstairs to see what had happened.

"You need to eat breakfast Taylor, otherwise you'll get sick," Tyler scolded her younger brother.

"Tyler, leave me alone. I don't have to do anything on the weekends but play."

"Taylor, I think you should eat some cereal, at least," Reyne said to announce her arrival to the melee.

"Oh Momma!" Taylor spun around when he realized she was behind him. He knew he was being unreasonable with his sister and bowed his head, whispering, "Yes ma'am."

"Thank you Taylor. Thank you Tyler for making sure our little guy stays healthy. Where is Lazarus?" Reyne knew today was going to be hectic and did not want to lose control. By knowing where everyone was, she could at least keep some sanity in her own mind.

"He is still sleeping. He got back late but needs to get up. He is playing with Taylor this morning while you, Leigh, and I go shopping for your date tonight." Tyler smiled an evil grin at her mother.

"Both of you are bad. I hope you know it," Reyne giggled.

"Yeah and we hope you will be bad too," Tyler replied.

The rest of the day was spent with Leigh and Tyler primping Reyne for her date. They went out and bought her an appropriate outfit that was on sale and shoes to match. They came back to the house and the real girlie time began. Lazarus and Taylor tried to stay in the basement or outside. At one point, they had actually not moved out of an area fast enough and ended up with their finger and toenails painted different colors to help Reyne choose the one she wanted for the night. After that episode, they did not let their escape route become blocked again for the rest of the day.

At 5:15 pm, Reyne was ready. She paced her bedroom floor until she heard the doorbell ring, and Leigh answered the door. Reyne knew it was Andy for two reasons; one, she could hear Leigh coming up the stairs to get her, and two, she watched the limousine pull up outside.

Leigh came into the room, "It's time to go, Sweetie."

"All right." Reyne left the safety of her bedroom and went down the stairs, praying she wouldn't trip and fall down the stairs.

Andy was at the door at the bottom of the stairs. He was extremely handsome even though his mouth had flopped open as she came into his view. "You are gorgeous. And no, I'm not pushing the 'gorgeous' thing." He said and took her hand and helped her down the last step. "Are you ready?"

"Almost. But first you must meet the most important man in my life." As Reyne said this, Lazarus came around the corner. Andy took a step back. Reyne giggled, "This is Lazarus, Tyler's boyfriend."

"Nice to meet you." Lazarus stuck out his hand to Andy. Andy reciprocated and they shook hands, easing Andy's tension at the sight of Lazarus. Reyne and Leigh laughed, knowing that the hand-shake had given Lazarus more information than Andy realized.

Taylor came around the corner, "Momma you look beautiful, but don't you think you are dressed wrong to go play?"

"Well, I might be, but I am only going to watch others play. I am not going to participate, at least not this time. Taylor, this is Andy. Andy, this is the most important man in my life, Taylor."

Taylor stuck his hand out to shake hands with Andy. Andy took his little hand and shook it as Taylor expected. "It is very nice to meet you. You must be nice to my Momma, and don't leave her sitting on the side of the play area for very long without checking in. She gets upset if you don't keep in contact with her. But you're not really dressed to play either. Are you just going to sit and watch, too?"

Andy gave Taylor a quizzical look, and answered, "Yes sir, I will take good care of your Momma. I promise. I don't know if I'll play, but at least I have flat shoes so I can if I want too."

Taylor gestured to Reyne to bend down for a secret. "I think I like him Momma."

Reyne stood up. "Thank you, baby. Now don't stay up too late and listen to Leigh."

Reyne watched Leigh and Taylor wink at each other before re-plying in unison, "Yes ma'am, we'll be good."

"I'll watch them, Mom." Tyler poked her head out to check Andy out and couldn't resist letting them all know she would tattle if she were not included in the fun tonight.

"Well, let's go." Andy took Reyne's arm and walked her to the limousine and for a night, he hoped, would become very special for her.

CHAPTER 11

The limousine took the scenic route into DC. Reyne knew without looking exactly where she was. It was the same route she drove to work on the days she did not take the metro. When they arrived in front of the restaurant, the limousine driver opened the door for them. As Reyne and Andy prepared to go into Maximus, the limousine driver pulled Andy to the side, reminding him that he needed to give him at 15 minutes notice to get to the door when they were done dinner.

Andy nodded and turned back to Reyne. Once inside, they were shown to a table. The waiter gave them menus and took their drink orders. When he arrived with their drinks, they ordered their appetizers and main entrée. They talked about their daily lives, their likes and dislikes, everything they could think of just to get to know one another better. Their dinners arrived, and they ate and talked some more, enjoying each other's company.

"Thank you for bringing me here. You would think with me working so close to here that I would eat lunch here quite often, but I don't." Reyne said.

"I am the same way. I don't eat here too often either. I prefer Quizno's, or Holly's Cookie Shop, or even Ben's Chili Bowl," Andy replied.

"Isn't Ben's a bit out of the way from here?" Reyne had heard of Ben's Chili Bowl, but had never been there or eaten the food. "I hear it is really good."

"Yeah, it's a bit of a hike, but it's the best. I'll take you there one weekend. You have never had a chili cheese dog like a Ben's chili cheese dog, and their chili cheese fries and homemade shakes are the best around. You'll love it." Andy reached across the table,

"Reyne. I need to tell you that I really like you and I enjoy your company. I would like to see you on a more regular basis."

Reyne was speechless. They had only had two dates, and this made three if you counted the lunch he left early a date. How was he so sure that he wanted to see more of her. "How do you know that? You barely know me. We've only seen each other two times, three with tonight."

"Reyne, I knew the woman of my dreams would let me know who she was as soon as I met her. I have taken it slow for you because I know you have been hurt. I was ready to commit to you after I met you at Chevy's. I will still take it slow until you tell me otherwise, but I know you are my perfect woman." Andy did not smile until he was done speaking. He was sincere, and he had wanted her to know it. He put his heart on the table for her to either take or stomp on. He wasn't afraid or at least didn't appear to be.

"You are incredible. I don't know what to say." Reyne sat there staring at Andy.

"Don't say anything, let me enjoy your company and let things happen naturally. Please don't feel that you have to do anything, just let me get to know you better and don't close me out. We will move at your pace, but I wanted to get this out in the open." He was almost begging her.

Reyne wondered how many times he had said this to other women. She decided not to ask and just to let him get to know her better and let things come naturally.

"Well, shall we go?" Andy asked her once they were finished eating. She nodded, and he pulled her chair out from the table. He took her arm and walked her to the door. The limousine was right outside the door as she exited the restaurant. They held hands on the short ride to the Kennedy Center, but did not speak. They just enjoyed the time being together and holding hands. The simplicities of life.

The limousine took them to the front door of the Kennedy Center. The driver again opened their door. Andy got out first and proceeded to help Reyne out. They walked into the theater and found their seats with the help of an usher. The seats were wonderful; they were in the center a little under halfway back. The stage was in full view.

They had just made it to the theater and got comfortable in their seats when the lights dropped and the show began. They sat there watching, holding hands, not saying a word. Reyne realized that since he had laid his heart out to her, they had said very little. She decided that during the intermission she would try to pull him out of the shell he was creating around himself, or at least find out why he wasn't talking to her now.

As the curtain fell for intermission, Reyne stood up and asked if Andy would like to join her for a stretch and drink. He smiled in agreement and they found their way to the bar area.

"Wait right here, I will get you a drink and be right back." Andy placed her by a column and went to battle his way to the bar for their drinks.

"Well, hello again."

Reyne spun around to stare into the eyes of her stranger. "You shouldn't sneak up on people like that. It's rude," Reyne said curtly, but then changing her tone, "By the way, hello."

Onyx laughed, "I didn't mean to startle you, but I saw you were here and was intrigued. You do get around, don't you? I don't mean that in a bad way, it is just that you must be a well-rounded person, versed in many areas of life to enjoy a Mexican restaurant one day and the theater the next."

"I guess you could say I am well-rounded. I call it usually too poor to enjoy the theater and the more exquisite things of life that I tasted when I was younger. Plus, having children changes a person's restaurant choices. You tend to get used to the ones you can take your children to." Reyne was telling this stranger way more than she had meant to. She looked around the stranger to see where Andy was. Unfortunately, he was still making his way to the bar.

"I just wanted to say hello and give you this." He handed her an envelope. "Thanks for talking with me. Maybe I will see you again." He turned and walked away.

Reyne was about to call to him and ask him his name when Andy arrived by her side. She quickly put the envelope in her purse, deciding she would read it later.

"The strangest thing just happened. I swear someone was making it impossible for me to get to the bar for about 10 minutes, and then it just opened up. Like there was no one else around. It was so weird. Are you all right?"

Reyne looked off in the direction she saw her stranger go but did not see him. "Yeah, I'm all right. I just have to powder my nose. I would have gone while you were at the bar, but I didn't want to worry you if you returned and I wasn't here. I'll be right back." She grabbed her drink and headed off to the bathroom.

Once in the ladies' bathroom, she took the envelope out of her purse and opened it. She pulled out the card that was inside. The front said simply 'Onyx.' She opened the card to see if there is anything written inside.

Hello Reyne,

My name is Onyx. At least that is what everyone I know calls me and has called me for as long as I can remember. I am giving you this card because I hope you will find the time to read it and not just throw it away.

I am not a stalker nor am I a mental case. I am, however, madly in love with you and have been for a long time. I decided that it was finally time for me to reveal myself to you. Other times have not been right for many reasons.

I am currently staying in DC. Should you wish to talk with me or meet with me, my number is on the card in this note. Just call the number. I will answer.

Please call me. I would very much like to talk to you again.

Your Eternal Lover,
Onyx

Reyne slowly put the card back into the envelope and placed it in her purse. He was the second man professing his love for her tonight. She was so confused. Since the two were almost identical, she couldn't go by looks alone. She would have to go by other criteria, which meant she would have to meet with her stranger, Onyx, eventually, so that she could make her decision. Obviously, Lazarus was right. The two men in his premonition were not necessarily whom she had suspected. It had become obvious to Reyne that Benjamin played no part of this. It was Andy and the stranger…No, Onyx.

She left the bathroom and found Andy. They returned to their seats and got ready for the next part. Andy watched the rest of the play, but Reyne did not notice much of the second half. She spent the time thinking about the two men and what this could mean to her.

The curtain fell and Andy stood to leave. "Reyne, what's wrong? Did what I say bother you so much that you didn't enjoy this evening?"

"No! My god, no! I mean it caught me off guard. I have thought about it tonight, but I have also thoroughly enjoyed myself. I haven't had this much fun in long time. Come on, let's get out of here."

Reyne grabbed his arm and pulled him through the crowd. They ran out the front of the Kennedy Center, laughing. She held his hand as they waited for the limousine to arrive.

Once they were seated in the limousine, Andy asked, "So what now? Do you want me to return you home, or do you have other plans?" He was so innocent. He truly wanted her to have a wonderful evening.

"Let's just take a nighttime sightseeing drive of DC. At night, it is a beautiful city, at least certain areas." Reyne giggled. If he only knew what she had planned for him. She had almost forgotten about it until he had asked her what was wrong.

"Sounds great. A nighttime sightseeing tour of DC." Andy told the driver as Reyne figured out how to close the glass screen between them and lock it.

She leaned toward Andy and touched his lips softly with her own. He reacted and followed her lead. He caressed her hair while he kissed down her neck and found his way into her blouse. Reyne leaned back and allowed Andy to kiss down her belly with every button he unfastened. His tongue slid back up her chest, stopping at each nipple, until he finally made it to her neck. Reyne's hands had been busy as well. She had loosened his tie and unbuttoned his starched shirt. She had just about gotten his shirt off when he interrupted her plan.

"Reyne, I don't think we should do this tonight. I don't want you to feel that you have to do this to keep me around, or because of what I confessed to you earlier this evening. I want it to be perfect when it happens, and this doesn't feel perfect, at least not to me. Does it to you?"

"No, it doesn't feel perfect. It does feel good and natural, but I understand what you mean. I have never heard a man talk like that before, it is usually me saying no and being the romantic. But not when I'm with you. You are just so romantic, you bring the excitement out of me. I am sorry. I shouldn't have pushed it this evening."

Reyne lowered her head, almost embarrassed that she had made the first move. She felt pushy and sleazy now.

"Don't ever be sorry for being passionate. Promise me. I just want our first time and every time thereafter to be everything you deserve, and I feel you deserve better than the backseat of a car, even if that car is a limousine." Andy smiled and pulled Reyne's blouse closed as he put his arms around her. They rode on for a while, looking at the lights on the Potomac and the people walking through Georgetown.

Reyne had started nodding off when she heard Andy tell the driver to head for home through an intercom. She knew her date was over and she figured so was her chances with Andy.

"Reyne…Reyne…We are almost to your house. You need to wake up." Andy stroked her hair and face while waking her.

"Mmm…Okay. I am so sorry…" Reyne said groggily.

"Ssshhh. I want to see you again, Reyne. I want to know if you'd like me to make dinner for you and the kids tomorrow."

Reyne sat up with surprise, "Andy, you don't know what you are asking. It is never just the kids and me. It usually includes Leigh and Lazarus. But if you want to make dinner for six, no seven with you, I will accept your offer."

"All I need to know is the time you would like to eat." He pushed.

"We like to eat around 7 pm. Then we still have time to get ready for the morning." Reyne wondered if she should let him into the family this quickly. "*Why not?*" she thought, "*I was gonna screw the shit outta him. Might as well let him into the family. But what about Onyx? I'll think about that later. Right now, I need to focus on Andy.*" Reyne suddenly got a motherly look about her and asked, "Do you want me to tell you the likes and dislikes of the kids? They are pretty picky. Hell, Leigh is picky."

Andy laughed, "Nope. They will love what I prepare. I promise. All kids like this surprise." Andy gave her a wicked smile and a wink.

When they pulled up to Reyne's townhouse, Andy got out and helped Reyne out. He walked her to her door, gave her a respectful kiss good night and walked back to the waiting limousine. Reyne watched him as he walked away. She turned to go inside when she heard someone say something. She turned around and saw a young blonde woman sitting a few houses down. It was the new neighbor. "I'm sorry. Did you say something to me?" Reyne tried to sound polite.

"Yes I did. I'm sorry, I was just saying that it was a beautiful night, don't you think?" the blonde woman answered.

"It is a beautiful night." Reyne answered. She was somewhat uneasy about talking to a stranger in the middle of the night, even if the stranger was a neighbor.

"My name is Elizabeth. My husband, Xavier and I just moved in a few weeks ago and haven't had a chance to meet anyone yet. I am sorry if I startled you, but I saw you standing there and more or less thought I would say hi. So… Hi."

Reyne started laughing. She walked over to Elizabeth's porch. "Hi Elizabeth. I am Reyne. It is nice to meet you."

"Nice to meet you too." Elizabeth was a petite woman, but had a very large presence and was almost hypnotic to the point that you couldn't ignore or refuse her.

"Well, it's late and I have to get up in the morning with my son. I'm sure I'll see you around again sometime." Reyne started back to her house.

"I am sure you will. I hope we can be good friends," Elizabeth smiled coyly.

"Goodnight," Reyne called back as she reached her door, but the uneasy feeling was creeping back

Once inside, she dropped her things in the kitchen and made her way to check on her family. She found them in their respective rooms. After ensuring everyone's safety, she decided to have a glass of wine before heading to bed. She quickly and quietly went into the bedroom and changed into shorts and a T-shirt, went back downstairs and poured a glass of wine before heading to the sofa. She started thinking about the evening and the two men recently entering her life. *"So, maybe the two I have to choose between are Andy and Onyx. But which one knows more about me than I know about myself? I am going to have to talk to Onyx more. I have to see him. How can I make a decision if I don't know all my choices, right? Right. I'll call him on Monday and set up a time to meet him and talk to him. Yeah, that's…what…I'll…do…."* Reyne fell asleep on the sofa and dreamt of Onyx and Andy.

CHAPTER 12

Leigh woke Reyne up the next morning. "Sweetie, Sweetie. You're on the sofa. Why didn't you come to bed last night? Reyne, Sweetie, Wake up." Leigh gently shook Reyne, trying to get her to wake up.

"I'm sorry. I saw you sleeping and didn't want to disturb you. You were sleeping so soundly. I figured I would drink a glass of wine and then come up to bed. I must have fallen asleep here." Reyne yawned and stretched.

"OK. I thought you were mad or something," Leigh said worriedly.

"Never with you," Reyne smiled and sat up.

The rest of the day went smoothly and uneventfully. The kids coming and going, people calling, music blaring, and video games blinking. Reyne did laundry and ironed her clothes for the upcoming week. She also had Taylor pick his clothes out early in the day so that they wouldn't have to be rude to Andy when he came over tonight.

Andy arrived at 6:55pm with dinner, which consisted of five large pizzas, three orders of breadsticks, soda, juice, and two bottles of wine. They made a picnic in front of the TV in the basement and ate their dinner. Andy cleaned up the dinner dishes with Leigh, while Reyne put Taylor to bed. When she came back downstairs, Andy handed her a glass of wine, and the three of them went to the living room to relax.

"So, how did I do with dinner? Do you think I won the kids over?" Andy smiled at Reyne when he asked her this. He had said the previous night that he would make a dinner that everyone would like, and technically, he did. It was just that she didn't expect dinner to be an order from Papa John's, but the kids loved it. Reyne did not allow junk food too often, so this had been a treat for them.

"Yes, I think you won over the kids. As for how you did with dinner, I would have preferred a more balanced meal." Reyne chided.

"What do you mean, more balanced? Pizza is perfectly balanced, there are the grains with the crust, the fruits with the tomatoes, vegetables with toppings, and dairy with the cheese. How is that not balanced?" Andy said in a hurt little voice.

"Ok, you have me there, it's balanced, sort of. Either way, thanks for dinner, Andy. We all loved it." Reyne tried to sound like she was sorry for complaining about his dinner. He was just trying to be nice to her. The least she could do was appreciate it.

"I hate to break up this party, but I've got to get home and get ready for work tomorrow. So I am going to put my glass in the sink and say good-bye." Leigh stood up and went to the kitchen.

"Yeah, I'd better go too. Can I call you later this week?" Andy stood with Reyne and took her hands into his.

"I would like that." Reyne tried to make it seem that she wanted to talk to him, but didn't want to seem too enthusiastic about it. Of course, after last night, it would be stupid to play hard to get now. Reyne giggled and thought, "Oh, what the hell." She giggled a little more than jokingly pleaded, "Please call. Please, please call. I love your company and would love to see you again. I figured I should be honest with you since you were so honest with me last night."

"All right then, I will," Andy said, laughing with her. He walked into the kitchen to put his glass in the sink.

Leigh was coming down the stairs with her bags in hand. "I had to get my stuff. I'll talk to you tomorrow, Reyne. Thanks for dinner, Andy. Bye."

"Wait up, I'll walk you out. I'm getting ready to leave too," Andy said to Leigh as she opened the front door.

"OK, I'll be right outside."

"Reyne, thanks for the wonderful evening." He said before kissing her goodnight. Andy's kiss was so gentle and yet burned with so much passion that it aroused Reyne.

"Good night Andy." Reyne kissed him back, hoping her kiss made him feel the way he had made her feel. He walked out and Reyne shut the door behind him.

She was alone now and could finally think about things. She could decide if she was going to see Onyx, and if she did see him, what she would say to him. She poured herself another glass of wine, walked out onto her deck, sat in a chair and lit a cigarette.

She sat there for quite a while thinking, when she heard the sliding glass door open behind her, "Now who could that be?" She waited for a moment for someone to say something.

"Mom, I thought you could use another glass of wine," Lazarus said as he placed the bottle on the table.

"Do you like to sneak up on people? You really freaked me out this time," Reyne scolded him.

"Sorry. You were just so deep in thought; I didn't want to bother you. I was just going to fill up your glass and leave the bottle," he explained.

"Thanks, I just have a lot on my mind, mainly the things you put on my mind," she said, smiling.

"Your two men? You must give each a chance to make an educated choice. You can't go by comfort level. You must know each road well before you chose," he reminded her.

"I figured it wasn't going to be easy. I am going to meet Onyx and have lunch with him. At lunch, I am going to tell him that I am seeing Andy and that I am honored, but the feelings cannot be reciprocated," Reyne stated.

"Who's Onyx?" Lazarus looked at her as if she was speaking a foreign language.

"Onyx…Oh, I haven't told you or anyone except Leigh, for that matter. I ran into him at the theater the other night. He gave me a card with his name and all necessary contact information. He is the stranger I met at Chevy's. He is my protector," Reyne started rambling.

"If this is your protector and your second man, do you really think you should blow him off?" Lazarus asked pointedly.

"What else can I do? I really like Andy." Tears welled up in Reyne's eyes. She was so confused.

"Get to know Onyx, before you tell him no. You will need him very soon. The danger I sensed is closer than I realized. I don't mean to scare you, but I am not strong enough to protect you and the family from this danger; none of us are. Most other dangers, no problem. Only your protector can handle this danger," Lazarus said firmly to make sure that Reyne understood the gravity of the situation.

"Okay. I will call him and meet him on Friday to have lunch and spend the afternoon with him. Get to know him. Then I will make my decision," she agreed.

"Mom, you will have to make the decision soon, but not just yet. Just let things follow a natural course. Promise me," Lazarus tried to emphasize that she should take things slow.

"I promise. However, I will still stick with my Friday plan. Okay?"

"OK. Go to bed now. You have to get up in a few hours," Lazarus ordered her in his way.

Reyne smiled, "Okay, Okay." Reyne got up and went into the house with Lazarus. She straightened up the kitchen and went to bed, knowing that tomorrow she would be nervous, but Lazarus was right, she had to know Onyx better. She had to do this, more so now, because she had promised Lazarus. She climbed into bed and fell asleep almost instantly.

CHAPTER 13

Reyne thought of her two men all morning on the way to work. She made her agenda for the day before she ever arrived at the Metro Station to begin her morning commute into D.C. The ride gave her plenty of time to think about things. She knew she couldn't and shouldn't make a decision between her two men without knowing both of them, but she continued to think of how Andy made her feel and what she thought of him. She knew she had to find out how Onyx made her feel and what she thought of him once she knew him.

Andy was stable, sweet, made her smile, and cared about her feelings. Onyx made the passion in her flow without even a spoken word, and that scared her since she didn't even know him. She hadn't even realized what scared her about him until this ride. He was too much, too passionate, too sexy. Everything she had never before attracted in her life. He was one of those people that would never have talked to her, but she would have adored from afar. The same as it was in high school and college. Why would he be interested in her? Maybe Leigh was right and all he wanted was sex. She would find out when she called him.

The train arrived at her stop. She got off the train and headed to work. As she walked down the street, she heard someone call her name. It wasn't a voice she recognized, and it wasn't very loud. It almost sounded like it came from within her head. She stopped and looked around, recognizing people, but none that matched the voice she had heard. She stood there for a moment then turned to start on her way again, when she heard her name called again, she thought, *"I'm going crazy. No one is calling me. What is going on? I just have to make it to work."*

Reyne began rushing down the street, eyes down and ignoring everyone and everything. She turned onto Pennsylvania Avenue headed towards 18th Street. She was passing Starbucks when a sudden urge made her go into the small café. She walked up to the counter and ordered a venti white mocha latte, paid, and took her coffee to drink as she finished her walk to her building. She turned to walk out the door and there he stood. Onyx. As she stared at him, it seemed as if everything around her vanished and the world consisted only of the two of them.

"Hello Reyne."

"Hello Onyx."

"You wanted to talk to me?" He smiled at her.

"How did you know? I haven't told anyone except Lazarus," Reyne frowned.

"I know a lot of things. Would you like to spend the day with me and talk?"

"I can't today. I haven't asked off from work. How about Friday? I will meet you at …." Reyne was going to finish but Onyx interrupted her and began to lead the conversation.

"I will be waiting for you in front of your building. We will go to lunch and talk."

"Yes. That sounds fine," she answered.

Onyx walked over to her and took her arm. He walked her through the door and down the street to her office building. "This is it. What time should I meet you on Friday?"

Reyne just stared at Onyx, "11:30 am."

"11:30 am it is." He smiled, "Have a good day Reyne."

"You too, Onyx. See you Friday."

She watched Onyx walk down the street to a waiting limousine and climb into the back of it. "Oh, wow. That was so weird. I have to tell Leigh." She ran into the building and up to her office.

She sat down at her desk, pulled out a leave request form, and filled it out for Friday afternoon. She wanted plenty of time to talk with Onyx, and time to maybe tell him to leave her alone, but she also knew she had to give him a chance first. She had promised Lazarus, but Onyx scared her so much. After she turned in her leave request, she called Leigh and pretended to work.

"Leigh Stein," came through the receiver.

Reyne immediately started rambling about the morning. "Hey Leigh, it's Reyne. You'll never guess what happened this morning on the way to work. I saw him again. He like called to me and I found him."

"What are you talking about, Reyne? Calm down and tell me." Leigh said.

"OK. I was thinking about Andy and Onyx. I thought about them all evening after you and Andy left and all morning on the ride to work. I was walking down to work when I heard someone call my name. I didn't recognize the voice, but I looked around. I saw people I knew, but the voice didn't fit any of them. Well, I started to walk again, and I heard my name again. It scared me. I focused on the ground and made my way all the way to Pennsylvania, when I got an urge for a white mocha latte, so I went into Starbucks, which in and of itself isn't really unusual as you know, and I ordered and got my coffee. When I turned around, there he was, standing in front of me. He walked me to work and asked me to have lunch on Friday. I told him yes." Reyne stopped and took a breath.

"Who asked you?" Leigh asked abruptly.

"Onyx." Reyne replied as if anyone else would have asked her.

"You did what? Why did you tell him yes?" Leigh asked, startled at Reyne's outburst.

"I need to tell him to stop bothering me and maybe sleep with him. He makes me hot with just a look. I don't understand this. It's scaring the crap out of me. I don't ever remember reacting like this with a man." Reyne sighed.

"OK. Well, just tell him to go away and leave it at that, Promise me." Leigh demanded.

"I can't. Not with him. I would love to promise, but I can't. Plus, I already promised Lazarus I'd give a chance and at least talk to him. This is something I have to do. I don't even know why I have to do it, but I do. Please understand. I'll call you on Friday, if not before." Reyne started to hang up.

"At least tell me where you are going to be, so if anything happens, we can find you."

"I don't know where I will be. Please trust me. I love you Leigh."

"I love you too, and I trust you. Just be careful."

"Always. Bye." Reyne hung up the phone, this time without waiting for Leigh to answer. Reyne knew she had withheld information from Leigh, but for some reason, she only felt comfortable talking to Lazarus about Onyx. She realized now that she should have called him not Leigh. Now, she plunged into work and hoped that the fear and anticipation would go away soon, otherwise she would never get her work completed.

By the end of the day, her leave was approved and the fear and anticipation had dissipated considerably. She packed up her things and began walking back to her Metro stop. The entire walk she hoped that he would find her again and yet she also feared that he would. However, the walk and ride home were uneventful. In fact, the rest of the week was fairly boring and mundane. She talked to Leigh once more and to Andy once, turning down dinner on Friday. She had lied to him, but she wanted to take care of this without anyone's input into her thought process. When she awoke on Friday, she realized the fear and anticipation were back, worse than they had been on Monday. As she was getting ready for work she kept thinking, "*How is this possible? Maybe it is because today is the day I meet with him. Yes, that's it.*" She got Taylor off to school and slowly prepared for her trip to work. She took the bus to the Shady Grove Metro Station because she was too nervous to drive. She rode in silence on the bus and she did not even open the book she was currently reading on the train. All she could do was sit, look out the window, and think about him. When she reached her stop, she again hoped he would meet up with her this morning. Today she would call in and tell them just to increase her request for the entire day. However, he did not materialize. She walked alone to her building and went up to her desk. She had not brought her briefcase today, so she just took care of little projects all morning.

At 11:15 am, she went to the bathroom to check herself. As she stood in front of the mirror, she saw a pretty woman, but definitely not beautiful. She fixed her makeup and straightened her clothes. She returned to her desk, popped her head into her boss' office, said good-bye and left for her date. She had chosen the perfect outfit to wear on a sunny, hot Friday afternoon in D.C., blue jeans, a white T-shirt with ¾ length sleeves, and the cutest pair of tan flats. She felt pretty. She walked out of the building and into the bright sunlit late morning. At first, she did not see him, but suddenly he was right beside her. It startled her and she squealed, before she realized it was him.

"You scared me. That isn't very nice." She scolded and then realized he had really done nothing wrong, it was more her own fears that made her jumpy. "I'm sorry. It's not your fault. I've been jumpy today. I guess I am a little nervous." She confessed before she could stop herself. She scolded herself as soon as the words left her mouth, "This isn't going well. You have a way of making me say things that I don't want to say out loud."

"I'm sorry. I'll block that for now." Onyx stated this so matter-of-a-fact that it seemed as normal as any conversation she would have with Lazarus.

"OK. You read minds. Any other tricks I should know about?" She was a little worried now but smiled at him to calm her own nerves and to make him think she wasn't frightened of him.

"Many. You will discover them all in time. I promise," He answered as if everything about him were mundane and normal.

"And what if I didn't want to spend time with you after today?" Reyne flirted as she said this. Onyx was gorgeous. He was tall and lean. His pants fit his hips snuggly and his shirt flowed with the breeze. She was getting excited and scared all in the same moment.

"You do, but even if you didn't, then you'd never know." He said this as either answer would have been acceptable.

Reyne started wondering whether he was just after her for sex of if there was more to it. She knew he was her protector, but was there anything more to it?

"Yes, I am your protector, and yes there is more to it. However, you will have to be patient and learn it all before you make your decision. Where would you like to eat lunch?" he answered her internal questioning of his motives.

"I guess Friday's would be great or Charlie Chang's. Which would you prefer?" Reyne replied.

"Charlie Chang's. I haven't eaten there in a long time. Please lead the way." Onyx took her elbow, and they began the walk to Charlie Chang's restaurant. Once there, they asked to sit away from others so they could talk in private.

They sat in silence until their food arrived. Reyne could stand it no longer. "OK. We are here to talk. I want to know what the deal is."

Onyx smiled. "The deal? What do you mean? I saw you at Chevy's and found you extremely attractive. I want to get to know you." He answered.

Reyne squinted her eyes, "Then why did you agree that you were my protector?"

"Because there are people close to you that would like to harm you. I am sure you know that there is danger around. If you didn't feel it, I am sure that your daughter's boyfriend has told you." He replied without really answering her question.

"How do you know about Lazarus?" Reyne stopped eating. She was getting worried about this man. He knew things that he shouldn't know yet. Then the thought ran through her mind *"One knows you better than you know yourself."* Onyx knew her better than she knew herself, but how?

"So that is his name. I didn't know the name; actually, I had never worried with it. He has strong feelings and can feel things others cannot. Just as you do, but you bottle yours up, because they frighten you. Is this not true?" Onyx smiled at Reyne.

"How do you know this?" Reyne was getting mad. This wasn't what she envisioned about their meeting.

"You already figured out my 'trick.' I read your mind." Onyx tried to use this as his answer for now.

"Let's start over. What danger are you going to protect me from if I let you stay near me?" Reyne asked directly.

"You have no choice. I am destined to be your protector. Whether you want me in your life, I will be there, because I have sworn to protect you from certain forces. If you like, I will never actually bother you again, but I will watch out for you from afar. But do not think for a moment that I will not protect you," Onyx admitted.

"OK, so I'm to be protected by you. Why are you so interested in me? And did you know I was the one you were to protect when you saw me at Chevy's," Reyne had to have the answers and she had to have them now. She was tired of his beating around the bush.

"I am interested in you because I find you beautiful. You are more than just a person to protect. There is a history here, but it is more detailed than you have time for in one afternoon. Let's get off this subject. Please let's get to know one another as any other two people would. Just spend time with me and get to know me as I get to know you. That is all I ask. If at the end of the day, you no longer want to see me, I will vanish from your sight, but I will forever protect you," Onyx said this with a conviction she had never heard before.

"You are right. Let's get to know each other first and then you can explain the rest to me. I have to admit, you have turned my life upside down. I don't know what is wrong with me. You scare me and excite me all at once." She admitted to him, knowing that she wanted him to know how he affected her.

"It is because I am unknown. Once you get to know me, I will no longer scare you. In fact, knowing me may alleviate any fears you have. Please, let's get out of here, walk the streets and talk."

"OK." It was all she could say. They had finished their food, and nothing was keeping them inside any longer.

They proceeded to walk the streets of northeast D.C. for the remainder of the afternoon. They talked and laughed and talked some more. Reyne realized this man was wonderful. He was everything she had wanted, minus one white stallion.

As they were making their way up Pennsylvania Avenue, Reyne looked at her watch. "Oh my god. It's 5:48. I have to go. I'm gonna be late picking up my son from day care," Reyne was getting frantic. She had never forgotten time as she had today, especially when it affected her children.

With a wave of his hand, a limousine pulled up beside Reyne and Onyx. The driver got out and opened the door for them. "Come, let me take you to the day care center. It is my fault you are late. I will happily take you there." Onyx reached out his hand for her.

"All right. I've got to get there and fast, so this would be the fastest way." She took his hand and let him help her into the back of the limousine.

He climbed in behind her. "Call your son's day care and tell them you are in traffic and will be there as soon as possible."

She took out her phone and made the call. She felt horrible for being late. How could she explain this to Taylor? She had never done this before.

"He will understand. He worries for you. He knows more than you realize." Onyx said without moving his gaze from out the window. "Tell the driver where your son is at, he will get us there."

Reyne leaned up to give the driver directions to the day care center. He nodded and told her he knew the area. She began to feel a little better and leaned back to relax. While leaning toward the front seat, she saw a pile of files and papers on the seat across from her. She knew she shouldn't look, but she couldn't resist. She had to see what they were.

Onyx's gaze came back to the limousine. When he realized where she was looking, he pushed the files away and put a briefcase on top of them. He stared at her. She blanked her mind, afraid he was trying to read her mind. "They are none of your concern." Onyx stated it plainly, boldly, and left it.

Reyne sat back and closed her eyes. "I'm sorry. I guess I'm just naturally nosy."

"There is nothing to be sorry about. They are my attorney's files, not mine. Therefore, I feel that I have to keep his confidentiality for him. I'm not upset." Onyx took her hand in his and squeezed it very gently. The ride allowed them more time to talk about things and get to know one another better.

Reyne smiled. She realized that they were turning into the day care center parking lot. "I can walk home from here after I go in and get him."

"What are you talking about? You think I would let him miss a ride in a real Limousine? Go get him and come back." Onyx said.

The driver had already gotten out and opened the door for her. She took his hand and got out of the limousine. She ran in quickly to get Taylor and was back out in less than five minutes, leading him to the limousine. He climbed in followed by Reyne and seated himself between the two adults.

"Hello Taylor. I am Onyx. I am a friend of your mother. It is my fault she is late and I wanted to apologize to you personally. Please do not be mad at her." Onyx told Taylor.

"I am not mad at her. I was worried about her. You are my mother's friend and protector. Keep her safe for me please." Taylor said as if he already knew Onyx.

Reyne was astonished with the conversation the two were having. How did Taylor know he was her protector? The conversation stopped and both of them stared at Reyne.

"He is an old soul, Reyne. He is older than you or I. He has abilities he doesn't even know of yet. He will learn them if you stop babying him so much. He will be a great ally in your future. Let him grow." Onyx said.

"Yes Momma, let me grow. Please." Taylor said to his mother with more understanding then Reyne could believe.

Reyne realized her mouth had fallen open and she closed it, swallowed, and then answered, "I will. I promise."

Without realizing it, the limousine had pulled up to the front of her house. She did not remember giving the driver directions, but she must have. They exited the limousine, and Taylor ran into the house to drop his things off and ran back outside. "Momma, can I go play?"

"Yes, but you know the rules. Stay nearby because Daddy will be here soon," Reyne yelled as Taylor took off.

"Okay Momma." Taylor ran off to play with the kids in the other houses in the row.

Reyne turned to Onyx. "Do you want to come in for a while? We could continue to talk."

"No, thank you. I have to be going. I have an appointment within the hour and have to prepare. I thank you for spending the afternoon with me." Onyx bowed to her.

"It was my pleasure. Can I see you again? I would really like it." Reyne asked so shyly that it made Onyx feel for her. Others had obviously hurt her, and this simple question was almost too hard for her to ask. He knew her history and vowed never to hurt her.

"I await your call. When you are ready, I will know." He climbed back into the limousine and then she watched it drive away.

CHAPTER 14

Reyne walked into the house and dropped her purse on the table. "You know he loves you, Mom."

Reyne screamed and turned all at once. There stood Lazarus. "Seriously Lazarus, you have got to stop scaring me like that. And what do you mean...He loves me?"

"He is the one who knows you better than you know yourself. Andy is the one who wants to get to know you better. Just wanted to let you know as promised," Lazarus explained. "Also, sorry to have scared you. Oh, I ordered subs for tonight. They should be here in about 45 minutes."

"Thank you for telling me, but I figured that out this afternoon. And thanks for ordering subs," Reyne said with a sigh. "Sometimes you really don't know more than you're saying, do you?"

"Let's go sit outside and enjoy the day." Lazarus knew that what he told her was upsetting, and he wanted to be here for her for a while.

"Okay, but let me call Leigh and let her know I'm home. She was worried about me." Reyne walked into the kitchen and picked up the phone.

"Hello?" Leigh answered the phone.

"Hello Leigh, it's Reyne."

"Where are you?" Leigh asked urgently.

"I'm at home and I'm safe," Reyne said curtly.

"Good. Let me call you back. I have company right now. OK?"

"Not a problem, go have fun." Reyne hung up the phone and went out to enjoy the evening with Lazarus.

Reyne sat on her front porch with Lazarus, watching the kids play in the grassy area by the house. As it grew dark, Benjamin arrived and picked up Taylor. He promised to have Taylor home by six on Sunday night.

After they were gone, Elizabeth came out of her house with a man. Reyne decided to make them feel welcomed in the neighborhood. "Hi Elizabeth. How are you this evening?"

Elizabeth looked startled at first, but realized that it was Reyne and smiled, "We're fine. Come down here, I want you to meet Xavier." Elizabeth turned to Xavier and whispered something to him.

Reyne got up and walked down to their townhouse. "Hi, I'm Reyne." She extended her hand to Xavier.

"Nice to meet you." He said, shaking her hand. "Elizabeth mentioned she had spoken with one of the neighbors, and now I finally get to meet you." He had a slight accent that Reyne couldn't place.

"Well, I just saw you out here and thought I would say hi," using Elizabeth's wording. "I didn't mean to interrupt. It was nice seeing you again Elizabeth and meeting you Xavier. Hopefully, we can talk again another time." Reyne turned to walk away.

"We are going to watch movies tonight if you want to come back over when we return from the store. He's getting movie snacks. You could watch them with us." Elizabeth offered.

"I don't want to intrude on your evening together, but thanks." Reyne walked back to her own porch. Lazarus had gone back inside with Tyler, but she decided to sit on the steps just a little longer.

She looked down at Elizabeth and Xavier's house. She could see them talking on their porch. Xavier turned to walk down the steps and go to their car. Elizabeth followed, but instead of going to the car, walked up to Reyne's porch.

"Do you mind if I sit here with you while he goes to get the snacks." Elizabeth asked as she arrived at Reyne's porch.

"I don't mind at all. Have a seat." Reyne scooted over on the steps to make room for Elizabeth. "I thought you were going with him?"

"He thought it would be good for me to make some friends. I don't always get to make friends. We move often with his work, so the fact that I have someone in the neighborhood I am speaking to is exciting for him. He hates that I never get to make friends," She explained.

"He is right; everyone needs friends. So what does he do that causes you to travel?" Reyne asked as Elizabeth sat down.

"He is an investor. He goes to different areas to see if there is anything worthwhile to invest in. He used to travel and leave me at home while doing his research, but we didn't get much time together and it was hurting our marriage, so now we spend about one year in a location and then move again. It makes for great but sometimes lonely adventures." Elizabeth seemed so sad behind her happy front.

Reyne realized this woman gave up her life for her husband to have his. "Well, hopefully, we will be friends, even after you leave this area. The world is getting smaller all the time." Reyne wanted her to feel that she was accepted and in the company of a friend. She wanted to alleviate any sadness Elizabeth may harbor for her choice. "I have a great idea. Why don't you two come to my house on Labor Day? I am going to have a barbeque. You can meet some other neighbors and friends of mine. Do you think that Xavier would like that?"

"We both would love it. Thanks so much. Well, it looks like Xavier's home. I had better go home now. I will let him know that we will be spending Labor Day at your house. I'm sure we will talk before then. Thanks again. Talk to you later." Elizabeth jogged down to her own house. Xavier met her at the porch as she arrived, kissed her, and they went inside.

It was completely dark now, so Reyne went into the house and found it cold and completely empty. Taylor was with his father and Lazarus had gone to his parents for the weekend with Tyler and left out the back door. She decided this would be the perfect time to call Onyx and invite him to dinner tomorrow night.

She found the card he had given her and was about to go to the phone to call him when the phone rang. "I told you I would know when you called me." It was Onyx.

"How did you get my…never mind I know. So do you want to?" she asked.

"Do I want to what?" Onyx asked sincerely.

"I figured you already knew why I was calling you." Reyne said.

Onyx gave a soft laugh, "Dinner, right? Of course, I will pick you up at 6:00 pm tomorrow night."

CHAPTER 15

Elizabeth entered the living room. The intensity in the air let her know Xavier was wound tight with anxiety. She slowly made her way over to her love, she reached out to touch him and let him know she was there for him.

He turned around and almost threw her across the room. "How dare you interrupt me? I'm trying to figure out a way to use that mortal to capture Onyx. She is his downfall and I want us to use her to that end."

Elizabeth pulled herself up from the floor and set the chair that had been knocked over back up. "Yes, my dear. I will help you. I wanted to let you know, she has invited us over for a barbecue on Labor Day. Your idea of moving into her neighborhood was pure genius." Elizabeth turned from Xavier. She stopped speaking and waited for the response and repercussions of her accepting the invitation.

Xavier turned her back around and she flinched as he pulled her into a hug, "You, my dear, are a genius. You have gotten us into her life. Of course, we will go to the barbecue."

"You…you're not…mad?" Elizabeth asked surprised.

"Of course not, my love. We know that she has met with Onyx on several occasions. Maybe he will be at the barbecue and at that point, we have him. He will not leave her, and he will not let us hurt her. He will come with us and we will destroy him. The lover he has followed throughout time will watch his demise." Xavier's eyes clouded with anticipation of the act.

"Why would she watch the demise? We will not need her after we get Onyx." Elizabeth asked.

"Elizabeth…she will have seen too much to return to normal life. Let's keep her. You can play with her for a while. When we tire of her, we kill her. I know you like having your playmates, or have you given up your obsessions with females?" Xavier gave her a little hug and a coy grin.

"You're right. She is pretty and would make a good playmate. All right, we will bring her to watch the torture and death of her lover and then we will play," she smiled and clapped her hands.

They both began singing and dancing around as children do when they are given everything they want. They had conspired not only to destroy Onyx, but now also to destroy his one obsession, Reyne.

CHAPTER 16

Saturday night at 6:00 pm, Onyx arrived at Reyne's door. The doorbell rang and Reyne went to answer it. "Hello M'lady. Your carriage awaits…"

The phone started ringing. "I'm sorry. Come on in. I have to answer it in case it about my son."

Reyne walks into the kitchen, followed by Onyx. "Hello?" Reyne answered the phone.

"Hey Reyne. How about you and I go out tonight for pizza and a movie?" It was Andy.

Reyne took a deep breath and slowly let it out. "Thank you Andy, but I can't tonight. I have made other plans."

"Oh, I figured you would like to go out, but Okay. Well, what have you been up to lately? I haven't spoken to you for days." Andy tried to pull her into a conversation.

"Andy, I am getting ready to walk out the door. I'll call you tomorrow. Bye." Reyne hung up. She hoped she did not hurt his feelings, but her Onyx was waiting for her. "Okay, let's go. I am starving, and we have a bit of a drive ahead of us."

They walked out to his limousine. He helped her into the back and climbed in behind her. She gave the directions to the driver and then sat back to enjoy the ride with Onyx. "We are going to this little place. It is actually a sushi bar, but they have a great space in the upstairs that we can sit in and not be bothered, unless you want to eat in the regular eating area."

"I'll call and reserve it. What is the restaurant's name?" Onyx asked.

Reyne gave him the name of the restaurant, and Onyx called and reserved the loft for the two of them. The person answering the phone was a little surprised there were only two in the party, but went ahead and reserved it for them.

Onyx poured both of them a glass of white wine and handed it to her. They sat beside one another in silence, drinking their wine and holding hands. It seemed enough for the moment just to be together. Reyne realized she had never felt like this before. This was a totally new, foreign, and scary experience for her. She had never felt this much, even with Andy. She did not like losing control of her emotions, but every time Onyx was near, her senses increased and she became more passionate, without anything more than the touch of his hand against hers. They arrived at the restaurant thirty-four minutes later and were taken up the stairs to the loft. As they sat on the floor by the table in traditional Japanese fashion and began reading the menu, Reyne couldn't help but wonder about the past they shared, at least that is what Onyx had told her earlier. This urge to know was distracting her. She had never been one to pry, but now she was becoming obsessed with knowing all about this man and her part in his life.

The waiter came and took their order. Reyne decided this was the perfect time to ask him about their past. "Onyx, I have to know. You said we have a past. Please tell me."

"This isn't the right time to explain it all. I have known my whole life that I was to be your protector. I have always seen you in my dreams and been told by my family that the dreams were telling me to protect you. I didn't even know your name until I met you a Chevy's, but I knew by your eyes that you are the one I am sworn to protect."

"This sounds too pretend, too fairy tale to be real. So, I am just supposed to let you into my life to protect me. What if I was involved with someone else? Would you still be here?" She sounded sarcastic even to herself, but she couldn't help it. Her feelings were so intensified when she was with him it was like having major PMS with the big mood swings. She was unable to stop herself from blurting things out that she did not mean and in tones that were not what she was going for. "I am sorry if I sounded terse or sarcastic. I didn't mean it. I am just trying to understand."

"It's all right. I have that effect on people sometimes. Let's just say that you only need me if you are unattached. If you were married, there would be no danger, but now that you are single, there is danger closer than you think. I'm here to ensure that you are not harmed by this evil," he explained.

"So, is my life in danger, or how exactly am I in danger?" She asked. She had to know to prepare things in case her life was in danger. "Maybe I should tell the police, too?"

"You definitely don't want to tell the police. That would be unwise for you and your children. Your life is in danger, but that does not necessarily mean death. It could just be an evil that haunts you during your lifetime to drive you insane, which would be worse than death. However, it could also push you to kill yourself, or cause you a slow, painful death. It is hard to tell until I know the next move of the evil. I am sure it will make a move very soon."

Their food arrived, but Reyne was no longer hungry. "Onyx, please be straightforward with me. I need to know everything, just in case."

"Nothing will happen to you as long as I'm near you. I'm near you even when you don't see me. During the time when danger could strike, I'm just a moment from you. I keep myself hidden from you as much as from the danger. If they don't sense me, they won't know what is coming. If I am not there, I have others ready to protect you. You are never alone."

"You said 'they'? Is it more than one person?" Reyne asked quizzically.

Onyx sighed, knowing he was going to have to tell her some things he was not ready to explain. He took her hands and looked straight at her. "It is not a person or more than one person. Actually, the danger is not from anything human. They are entities that lean toward evil. No more talk about this. I want to enjoy my dinner with you and the time we share together, and not worry about those things right now. Just be with me." He almost begged her.

She agreed to drop the subject and throughout the rest of the dinner; they chatted and talked about their dreams and goals. Reyne told Onyx about her past trouble with men and how that affected her relationships now. Onyx told her that it had been a very long time since his one true love had died and he knew it was time to move on.

As they rode back to Reyne's house, Onyx played a CD that was a type of music Reyne had never heard before. It wasn't Classical, Country, Hip Hop, Rap or Rock. "I like the music. May I ask what type it is? I've never heard it before."

Onyx smiled and stroked her hand while looking into her eyes. "It is Techno. There are several basic kinds of Techno. First is Trance, which is mellow and pulls you into it. Second, is House, which is easy to dance to and has incredible rhythms. There is also Industrial, which is harder and heavier than House. There is Drum and Bass, which is obviously drum and bass rhythms. Of course, there are other variations, but these are the basics. We are listening to ATB Two Worlds right now. It is older, but it is one of my favorites. This would be considered Trance. Do you have a CD player at your house?"

"I know it's old school, but of course I do," she answered. "Why?"

"I am going to give you some CDs to listen to so that you can hear the different styles of Techno," Onyx explained.

"I'd like that. Thank you."

Onyx pulled the CD binder from the other side of the limousine and pulled out several CDs.

Reyne giggled when she saw the binder. "I haven't seen one of those in years."

"Most people haven't, but it is still the best way to travel with CDs, and not all music is on the internet." He answered before explaining each CD's style as he handed them to Reyne after putting them into jewel cases.

"This is a House version of Techno. This one is European House. This one is by a group called Lords of Acid. It is not really techno, but it's the closest thing I have to Industrial with me. This is a Perfect Trance by Suzy Solar. Again, an older CD, but one of my favorites, and obviously, it is Trance. I hope you enjoy them. They should at least get you started."

"If they are all like this one, I am sure I will." Reyne was so excited. He was introducing her to new things, and that was always exciting to her.

"Reyne, you really know nothing about Techno, do you?" he asked her, not quite believing she really knew nothing about the music. He already knew the answer. She was a single mother of two. Her daughter probably had been to a rave or two, but not Reyne.

The limousine stopped. They had arrived at Reyne's house. The driver opened the door and waited for Reyne to emerge from the car. "Would you like to come in and talk some more?"

"I would love to, and if you like, I can explain the CDs you hold in your hands to you as you listen to them. They are not all like the one we listened to on the way here." He reached over, took the CD from the player, and put it in a jewel case.

Reyne got out of the car and Onyx followed her. He stopped to give the driver instructions and followed her to her door.

She looked over and saw that Elizabeth was out on her porch. "Hello Elizabeth." Reyne called and realized that Onyx was already at her door waiting for her to open it.

"Hello Reyne. How are you tonight?" Elizabeth replied.

"Pretty good. I'll talk to you later." Reyne opened the door, and she and Onyx entered the foyer. "You seemed in a rush to get into the house. What's wrong?"

"I'm shy. I don't want your friends to meet me until you decide that I am going to be around for a while. That way, they won't ask you what happened or anything. You have only yourself to help you decide if you want to be with me or not."

"You are always surprising me." She gave him a smile and pointed to the living room, "My CD player is in here. Let's start my education of Techno." Reyne grabbed his hand and pulled him into the living room.

Onyx smiled that she was taking the initiative. Usually the women just looked his way and danced for him, hoping to be the chosen one. She knew nothing of that type of life and he quite enjoyed it, but eventually she would have to know it all. She would have to know what he was and at that point, she would either accept him or tell him to go away. He could not let her know until after she knew him as a person. Then maybe she would accept him better for his true self. "OK. Here is 'The Perfect Trance.' Put it in and let's listen to a few songs. I will explain more as we listen more."

Reyne put the CD in the player and pressed start. The music began.

"Hold on, we are missing some things. I have to get the driver to run an errand for us. I will be right back." Onyx walked out to the kitchen and made his call to the driver. When he returned to the living room, he smiled at Reyne. "You are going to be really surprised tonight. I want you to go get on some clothes that are easy to move in. I am going to teach you to dance to Techno and eventually I will take you to a Rave."

"A Rave? Those things are illegal and are full of drugs. Why would we want to go to a rave?"

He laughed, "That is where Techno is at its best. However, if you would prefer, we can go to a club that focuses on Techno instead, but it is not as good as a true Rave."

"You mean this music is what is played at raves?" Reyne suddenly wondered what she was getting herself into.

"It is not all that bad. Go get on some leggings or shorts and a t-shirt. It's going to get hot, and we are going to have fun." Onyx looked at her, staring straight into her eyes. She could barely breathe from his stare. "Trust me."

Reyne mouthed the word "Okay" and went upstairs to change. When she returned, she wore a pair of black leggings and a tank top with no bra. It was almost too much for Onyx, but he buried the urge quickly when he saw her.

"OK, do you have any cigarettes?" He asked.

"Yes, but we don't smoke in the house."

"We aren't going to smoke, we are going to dance. It'll be the easiest way to teach you. You do the move incorrectly and you burn yourself with the cigarettes, and you can see what you are doing…" Onyx said grabbing the pack of cigarettes.

There was a knock on the door. It was obviously the driver, so Onyx when to the door, got the items, thanked him, and gave him instructions. He returned with his CD binder and glow sticks.

"What in the world are you doing with glow sticks?" Reyne asked.

"You'll see. First of all, you have experienced only one Trance CD and part of a second one. Now light two cigarettes and I will show you one of the ways to dance to Techno." He instructed her and she willingly followed those instructions.

The rest of the night, he spent teaching Reyne to dance to all types of Techno. Before he put on each CD, he would explain the idea and variation behind the CD. He knew that she was not comfortable with all the references to new drugs she did not understand in some of the songs, so he tried to instruct her in that area of things too. However, after a while Reyne realized there was a difference between those that condoned drug usage and those that did not touch on it. They were like two different variations of the same thing. He also started introducing her to Goth Music, but soon realized that she would have to learn about that another night. Onyx could see her getting tired. He had forgotten that she was mortal.

After hours of dancing, learning about Techno, and starting in with Goth, Reyne went to the kitchen to make coffee. Rasputina played on the CD player. She brought two cups into the living room and sat down on the floor with Onyx.

She lit a cigarette and took a sip of coffee. "I know I don't smoke in the house, but I'm too exhausted and don't feel like going outside right now."

"Well, let us go outside, anyway." Onyx helped her up and opened the sliding glass door for her. They stepped out on the deck.

"Oh, isn't it beautiful? I love watching the sunrise. How about you?" She asked Onyx.

"It is one of my favorite things, but I think I should prepare to leave you for now. If you would like to see me again, you have my number. I will leave that decision to you."

"Why are you being like this? I mean, it isn't a bad thing. I'm just not used to a man letting me make the decisions on whether I want to see him again or not," she said.

"I have waited for you this long, I can wait a while more," he confessed.

Reyne finished her cigarette, and they went back into the house. She helped him get his CDs together and walked him to the front door.

"You know you should be hearing from me very soon. You make me very happy." Reyne smiled up at Onyx. He was a full foot taller than she was. He picked her up and placed her on the bottom step of her stairway. It made them almost the same height. She could look into his eyes from this viewpoint.

"I only want you to be happy." He leaned into her mouth and kissed her. His kiss penetrated into places Reyne did not know had nerve endings. It filled her completely with its hot wetness. As he pulled away, she tried to pull him back. "No. I will not have things happen faster than they should. Let us take our time. When the time is right, we will both know and it will be beyond any normal comprehension of pleasure, I promise you." He opened the door and left.

Reyne watched him get into his limousine and leave. She walked into the kitchen, refilled her cup of coffee and went out on the deck again. She sat there smoking and drinking coffee until the sun was full in the sky.

CHAPTER 17

Reyne awoke to the ring of her telephone. She slowly got up from her chair and made her way inside. By the time she reached the phone in the kitchen, the caller had hung up. "Thank goodness for caller ID," she thought, checking the little caller ID box.

It had been Andy. She picked up the receiver and dialed his number. As the line began to ring, she realized that her whole body still burned from the passion of Onyx's kiss.

"Hello?" Andy answered his phone.

"Hello Andy. You just called me. By the time I got to the phone, you had hung up. What's up?" Reyne tried to sound awake, but she felt she did not give a very good performance.

"I was calling to see if you wanted to go to brunch. When you didn't answer, I started getting worried and was going to come over and see if you were OK." He sounded relieved to hear her voice.

"I'm starving. I'd love to go to brunch. Can you be here in a half an hour?"

"Less. Bye." Andy had hung up.

Reyne took a quick shower. Her body enjoyed the hot water falling onto it. She ached all over from her night of dancing. When she finished her shower, she brushed her teeth and hair and got dressed.

She was putting on her shoes when she heard a knock at the front door. She ran down the stairs and opened the door.

"Hey Andy," She blurted as the door flew open completely.

"Reyne? What is up with you? You seem different or something." Andy looked at her suspiciously.

"Just hungry. Let's go. By the way, where are we going?" Reyne tried to be calmer, but her body and mind were not responding to her.

"I was thinking Martingales, or we can go any place that serves food. We just need to get you fed," He smiled softly at Reyne.

"What time is it, anyway? I haven't even looked at a clock since yesterday evening," Reyne said before she could stop herself.

"It's 10:45." Andy looked at her with a strange expression. She knew that he realized her not knowing the time was strange. She was never this negligent about time.

"I love the way Martingales does the omelets to order at the buffet," she said quickly.

"Sounds great. Let's go."

They walked to his car and headed to the restaurant. Once parked, he walked around to open the door for Reyne, and they walked into Martingale's. The theme of the restaurant was horses; hence the name Martingales. It was full of pictures of horses, real saddles, reins, and riding crops, all of which adorned the walls of the restaurant. As they waited to be seated, Reyne glanced to the back right hand corner of the dining area trying to see what was available on the huge open buffet.

Andy ordered them each the buffet and a cup of coffee before they headed to the buffet to fill their plates. Reyne returned to the table to sit down when she saw Elizabeth and Xavier enter the restaurant. She waved and walked over to them. "Hi Elizabeth, hi Xavier. How are you two doing?"

"Hi Reyne, you seem to be in a great mood this morning. Does it have anything to do with the handsome man you were with last night?" Elizabeth smiled and winked at Reyne.

"No, nothing like that. Why don't you join Andy and me for breakfast? Oh, and don't mention last night in front of him. Please?" Reyne's happiness seemed to fade as the last sentence came from her mouth.

"Not a problem, and we would love to join you." Xavier responded, as he took Elizabeth by the elbow and followed Reyne to the table.

Andy had just sat down and began eating as the three arrived at the table. When he saw Reyne, he stood up to meet her friends.

"Andy, I would like you to meet Xavier and Elizabeth. They just moved in to the townhouse few doors down from me," Reyne said, introducing them to Andy.

"Hello, nice to meet you. Please have a seat." Andy waited for them all to be seated before he sat down again. He called the waiter over to the table. "Two friends have joined us for brunch."

"What would you like to drink this morning?" The waiter asked of Elizabeth.

"Xavier would like a cup of coffee and I would like a cup of hot tea. We will be having the buffet too. Thank you." Elizabeth told the waiter. She and Xavier proceeded to get up and go to the buffet. Their drinks arrived by the time they had returned.

Reyne and Andy spent the whole meal telling Xavier and Elizabeth about all the interesting places to visit and things to see and do in the area, including which areas to avoid and which areas were the safest in Washington D.C. Reyne told Elizabeth about the smaller towns to the north and talked about the different craft shows that were held in Frederick and Thurmont.

By the time the four of them had finished eating, it was early afternoon.

"We've imposed on the two of you long enough. We're gonna go now. I'll see you later, Reyne. Come on, Xavier." Elizabeth stood up and gave Reyne a hug. Xavier shook her hand, then turned and shook Andy's hand.

"Nice meeting you, Andy. Have a good day, Reyne." Xavier turned and followed Elizabeth out of the restaurant.

Reyne looked at Andy. "I'm sorry. They are just new to the area and she doesn't have any friends..."

"It's okay. I love you for who you are. Let's go. Is there anything else you want or need to do today?"

"Just laundry and get myself together for work next week. Why?" Reyne flirted with Andy as she said this.

"Just wondering. I was going to help you do errands or whatever. That's all," he replied.

"Thanks, but I got it all done early Saturday."

Andy stopped and looked seriously at Reyne. "Reyne, is everything okay?"

Reyne did not respond. They had reached the car. Andy opened the door for Reyne and held it until she was seated. He then got into the car himself. He drove in silence. When they got to her house, he walked her to the front door.

"Give me a call sometime. I'd love to see you again." Andy pulled her close. He stared down into her eyes and slowly dropped his mouth to hers. Her lips parted to take him into her. Reyne felt the electricity between them and prepared for more. Slowly, he withdrew from her and started walking back to his car.

Reyne went into the house and straight into the kitchen, thinking about the differences between the kisses. She turned to put her purse on the table so she could brew some coffee when she saw Leigh sitting at the little table. "Reyne, where have you been? You haven't been home for almost 24 hours. I haven't heard from you recently, and you went out last night and never told me about it. I had to hear about it from Andy. What is going on?"

"First thing, Leigh, you are not my mother. I have been home. In fact, I was home all night. I went out to dinner with ..."

"Onyx. I know. I figured it out when Andy called and told me you blew him off. I couldn't tell him about Onyx because you haven't told me much lately. I thought you were going to stay away from the guy?" Leigh gave Reyne a look of worry and exasperation.

Reyne felt that Leigh was overstepping the line of friendship. She had to stop her now or their friendship would be over. "Listen. I don't have to explain myself to you, and I told you already, I wouldn't just blow him off. I'll tell you now because you're my friend.

My best friend. I love you and I know you worry about me and that is why I'll tell you, but do not demand me to do things. Now shut up and listen." Reyne took a breath and continued.

"Yes. I went out last night with Onyx. We were back here by 10 pm listening to music. I checked caller ID when the phone rang. I had decided to take an evening to myself and only answer if it was Benjamin, Tyler and Lazarus, or Taylor. Onyx and I listened to music all night. He had been playing Techno in the limousine, and I was interested in it. So, he came in with some CDs and taught me about the different types. This morning, I went to brunch with Andy. We went to Martingales at the Marriott. We ran into my new neighbors, Xavier and Elizabeth, and had them join us for brunch. That is where I am currently coming from. As for not talking to you, the last time I tried, you told me you were 'busy.' Well?" Reyne finished her little speech. She had made herself a cup of coffee and sat down at the table staring at Leigh. She was furious that Leigh was trying to run her life, but she did not want to lose Leigh's friendship either.

"I'm sorry Sweetie. I was just worried. When Andy called me..."

"Andy should never have called you!" Reyne screamed. Now she was furious at both of them.

"Reyne, he was worried. He really cares about you. He is a good man."

Reyne was still mad, but she began to calm down as her mind drifted to thoughts of Onyx, "*How can this man calm me down and excite me all at the same time?*" Reyne sat for a moment, thinking of what to say next. "Leigh, I know you are just worried about me. I forgive you."

Leigh hugged Reyne, "You're right. I overstepped. I'm sorry. Now something else has been bothering you. Let's talk." Reyne couldn't speak, but nodded. They filled their coffee cups and grabbed their cigarettes, and headed to the back door when the phone rang.

Go on out. I'll be right there." Reyne pulled the sliding glass door open for Leigh and went to the kitchen to answer to phone.

"Hello?"

"Hello Reyne. It's Benjamin. I wanted to know if Taylor can stay the week with me. I have taken off from work to move and would enjoy his company. I know this is short notice, but please consider it.

"Let me talk to Taylor."

"Ok." Benjamin called to Taylor and told him to pick up the phone.

"Hey Momma." Taylor's cheerful little voice came across the phone line.

"Hey, baby. Daddy wants you to stay with him this week. What do you think? Do you want to?" Reyne asked him as objectively as she could.

"Yeah, Momma. It's all right now. We are moving Daddy into his own apartment," he answered, then asked, "Is your protector with you?"

"He isn't here with me, but he is watching me, so I'm safe. If you want, you can stay. I love you and I'll call you back later," she answered him.

"OK Momma. Since Onyx is with you, and you are safe, I would like to stay and help Daddy. I love you. You wanna talk to my daddy?"

"Yes, baby," Reyne smiled to herself.

"Hello, Reyne. So can he stay?" Benjamin asked.

Reyne sighed, "You've got to stop changing things on me last minute, but yes, he can stay this time. Are you going to use daycare at all this week?"

"I don't know. I'll call them and let them know. I'll get a check to them too." Benjamin promised.

"Okay. I'll call back later to tell him goodnight. Bye."

Reyne hung up the phone. *"So that is what was bothering Taylor. Benjamin's parents must have said something to my baby. Well, at least now, Benjamin is getting his own place and I don't have to worry about Taylor around his grandparents."* Reyne opened the sliding glass door and went out onto the deck with a tray she had prepared of creamer, sugar, and a big thermos of hot coffee. She placed the tray on the table in front of them.

"I started brewing another pot, just in case." Reyne told Leigh as she sat down and lit a cigarette. "Okay. You want to know what is bothering me. Here it is. The night I met Andy, Lazarus told me to be open to people. He said I would be meeting someone who was to be my protector and that I would need this person. He also told me it wasn't Andy. I went to the restaurant to wait for Andy and met Onyx. Of course, I didn't even know his name at that time. Andy and I had dinner and enjoyed ourselves. I didn't think of the stranger after that night for the most part. I saw him one day in a restaurant in D.C. But even after seeing him there, it didn't keep him in my mind enough to be a major distraction. Lazarus told me several days later that two men were in love with me. He said one wanted to get to know me and the other knew me better than I knew myself. I told you that part. I figured it was Andy and Benjamin, like we had discussed. It was during this discussion he mentioned my protector, the stranger. Again, we talked in brief, but I focused on the two men as Benjamin and Andy, and that Andy was my choice. Ok. So, I met him at Chevy's and then I saw him at TGI Friday's, but it really wasn't a big deal. However, when he came up and talked to me at the Kennedy Center, I knew he was to be more than a protector. He gave me a little note with his name and number on it. From that point on he has been on my mind. I finally called him and asked him to lunch..." Reyne hesitated, wondering if she should remind Leigh about the Starbucks incident and how he had walked her to work that day. She decided not to tell her and continued. "...we met for lunch a few days later, but you know that. We went to Charlie Chang's and then walked around D.C. talking all afternoon. He gave me a ride to Taylor's day care that evening because I was running late. After that day, I knew I had to see him again. So we went to dinner last night. I knew I had misjudged who the two men in my life were. I was right about one being Andy, but the other was Onyx. We went to dinner and then listened to music. I originally went to lunch to on that Friday to meet him and then tell him I was dating someone else, but the more we talked, I knew I couldn't do it. Then the clincher comes. I kissed Andy the night he took me to the Kennedy Center, and I felt electricity between us. There is definitely chemistry there. But when I kissed Onyx, oh my god. He had never kissed me before last night and it was only one kiss before he left, but he made every cell in my body vibrate. I have never had a kiss like that before. Leigh, I have spilled my guts to you. Now help me. What am I going to do?" Reyne had a desperate look at her.

Leigh looked and Reyne and knew the woman was confused and really needed her friend, "Ok. Here's what you are going to do. You are going to call each one and invite them to your Labor Day Barbecue. You will tell each of them that you have been seeing both men and now have to decide which one you want a relationship with before emotions go too far and someone gets hurt. Then you tell them not to contact you by phone, letter, email, or in person until they arrive at the party, at which time you will tell them of your decision. Well? What do you think?" Leigh sat back and waited for Reyne's reply.

"But that's 3 weeks. I can't be without him for that long." Reyne felt so lonely and hated having to make this kind of decision.

"Which him?" Leigh asked Reyne and smiled. They both knew who she meant.

They finished the pot of coffee and took the tray back inside. Leigh helped Reyne clean up the mess and then prepared to leave.

"You're not staying for dinner?" Reyne questioned Leigh.

"Nope. You've got things to do and think about. I'll give you a call in a few days." Leigh picked up her purse, hugged Reyne, and said, "I love you Reyne, and I support you no matter what your decision is," then she left.

133

CHAPTER 18

Reyne sat in her living room thinking of the perfect way to tell each of the men about this. As she sat there, the phone rang. She got up and answered it.

"Hey Reyne. I wanted to make sure you enjoyed today." It was Andy.

"I did. But there is something I have to tell you," Reyne tried to sound normal, but she knew she wasn't doing a good job of it.

"What is it?" Andy asked, the worry in his voice.

"I have to tell you that I really like you and enjoy being with you. However, I have also been seeing someone else too. Emotions are beginning to be a part of these relationships, so I have decided it is time for me to decide what I am going to do before things go any further and someone gets hurt. I'm asking you to please come to my Labor Day Barbecue. If you are willing to wait, I'll have made my decision by then. In the meantime, please do not contact me in any way. I need the next few weeks to think. If you cannot wait, I will understand, but please do not hate me," Reyne stopped. She waited for Andy's reply.

"Reyne, I understand completely, and I appreciate your honesty. I'll do as you ask. What time should I be at your house on Labor Day?"

Relieved, Reyne answered "2 pm. Thank you Andy. Goodbye." Reyne hung up the phone. *"One down and one to go,"* Reyne thought to herself. She got up from the kitchen table, where she had been sitting while talking to Andy. She went through the house, gathering all the laundry and took it to the laundry room. She started the laundry and then began cleaning the house.

By that evening, the laundry was complete, and the house was clean. Reyne drew herself a bath and had just climbed in when the doorbell rang. She grabbed a towel and headed to the door. She was startled to find Onyx standing on her doorstep. She thought, "Didn't I call him? Didn't I tell him not to contact me until Labor Day? Oh my God, no I didn't. I told Andy but not Onyx." Reyne stopped staring at Onyx, "Please come in. Excuse the way I look, I thought you were my daughter. She and her boyfriend are due home soon."

"Thank you, but I can only stay a minute. I wanted to tell you that I have to leave town for 3 weeks on business, but then I will be back. I didn't want you calling me and hear I had checked out of the hotel. I thought I should just stop by on my way to the airport to let you know. The phone felt impersonal. You will be in good hands while I'm gone, so have no fear. You are still under my protection and nothing will happen to you. My father's personal bodyguard will be watching you until I return, which will be soon."

They were still standing in the hallway by the front door. All Reyne could do was stare at him. He was wearing tight black jeans, a black tank top, and black books. He looked like one of those bad boys that all young girls are crazy over, but can never have.

Reyne's heart began to race with dread. *"How can I stand to be without him for three weeks?"* When Reyne was finally able to speak, she asked Onyx, "Well, will you be back in time for my Labor Day Party? And what do you mean your 'father's personal body-guard?'"

Onyx smiled and answered her first question. "Yes, I'll be back for your Labor Day Party. I wouldn't miss it for anything. I await your decision as well. That is why I am attending to this business now. I will see you upon my return. And my father's personal bodyguards are just that. They are the people that guard my father. He is lend-ing them to you." He leaned down, kissed her gently on each eyelid, the tip of her nose, and then delved deep into her mouth. The towel slipped from around Reyne's body and fell to the floor, but she did not care. All that she cared about was living the passion of the kiss as he picked her up and carried her upstairs.

Reyne's mind was so high with excitement and passion. Her body felt like it was floating. She felt the warm water of her bath surround her. When she opened her eyes, he was gone. The towel lay folded on the toilet seat and she was back in her bath. "Did it really happen, or was I dreaming? And his father's bodyguards being lent to me? I must have been dreaming." Reyne said aloud to ensure she was truly awake.

The bath water was beginning to get cold, so Reyne decided it was time to get out. She stepped out of the tub, drained it while drying off, and got dressed. She went downstairs, dumped the coffee she had brewed earlier that she didn't drink, set up coffee for the morning, and made her lunch. As she placed her lunch in the refrigerator, when the front door opened, Tyler had finally arrived home.

"I'm glad you guys are home; I was getting worried." Reyne yelled from the kitchen.

"Sorry we are late, but we ate with his parents." Tyler looked tired and irritable.

"Where's Lazarus?" Reyne looked behind her daughter to see if Lazarus was still coming in.

"He'll be back later. He had something to take care of and since we are returning late, he dropped me off so I could get sleep before work tomorrow."

"That was nice of him." Reyne smiled at her daughter.

"Yeah, I guess." Tyler turned away and walked toward the basement. "See ya tomorrow, Mom."

"See ya, Baby Girl," Reyne watched her daughter go into the basement. She turned, walked up the stairs and into her bedroom. It was already well past her bedtime. She had told Taylor she would call him this evening, and she had forgotten. "What is happening to me? I am losing track of time really bad." She thought as she turned her bedding down. There on her bed laid a piece of paper. She opened it and read it.

Dearest Reyne,

I will do as you wanted to ask of me. I will return to you on Labor Day to receive your decision, as I said. I thank you for your honesty in this situation and only pray that you choose me. You are protected while I am gone, so do not worry. You will always be with me in my heart and my mind until we are in person again very soon.

With all my Love
Onyx

P.S. The kiss was beyond words.

Reyne laid down in her bed, holding the note. She smiled to herself and fell asleep.

CHAPTER 19

For the next three weeks, Reyne kept herself busy preparing for the Labor Day Party and thinking of the two men in her life. Other things had happened as well. Leigh had started seeing someone, and she didn't stop by as often as she used to. Reyne was used to this though. Every time Leigh got a new boyfriend, she did this for the first few weeks, and then things returned to normal. Leigh had promised that she would help prepare everything for the party, so Reyne expected to see her the Sunday prior to Labor Day, but Reyne really wished she was here now.

One of the effects of Leigh not being around was that Reyne and Elizabeth became very close in a very short time. The two women spent time together each day and would talk for hours. The Monday before Labor Day, Reyne and Elizabeth made invitations and handed them out to the neighbors and friends. Everyone agreed to come and asked if they should bring anything. Reyne always replied the same… "Drinks!"

Reyne awoke early the Sunday before the party. She was just walking down the stairs when the doorbell rang. By the time she got to the door, someone was unlocking it with a key. The door suddenly flung open, "Hey Sweetie. Look who I found to help us." Leigh jumped through the doorway and hugged Reyne. Elizabeth followed her into the house.

"Hi Reyne." Elizabeth smiled. "I hope you don't mind me helping out."

"Not at all. The more the merrier. Plus, you've been helping the past couple of weeks, why not today too? Coffee anyone? I was just coming down to brew some." Reyne answered, smiling.

"Yes," the two women answered in unison.

"So, have you made you decision, Reyne?" Leigh asked. "I need to know."

"Of course I made my decision. I am choosing…"

"What decision? What are you all talking about?" Elizabeth looked at Leigh and Reyne with puzzlement.

Leigh poked at Reyne. "You haven't told her yet, Reyne? Bad girl. Reyne was seeing two men. Tomorrow she lets them know which one she has decided to go to the next level with and start a monogamous relationship with."

"Don't worry Leigh. I didn't pick Andy." Reyne giggled.

"What do you mean?" Leigh asked anxiously and a little too fast.

"I figured out that you two were seeing each other about two weeks ago. I tell him I can't see him for three weeks and all of the sudden, you start seeing someone all the time. Of course, I could have been wrong, but I didn't think so. Reyne smiled and waited for Leigh to deny it.

"You got me. It just kinda happened," Leigh started to explain.

Reyne laughed, "I've known from the day I told them both about the party, whom I was going to pick. You knew who I'd pick the day you gave me the idea. Now, coffee's ready."

The three women got mugs, poured their coffee and started taking inventory of the items they needed to purchase at the grocery story. As soon as they finished their coffee, the three headed to the grocery store. When they returned, they took inventory again to make sure they did not forget anything. Elizabeth and Leigh moved furniture around to make room for guests, while Reyne started to prepare the food. Elizabeth offered to let Reyne use some of her chairs for more sitting space. Reyne gladly accepted the offer. They all went to Elizabeth's house to help bring back chairs. After three loads of two chairs each, there were plenty of seats for the guests. They finished preparing the food to the point that all that needed to be done was to heat up all the dishes in the morning and grill the hamburgers and hotdogs. They cleaned up the kitchen, grabbed some glasses, a bottle of wine, and headed for the living room.

Leigh poured the wine and lifted her glass, "Cheers, girls. We've done an awesome job."

"Cheers." Reyne and Elizabeth joined in, lifting their glasses with Leigh's glass.

"Well, I'd better be going. Xavier is going to be wondering if I'm ever coming home." Elizabeth smiled. "Plus, we're going out tonight." She got up to leave.

Reyne followed her to the door. "If you wanted to, you could have left earlier since you have some place to go."

"I wanted to stay. He'll understand." Elizabeth patted Reyne's hand.

"Thanks for all your help today and for letting me borrow your chairs. I really appreciate it," Reyne said.

Elizabeth smiled, "Not a problem. It is what friends do. If you need help in the morning, just give me a call. Otherwise, what time should we arrive?"

"Around three would be good. See you then." Reyne shut the door behind Elizabeth and returned to the living room.

"Reyne..." Leigh hesitated.

"Yes, Leigh." Reyne answered as straight-faced as she could muster.

"Are you sure you aren't mad? I mean let me explain. He came over..." Leigh started.

"What is there to explain? I knew you liked him when you first told me about him. I couldn't understand why you didn't date him. He came to you upset because of what I had said. You were already friends, and you were there for him. I am grateful for that. But how would you like to tease him a little tomorrow?" Reyne grinned wickedly.

"I'd love it." Leigh smiled, but something was still bothering her. "You know, if you were to pick him, I think he would leave me for you. He still thinks you are his Ms. Right."

Reyne now understood. Leigh was afraid he would leave her for Reyne. "I'm not Ms. Right for him, but I do believe I am Ms. Right for Onyx." Reyne leaned over and hugged Leigh.

Leigh seemed to relax, "Well then, whatever you decide to do to him, I will follow you lead. This should be fun. But right now I'm gonna go home. I am exhausted. I'll see you tomorrow. Are you sure you don't want me to come over earlier?"

"Nope. I can manage until 2 pm with Tyler and Lazarus. Thanks for all your help today. You've been great." Reyne hugged Leigh again.

Leigh got up and went to the kitchen. Reyne followed with the glasses and bottle of wine. She walked Leigh to the door, said good-bye, and went to bed. As she laid in bed, feeling her exhausted body caressed by her mattress, she drifted off to sleep thinking *"Tomorrow I see my Onyx."*

CHAPTER 20

Reyne awoke early and started heating up the food. At 11 am, she hopped into the shower and got ready for people to start arriving. When Leigh and Andy arrived at 2 pm, they found Reyne in the kitchen, working on putting platters together with finger foods.

"Hey Sweetie, we're here." Leigh yelled as they walked in the door. "What do you need done first?" Leigh said, smiling at Reyne.

"I guess the first thing would be to talk to Andy. I am sure he is awaiting my decision." Leigh made a move to leave. "No Leigh, please stay. I want you to hear this." Reyne looked at Andy and Leigh. They did make a cute couple.

"OK, Andy, I have made my decision…" Reyne started.

"Before you say another word, I need to say something." Andy interrupted.

Reyne and Leigh looked at one another as if to say, "What is he doing?"

Andy continued, "I do not want to hear your decision. In the beginning, I told you I believed you were Ms. Right, but I am not so sure now. You may have been at that time, but after you told me about seeing another man and that you would decide if you wanted to continue seeing me, well…" he started and then just blurted out, "I've been seeing Leigh. I'm sorry Reyne. I didn't mean for it to happen, but it did. I hope you can forgive me, especially if you picked me, because I am going to stay with Leigh."

Reyne smiled. Leigh looked shocked. It was perfect. Reyne giggled at the irony of the situation. They were going to scare poor Andy, and he had turned it around and floored Leigh.

Reyne shrugged and said, "OK."

"OK? Just OK? What do you mean by that? How dare you? I pour my heart out! I worry that you are going to be upset and you say OK!" Andy seemed confused and furious all at the same time.

"What do you want me to do? I have thirty plus people due here anytime now and you want me to cry. Get real. That isn't me at all. I'll cry when I'm alone and not before. Plus, I probably won't cry because I have known for a little over two weeks that you two have been seeing each other. In addition to that, I didn't pick you. So 'OK' seemed an appropriate response." Reyne finished her speech with a smile. Andy's expression of disbelief was priceless. Reyne and Leigh began laughing hysterically.

Leigh gave Andy a hug and kiss, "It's all right, baby. Let's help her finish setting up and thank you for choosing me."

Andy was speechless and totally caught off guard; all he could do was nod his head in acknowledgment and start helping with the preparations. People started arriving as soon as the last of the party platters had been set out. The music was turned on and people were all over the house, talking and laughing with one another. They all seemed to be having a great time.

Xavier and Elizabeth arrived a little after three. Reyne grabbed them and pulled them into the kitchen. "Are you okay, Elizabeth? You don't look so good."

"I will be fine. We were up late last night and I overslept today. Once I completely wake up, I will be fine. Any coffee?" Elizabeth smiled a dull smile.

"Fresh-brewed. Help yourself." Reyne got a mug for Elizabeth and handed it to her. Elizabeth looked at Xavier after the first cup and said, "Let's go mingle. I'll feel much better."

"Sounds good to me, baby," Xavier answered. Taking her by her hand, they left the kitchen.

"I'll introduce you to people if you like," Reyne offered.

"No thanks, we can do it and I have met many of them when we were handing out the invitations. You have enough to take care of. You do not need to worry about us," Elizabeth stated as she and Xavier went to mingle with the other guests.

Reyne spent the next hour and half walking around making sure all the food trays were full, sending Andy on ice runs, and ensuring everyone was having a good time. However, all during this time, she worried that Onyx had decided he did not want to wait either, and wouldn't return to her.

Reyne found Andy and asked him to light the grill. It was about time to start making the hamburgers and hot dogs when Taylor and the neighborhood kids came running in yelling about a limousine out front. All the guests on the first floor went to the front of the house to check out the limousine. Reyne stood on her front porch, waiting to see if it was Onyx. Everyone watched the man climb from the back of the car. He was exquisite. His leather pants sat on his hips and accentuated the muscles of his thighs, his white ruffled shirt opened halfway down his chest, allowing enough to be seen to create curiosity. The guests had congregated in groups on Reyne's front lawn and had started whispering to one another about this man who intrigued them. The stranger walked straight up to the front porch and bowed to Reyne.

"I have returned to you as I promised. May I please enter your home, or are you going to break my heart and turn me away?" He stretched his hand to her.

"You may enter my house and my life" She took his hand and pulled him up the front steps. They stood on the front porch entwined, lost in the moment, until they realized the guests were clapping. Reyne turned and smiled to her guests. "Come on back in, everyone. Andy is gonna start cooking the burgers and hotdogs."

As Reyne and Onyx entered the house, she tried to pull him to her to kiss him, but he wouldn't let it happen. Onyx looked down at her and smiled, "First, we talk." He guided her up the stairs and into her bedroom.

Once inside the bedroom, he leaned down and kissed her gently on the cheek. When he finally let her go, he asked, "So I take it you made your choice? You have chosen me."

"Yes, if you will have me." Reyne answered.

"I love you Reyne. I will never leave your side if I can help it. I promise." He grabbed her close again, and this time placed his mouth gently on hers. She felt his tongue enter her mouth. The sweetness and tenderness flooded her again. She began to fly and lose track of her surroundings, but he stopped before all her senses left her. He helped her sit on the bed until she was feeling herself again and only then did they return to the party.

Reyne took him around to all the guests and introduced him. She introduced him to Andy and Leigh. Andy offered his hand, and Onyx took it. The two men could have passed for brothers, but there was definitely something different about Onyx, something that made a person gravitate toward him.

"Onyx, there are two more people you must meet. They are new to the neighborhood." Reyne and Onyx walked through the house until Reyne spotted them on the patio in the backyard. Reyne called to them, "Xavier, Elizabeth. I have someone for you to meet." Reyne felt Onyx's hand tighten around hers when she called their names. As she and Onyx made their way to Xavier and Elizabeth, the three just stared at one another.

Finally, Elizabeth smiled slyly, "So is this the one you chose?"

Reyne blushed. "Yes. Xavier. Elizabeth. This is Onyx. Onyx this is Xavier and Elizabeth. Elizabeth has helped me a lot through the last three weeks, both personally and with the party."

Onyx stared flatly at the two and pulled Reyne closer to him, as if to protect her. "Nice to meet you." He said stiffly.

"Likewise." Xavier responded just as stiffly.

"Reyne, I am really enjoying meeting everyone, but I have just come from the airport and I'm starving. Please excuse me while I go get something to eat." He released her and started up the stairs to the kitchen.

Onyx went in search of Leigh and Andy, instead of the kitchen, as soon as Reyne was out of sight. He had to talk to them. They both cared for Reyne. Leigh was her best friend, and Andy was the other man and should still have feelings for her. He had to tell them, and the sooner the better.

Elizabeth watched Onyx leave and smiled at Reyne, "He sure is handsome. You are very lucky, Reyne."

"Thank you. I feel very lucky when I am with him. I'll talk to you all later. I've got to fill up some trays and check on the ice situation." Reyne turned to leave them. She started thinking about the response she got from Onyx when she said their names and the formality and tension she had sensed when the three were together. She thought, "All their reactions were strange, but maybe I have just overwhelmed him."

Onyx found Leigh in the living room and made his way to her. "Leigh, I need to talk to you. It is very important."

"You're not going to hurt her and leave her, are you?" Leigh asked defensively.

"Never. I love her, and that is why I need to talk to you and Andy. Please find him and meet me in the laundry room. We need to speak in private. I will be there in 5 minutes waiting for you." Onyx turned and left her standing in the living room. She had seen a look of urgency in his eyes, so she immediately set off to find Andy.

Onyx went straight to the laundry room. As he opened the door he saw Xavier and Elizabeth. They seemed to be waiting for him.

"Hello again, Onyx." Xavier smiled evilly as he said the words.

"Hello Xavier. How is your father?" Onyx asked civilly, as he shut the door to the laundry room.

"My father, your uncle, is fine. You have not said hello to my beautiful Elizabeth."

"Hello Elizabeth." Onyx gave a slight bow toward her.

Leigh had searched for Andy and found he had run to the store to pick up more ice and soda. She went to the laundry room and was about to open the door, but heard voices and thought better of it. She decided to listen instead. Obviously, someone was in there with Onyx. She had to find out what they were talking about. Leigh still did not trust Onyx completely. If he was hiding any secrets, she would have to tell Reyne to protect her from this man.

"Give up Onyx. We found her first. She is ours." Xavier stated.

"Never. If I do that, she is dead. I will not let you have her." Onyx's fury was building in his voice.

"What choice do you have? Elizabeth has become a close friend of hers. Reyne will become her toy before too long. I can ensure that you are not around to protect her. You know, working for my father can require a lot of traveling." Xavier and Elizabeth both started laughing.

Leigh stood outside the door, totally shocked. "So Onyx is her protector. He is protecting her from them." Leigh was ashamed that she did not trust Onyx without even getting to know him. She put her ear back to the door and listened.

"Listen, to save her, you know what you have to do. Just do it and we will leave her alone."

Elizabeth finally spoke. "Maybe. I have come to crave her. I want her and I am going to have a hard time curbing that desire. She is beautiful and I want a taste." She smiled at Onyx, licking her lips.

He understood perfectly what she meant to do to Reyne. "That is it. I will finish this and finish it soon. Leave Reyne alone. I have come into the picture and you have to leave." Onyx demanded.

"As you said earlier, never! Let's just say may, the better immortals win. Oh, but that is right. You have not taken your gift yet. You are still mortal. So, I guess the immortals will win again this time." Xavier started laughing. He flung the door to the laundry room door open.

Leigh jumped behind the flung open door quickly so she wouldn't be discovered. "If they want to kill Reyne, they may want to kill her too, if she knew. I have to tell Reyne this evening."

Onyx stormed out of the laundry room and passed by Leigh without noticing her. She started to call out to him, but decided she should let it be for the moment. Onyx ran up the stairs and out the front door, pushing past Reyne without saying good-bye. Reyne watched him leave.

Reyne stood at the door when Xavier and Elizabeth came up behind her. Elizabeth stopped for a moment as Xavier left. "We have to leave…" Xavier came back, grabbed Elizabeth's hand and started pulling her out the door. Elizabeth looked at Reyne apologetically and left with Xavier.

Leigh stood with Reyne at the front door. Reyne ran up the stairs to her room. The party ended abruptly because of the disruption of the departures of the three people.

Leigh went upstairs to console Reyne. As she entered Reyne's room, she could hear her crying. "Sweetie. It's me."

"Oh Leigh, he left me. He didn't even say good-bye. And something happened between him, Elizabeth, and Xavier. I am humiliated." Reyne sobbed.

"No Sweetie. You are not. People just think he is an asshole. They think he hurt you and he doesn't deserve you." Leigh pulled Reyne's head to her shoulder and let her cry. "It's not what you think. Give him a chance. I'll take Taylor home with me. You need time to calm down."

"No, he can stay. We will be fine." Reyne wiped her eyes.

"Are you sure?" Leigh asked.

Reyne could only whisper, "Yeah."

"Andy is downstairs cleaning up. Once we are done, I'll be back up to check on you. Okay?" Leigh laid her down on the bed.

"Thanks," Reyne turned over and started sobbing into the pillow.

Leigh decided to call Benjamin and asked if he could take Taylor for a few days, because Reyne was very sick. He promised he would be right over and keep Taylor at least that night. Leigh told Taylor his Momma wasn't feeling well and that he needed to pack to spend a couple of days with his daddy. Taylor ran upstairs. Leigh thought he was going to pack, but Taylor had other ideas.

"Momma, do you feel bad?" Taylor asked innocently as he stroked Reyne's cheek.

Reyne looked at Taylor and held out her hands to him. "Yes. Momma doesn't feel so good."

"Leigh called my Daddy. He is coming to pick me up. Should I go, or do you need me to take care of you?" He sounded hurt.

"Why don't you go with Daddy? It will only be for a day or two. You can play with your cousins and Momma can feel better faster if she sleeps a whole lot. You know how you like to sleep when you're not feeling well, right? Well, Momma needs sleep. Do you understand?"

"Yes Momma. I love you. By the way, Onyx loves you. He did not mean to hurt you. Trust me. Please forgive him, Momma. I like him. I've got to go pack. I'll be back to say good-bye before I leave." He ran out of her room. She couldn't help but smile. He cared about her, and that should be enough. She should have left well enough alone. She did not care if Onyx loved her. She vowed again to forget men and just worry about her children. She thought, "*I should have realized he wasn't the one. There was no white stallion he rode in on.*"

By the time Benjamin arrived, Leigh and Andy had finished cleaning up the house. Taylor said good-bye to Reyne, kissed her, and went downstairs. He left with no problem, but with instructions to Leigh to 'take good care of my Momma, and make sure she talks to Onyx.' Once Benjamin and Taylor were gone, Leigh went back upstairs to check on Reyne.

"Do you want me to stay, Sweetie?" Leigh asked softly.

"Please. Would you call my boss's voice mail and leave a message that I am very ill and won't be in tomorrow?" Reyne whispered her request.

"Of course, Sweetie. I'll be right back." Leigh left the room. She went downstairs and found Andy preparing to leave.

"Come on baby, let's go home." Andy held out Leigh's purse for her.

"I'm gonna stay. She needs a friend right now. You understand, don't you?" Leigh looked longingly at Andy.

"Yes. Do you want me to stay too?" He asked?

"No. I am going to take tomorrow off with her. Stop by after work." Leigh kissed him good-bye and walked him to the door. After he left, she locked up the house, made the call to Reyne's boss and her own boss, and went back upstairs.

Once Andy was gone, she realized Reyne was asleep. Leigh pulled the blankets up around her and left the room. She went down to the living room to watch some TV. While watching the news, Tyler and Lazarus returned home.

"Hey Leigh, what's going on? Where's the party?" Tyler asked with astonishment that the house wasn't still full of people.

Leigh explained most of what had happened, including the departures of Onyx, Xavier, and Elizabeth, but not telling them about the conversation she overheard. Lazarus sat down on the sofa with Tyler while they listened to the story.

"Serves my Mom right. She falls for this loser, from what I can tell, and then he treats her like this," Tyler exclaimed.

"It's not like that at all. He isn't a loser. He is really good for her and seems to want only the best. There are other things going on you do not know about. Your mother doesn't understand yet, because she is too hurt, but she will soon. Right now she just needs her time to heal the wounds," Leigh tried to change Tyler's view with the explanation.

"It's not going to work, Leigh. I know my mother. She's into losers. Oh well. It's her life. I'm old enough to go on my way. Lazarus, this is your fault too, for telling my mother he was her protector. You can sleep up here tonight," Tyler stomped off to her room in the basement.

Lazarus looked at Leigh. "All will be okay. I know it."

Leigh nodded in agreement. "They want to hurt her, Elizabeth and Xavier. Hurt her to hurt Onyx. I overheard them talking in the laundry room. He is protecting her from them. What are we going to do?"

Lazarus took it all in, then said, "You and I will do all we can to protect her until we can get Onxy back in her life. We have to or she is dead."

CHAPTER 21

When Xavier and Elizabeth arrived home, Xavier grabbed Elizabeth, hugged her and spun her around and around, laughing. "We did it. We may not have captured him yet, but he knows that we are close to her and to him. His destruction is within our reach."

Elizabeth smiled and kissed Xavier. "What is our next step, my lover?"

"We have caused friction between the two lovers. You move in and take her. She will need a friend right now. Her friend Leigh has obligations and a boyfriend. Your only goal is the same as mine. Therefore, I won't have a problem with you spending lots of time with her, at least for a few days. Starting tomorrow, you make your move." Xavier kissed her again. "Let's go hunt. You will need to be extra sated so you can devote time to her and not hunt."

Elizabeth nodded in agreement. The two left to hunt, feed, and sate themselves to celebrate.

CHAPTER 22

Onyx climbed into his limousine and just sat for a minute. "Maybe I should go back in and take care of this now. No. But I should talk to Reyne. Not now. I am too emotional and things would be said that she doesn't need to know at this time." He tried to clear his mind, "Driver, let's go."

"Where to, sir?" the driver asked.

"Just head back toward DC. I need time to think." Onyx instructed him.

As the limousine pulled away from Reyne's house, Onyx called Brian to tell him to get ready. The bodyguards needed to be at Reyne's house because he and Brian were going out. Brian was waiting out front of the hotel when Onyx arrived. He entered the limousine and Onyx immediately started to tell him about the events of the day. The two rode around D.C. and northern Virginia, making plans to protect Reyne and take care of Xavier and Elizabeth for most of the night.

CHAPTER 23

Reyne had been lying in bed just staring at the wall since the sun had come up. It was now mid-morning, and she had not moved in hours. Leigh had stayed the night, but Reyne knew she couldn't keep her forever. Tyler and Lazarus had gone to work and Taylor was due back this afternoon. She had to get over this depression. She had to get up and get over it. She had too many responsibilities in her life to just keep lying here feeling sorry for herself. She started to cry softly again.

Reyne heard the phone ring beside her bed, but decided to ignore it because she did not feel like talking to anyone except Onyx. Leigh walked into the room, phone in her hand, and sat on the bed beside Reyne.

"Sweetie?" She rubbed Reyne's back to get her attention, as well as to soothe her raw emotions. "It's Onyx, Sweetie. Do you want to talk to him?"

"Yes. But only for a moment." Reyne whispered as she took the receiver from Leigh. "Hello Onyx." Her voice was flat and lacked emotion, and she knew it.

"Hello Reyne. I'm calling to apologize for my actions yesterday. I'm sorry I hurt you. I never meant to." He hated to hear the wounded sound of her voice. He had to alleviate her sadness and give her back her life with him.

"What happened? Why did you leave so fast? What is going on? Please explain it to me." There was desperation in her voice. She wanted Onyx to give her an explanation she could readily accept. She wanted to automatically forgive him for everything that had happened.

Onyx hesitated for a moment, "I promise to tell you everything very soon and in person, but right now I need to know you are okay and hope that you forgive me." He hoped she would give him the time he needed, but he was not sure at the moment.

Reyne's fury began to build. She couldn't believe that he had asked her for forgiveness and yet had not explained why he had acted that way. She sat up with a new fire in herself, "What did you say? You want my forgiveness? Why should I forgive you? You left me! You left without even saying good-bye, screw off, bite me, or anything, and you want forgiveness. I believe I deserve an explanation before you ask me for forgiveness. I cannot..." Reyne stopped. She sat on the bed, shook her head and thought, *"Are men really this stupid? This was a first. Forgiveness without an explanation. Boy, can I pick 'em."*

Onyx sighed in understanding and frustration, "Okay, don't forgive me. But promise to give me a chance to explain everything upon my return. I have to leave for a few days, but I will come to see you as soon as I return. Is that okay? Please promise me."

"I will wait for you to return to hear your explanation. I want to hear everything, not just parts of the story. Then I will decide. Good-bye." Reyne hung up the phone and started crying all over again.

Leigh hugged her and tried to comfort her. She finally got Reyne calmed down enough to rest. Leigh was exhausted and had just laid down for a nap when the doorbell rang. Leigh rushed to the door before the visitor could ring the doorbell again and opened the door. "Hello?" Leigh said with a mixture of frustration and exhaustion.

"Hi Leigh. How is Reyne doing?" Elizabeth asked as Leigh opened the door for her to come into the house. Elizabeth could see the fatigue and anger in Leigh's face. "How are you doing?"

"I'm okay, just really tired. Reyne had a rather sleepless night. She tossed and turned, which made it hard to sleep. I'm really worried about her." Leigh allowed herself to be drawn into Elizabeth's arms, even though she knew that Elizabeth was a threat. She was too tired to fight right now, and if she said anything, she would give away her advantage. She had not been able to tell Reyne, because it would have just upset her more. She had to keep it between her and Lazarus for now. She had to get Reyne well; that was her focus for the moment.

"I wanted to apologize for the way Xavier acted yesterday. Do you think I could go up and talk to her?" Elizabeth said sincerely.

Leigh, in her tired state, thought she sensed true concern in Elizabeth's request, "Yeah, I'll go with you."

Leigh and Elizabeth walked up the stairs. Elizabeth knew Leigh was tired and wanted to see Andy, and she wanted Leigh out of the way. *"This could work to my advantage,"* she thought to herself. She turned to Leigh, looked deep into her eyes, and said, "Leigh, you are tired. Why don't you go home? I can help Reyne, and you need the rest. Xavier feels horrible that he hurt her and feels that we need to make it up to her. I could do this for her as my way of apologizing. I'm only too glad to help. Plus, she is the first friend I've had in a long time. I won't have my husband messing this up." The intent and influence pushed into Leigh.

Leigh smiled as she sensed Elizabeth seemed genuinely worried about her and Reyne, which made her forget Onyx's warning in her weariness and the actual conversation that she overheard. All concern of the threat Xavier and Elizabeth posed was instantly gone. "Yes, I am exhausted. Thanks. We will tell her when you apologize. I think we should make sure it is okay with her, don't you?" Leigh said stiffly. She also knew she couldn't just leave; Reyne had to be okay with the plan too.

They entered Reyne's room and approached the bed. Leigh sat on the side of the bed and stroked Reyne's arm, while Elizabeth made herself comfortable on the floor beside the bed. Reyne stirred and turned over to face the women.

"Hey Sweetie. Elizabeth is here. I thought you might like to say hi," Leigh spoke softly to Reyne.

Reyne looked from Leigh to Elizabeth and gave a small smile. "Hi Elizabeth," she said in a barely audible voice.

"Hi Reyne. How are you?" Elizabeth reached up and took Reyne's hand into her own. Touch always strengthened her influence.

"Not so good." She gave another small smile as the tears welled up in her eyes.

"Please don't cry. I just wanted to apologize for Xavier and myself. We feel terrible." She looked into Reyne's gentle, blue eyes and thought, "*She really is beautiful, even with puffy eyes and a red nose. I can't wait until she is mine. I will protect her and keep her for a very long time, maybe forever.*"

Leigh stroked Reyne's hair from her eyes. "Reyne, Elizabeth has offered to stay with you while I work this week. I'll come by every evening and you can call me during the day if you need me. I will be back on Friday night to spend the weekend with you. Do you mind?" Leigh yawned the question.

Reyne remembered that Leigh had to go home and take care of her own responsibilities. "It is okay, Leigh. Go be with Andy and take care of yourself. I will be fine and back to work tomorrow. You know I bounce back pretty fast." Reyne also replied stiffly and gave Leigh a weak smile.

"All right, well then, I'm going. Elizabeth, please take good care of her. If you come downstairs, I will show you where everything you may need is located," Leigh stood up, gathered her bag, and headed downstairs.

Elizabeth stood up, "I am going to let Leigh out and call Xavier and let him know I won't be home tonight. I will be right back." She went down the stairs and found Leigh in the kitchen.

"Okay, here's the scoop. Tyler is at work. She and Lazarus will be home about dinner time. Taylor needs to be picked up at day care, the one at the end of the street, before 6 pm unless you hear from his father. Here is Reyne's address book. Benjamin, Taylor's dad's number is in there, Tyler and Lazarus' cell phones are in there. Andy and I are in there too; if you need one, both, or all of us, call. The kids can fill you in on the rest of their routines when they get home. I'm going home and fall into bed. See you later and thanks." Leigh opened the door and left knowing she was forgetting something, but too tired and foggy to remember anything but her need to sleep.

Elizabeth smiled as she shut the door, thinking to herself, "*No Leigh, I should thank you. You are helping us more than you know. In the end, we will promise to take care of you for helping us so much.*" She went back upstairs to check on Reyne.

Reyne was sitting up in bed when she got to the room. "I'm gross. I'm the worst person in the world."

Elizabeth knew humans were weak, but this was pathetic. It made her want to protect Reyne even more. "No, you are not. Let's get you up and showered. That always helps. It may not help completely, but it does help. True?" Elizabeth smiled and took Reyne's hands.

"So true." Reyne allowed Elizabeth to help her into the bathroom. She turned on the shower and got undressed while the water warmed up. She climbed into the shower and let the water slide over her body. She pretended that it was washing all the hurt and depression away.

After a few minutes, she turned off the shower and climbed out to dry off. She opened the bathroom door and walked back to her bedroom with the towel wrapped around her. She dressed and made a quick phone call to work. As she replaced the receiver on the phone, Elizabeth walked into the bedroom.

"Why don't you and the kids come to my house for dinner? You need to get out of the house and clear your head."

"Thank you, but no. I am not ready to leave the house yet. In fact, before you came into the bedroom, I called work and requested the rest of the week off. You really don't have to worry about me. I'll be fine. The worse is over. Tyler and Lazarus can help me. You can go home, but thanks for the offer." Reyne knew she could use the help, but did not want anyone to know how bad off she truly was.

She always did whatever she had to do to survive, and if it meant taking care of the kids and house, she would. She just couldn't face her co-workers, yet after many of them witnessed Onyx's arrival and abrupt departure.

Elizabeth was touched by Reyne's independence, but she had her own motives, "Nope. I promised Leigh, I would help you and I will. Since you won't come to my house for dinner, I'll make dinner here. Oh, Taylor is outside playing. I went and picked him up while you were in the shower. I hope that's OK."

Reyne smiled and was glad that Elizabeth had refused her. "It's fine. Thanks."

"Good, we're done with the argument. Now... What did your work say?" Elizabeth wanted to know because she really did care about Reyne, but also to know how fast she needed to work.

"I was told that I could take this week off, but I have to return on Monday. I hate my job! I hate it!" Reyne sobbed and collapsed back on the bed.

"It's not that bad. I think I can work it so you can work from home. OK?" Elizabeth prompted her.

"How?" Reyne wiped the tears from her eyes.

Elizabeth continued, "Xavier wants to open an office in this area. He needs someone to set up an office, keep track of his investments in this region, look into new opportunities, and keep him apprised of things in the area. More or less be him in his absence. Why not you? You have an extra room for the office and we would provide all the necessities. Think about it and rest. I'm going to go start dinner." Elizabeth left the room.

Reyne sat on her bed in disbelief as Elizabeth went to the kitchen. *"Work from home for Xavier?"* She thought. She could hear

Elizabeth moving around in the kitchen, looking for food, pots, spices, etc. trying to cook a meal. "Maybe I should go down with her and help?" but she couldn't rally enough courage to get out of bed again. She felt useless. But what about the job offer? Of course, Xavier would have his say, so he probably wouldn't hire her. Elizabeth was just trying to make her feel better. She was sure of it.

Reyne heard Elizabeth yell for Taylor to come in for dinner. "My god, is it really that late?" Reyne said aloud as she looked at her alarm clock. The front door opened, and she heard Tyler and Lazarus make the announcement that they were home. "I guess it is." Reyne rolled over, stared at the wall and cried herself to sleep.

Elizabeth made a dinner of burritos and tacos, set the table, and called Taylor to dinner. Tyler and Lazarus arrived just in time to sit down with Elizabeth and Taylor for dinner.

As they all sat at the table eating, the doorbell rang. Elizabeth went to the door. "Hi Honey. Come on in. Would like to join us for dinner?" It was Xavier. He knew that Elizabeth was making her move and wanted to check her progress.

"I would love to, thanks." Xavier came into the dining room and sat at the table. Elizabeth brought another place setting to the table and sat back down.

After dinner, Lazarus and Tyler offered to clean up the dishes while Elizabeth got Taylor ready for bed. He was not happy about this new arrangement. He would have to talk to Leigh about it soon.

Elizabeth and Taylor went up to his room. Taylor got his pajamas and a towel while Elizabeth started his bath. She got him into the tub and washed his hair. "I'm gonna check on your Momma. I'll be right back." She smiled as she left Taylor playing with his bath toys. She stopped at the top of the stairs and listened to Lazarus and Xavier talk and thought, "*Lazarus had grown into a fine young man. Xavier should offer him a job, before he finds out the truth. I'll mention it to him later, but right now, our focus is*

Reyne." She turned from the stairs and went into Reyne's bedroom. The thought completely left her when she walked into Reyne's bedroom and found Reyne was sleeping soundly.

Elizabeth gathered up the laundry in Reyne's room and went back into the hallway. She put the laundry on the floor and went into the bathroom. "Come on Taylor. Let's get out of the bath. We'll get the laundry together and go watch some TV." She opened the towel for Taylor to walk into as he exited the tub. She helped him dry off, got him dressed, and gathered the laundry from his room. The two of them went to the basement, and he showed her how they sorted the clothes into piles. She let Taylor pour the laundry detergent into the washer while she added the clothes. When the laundry was started, they walked into the family room and started watching TV.

Xavier, Lazarus, and Tyler came into the family room after they had finished cleaning the kitchen and dining room area. Tyler sat down beside Elizabeth. "Thanks for everything, Elizabeth. How is Mom? I don't like to see her like this, but I'm glad that the asshole showed his true colors now."

"She is sleeping. She has done a lot of crying, but she will be better soon. I told Reyne I would take care of Taylor until she felt better. I also promised Leigh I would help out around the house."

Taylor smiled at Elizabeth, "Thank you for being her friend." Then she and Lazarus headed to her bedroom.

After a couple of shows Xavier got ready to leave. He and Elizabeth walked up stairs with Taylor following.

"Wait here, honey. I've got to get Taylor into bed. I'll be right back." Elizabeth turned to Taylor. "Come on, I'll tuck you in."

Taylor took her hand and walked up the stairs with her. She opened his bedroom door and followed him in. The blankets had been pulled back and the night light was already on. Reyne sat on the bed waiting for her son.

"Hey Baby. You ready for a story?"

Taylor ran to Reyne and hugged her. "Yes, Momma, are you feeling better?"

"Not completely, but I feel well enough to read to you and finish our nightly routine." She hugged Taylor with all her weakened ability. "Thank you Elizabeth. I can tuck him in from here. I'll be down when I'm done here. I really appreciate everything you are doing." She smiled at Elizabeth as she picked up the book she and Taylor had been reading.

Elizabeth looked at her warily, "Why don't I come back up in about an hour and check on you?"

"All right. I'll see you in an hour." Reyne turned to Taylor and continued reading.

When Elizabeth left the room, Taylor said, "Momma, I don't like her. There is something wrong with her.

Reyne gave him a weak smile, "Really? When you figure it out please tell me. I will believe you, but until you figure it out, you have to be nice to her and let her help. Okay?"

"Okay, Momma." He answered and listened to the rest of the story. Then, Reyne gave him a kiss, tucked him in and went back to her room.

Elizabeth met Xavier at the front door. She kissed him good-bye and locked the door behind him. She turned around and was startled to find Lazarus standing right behind her. "Oh, Lazarus, you startled me."

"Why are you here? Where is Leigh?" He stared down at her.

"Aren't you nice?" she sneered, but quickly regained her composure. "Leigh was exhausted. She had stayed up with Reyne all last night. I offered to stay with Reyne during the week and Leigh will come over the weekends. We agreed, and Reyne agreed as well. Reyne took off all week and needs the company. I don't work, Leigh does, so it seemed only natural that I help out. It was Xavier's fault that Onyx left and put Reyne in this mood. What else could I do?" Elizabeth stared hard at Lazarus. She knew his secret of being able to tell things about people, but she felt certain that she had hidden her true agenda from him.

"Tyler and I are here. I'm sleeping on the sofa, here in the living room, so if you want to go home and get some sleep, I can listen for her. I guess you could come back in the morning, though. Tyler and I are usually on our way to work by 7 am." Lazarus did not trust her for good reason, but didn't know what else to do. Even after what Leigh told him, she trusted Elizabeth, so if Leigh now trusted her, maybe he should, but it was going against every fiber in his body. He definitely needed to talk to Leigh.

"Then I'll be back at 6:45 tomorrow morning that way Reyne and Taylor aren't alone. I don't think she is up to trying to handle Taylor alone right now. She is really depressed. I feel so bad for her." Elizabeth did feel bad that Reyne was suffering, but it was necessary and Elizabeth would allow it to continue. "*After Onyx is gone, Xavier and I will relive her pain with an eternity of pleasure.*" Elizabeth wanted to gain his trust but realized she would have to do it without influence. Her influence was not working. "Let me check on her and change the laundry, then I will leave for the evening. Okay?"

Lazarus nodded. She went upstairs. Reyne was back in her own bed. Elizabeth checked to see if she needed anything. She let Reyne know Lazarus was in the living room. She would be back in the morning before Lazarus and Tyler left for work.

Elizabeth returned to the living room after changing the laundry, "See you later Lazarus. And thank you." Elizabeth walked to the door and left.

Lazarus laid on the sofa for a long time, waiting and listening for Reyne before falling into a very light sleep. His last thoughts before he fell asleep were that the danger was so close, but there was nothing he could do. They were strong enough to fight it without Onyx.

Elizabeth arrived promptly the next few mornings. She always checked on Reyne before getting Taylor up for each day. Most mornings Reyne was just lying in her bed staring at the wall, but on Friday she was in the shower when Elizabeth arrived.

Elizabeth woke up Taylor, went downstairs, and started breakfast for Reyne and Taylor. It was good to see Reyne up and moving. Elizabeth was packing Taylor's lunch when the phone rang, "I wonder who it could be this early in the morning?" She said aloud before picking up the receiver. "Hello?"

"What are you doing there?" Onyx asked with fear and hate intermingled in his voice.

"Protecting and caring for someone who has become very special and very close to me. You ran out on her. I stepped in." Elizabeth smirked, knowing this would hurt him.

"Where is she? What have you done to her?"

"I have done nothing but be her friend when she was so hurt by you. She is in the shower. I'm making breakfast for Taylor and her. Because of you, this is the first time she has been out of bed since Monday. I think I should be questioning you about what you want. I'm not letting you near her again. She is mine now." Elizabeth said stinging him again with her tone.

"Where is Leigh?" Onyx growled.

"Leigh calls daily. She has to work, unlike Reyne, who has been offered a job where she can work at home when she is ready to return to work. Xavier is going to hire her." Elizabeth knew this bit of information would send him over to anger completely. This would bring his vampiric tendencies out and would prove to be his downfall.

"Please let me talk to her." Onyx asked calmly.

"No." Elizabeth hung up the phone. The shower had stopped and she could hear Reyne walking around upstairs. Elizabeth made Reyne a cup of coffee and took it to her bedroom.

"Good morning Reyne. I was beginning to worry about you. I am glad to see you are up and moving. Here is some coffee. I have gotten Taylor up and moving. His breakfast is ready." She handed Reyne the coffee and left the room.

Once she had taken Taylor to daycare, she returned to Reyne's bedroom. "How are you feeling today?"

"I'm still depressed, but I have to start moving. I have to go back to work in two days, and if I don't move today, I will never be ready. Did I hear the phone ring? Who was it?" Reyne sighed and started curling back into bed.

Elizabeth grabbed her, "Yes, it was a wrong number. And there is no way you are getting back in bed. We are going out. Finish getting ready."

Reyne smiled, "OK, give me 20 minutes to get dressed." Reyne came into the kitchen exactly 20 minutes later. She was dressed, hair brushed, makeup on, and shoes on her feet. "I'm ready to go. Where are we going?"

"We are going to see Xavier. He wanted me to bring you to the house to discuss with you the job opportunity I had discussed with you before. He told me to bring you over as soon as you were up and moving on your own." Elizabeth smiled. She refilled Reyne's coffee mug and turned off the coffeepot. "Let's go."

Reyne was completely floored. She had been sure that Elizabeth had just told her about the job to make her feel better. When Reyne didn't move, Elizabeth grabbed Reyne's hand and pulled her out the door. They walked down to Elizabeth's house to meet with Xavier.

As Elizabeth opened the door, she yelled, "She is here, honey. She is up on her own and wants to know more." She turned to Reyne, "Go have a seat in the dining room. He will be right in. I will go get him."

Elizabeth ran up the stairs while Reyne made herself comfortable in the dining room. Xavier came down a few minutes later with papers in his hand. He greeted her and asked if she needed more coffee. After she declined, he proceeded to tell her about the job opportunity he hoped she would accept. Two hours later, Elizabeth and Reyne were walking back to Reyne's house.

"Did you take his offer?" Elizabeth asked.

"Well, Elizabeth, as soon as we go in, I am going to email my boss and let him know that I am giving my two weeks. I took Xavier up on his offer." Reyne felt the stress leave almost immediately, and she smiled at Elizabeth.

"I am so happy. This way, I may be able to hang around here more often when he is on business trips. Maybe, now, I'll get him to settle down and start a family." She said, and smiled wickedly. Little did Reyne know that they were going to make her the start of their family.

CHAPTER 24

Onyx called Leigh's home number soon after Elizabeth hung up the phone. He knew he had to tell them everything, too. He would need their help protecting her.

The phone on the other end rang several times before voice mail picked up. Onyx left a message and hung up. He proceeded to call Leigh at work.

"Leigh Stein's desk," she answered.

"Hello Leigh, it's Onyx." He hoped she did not hang up on him.

The fog that had been hiding the missing piece vanished as he spoke, like breaking a spell. The realization of what she had done hit her all at once and she sobbed, "Onyx, I need your help. I am scared for Reyne." She had terror in her voice. "What have I done? I couldn't remember until I heard your voice."

"Well this is a surprise, because I was going to ask you to help me, because I am afraid for Reyne...but why are you afraid and what do you mean by 'what have I done?'" Onyx needed to know what happened before he could ask for her help.

"Don't be mad at me, Onyx, but I overheard your conversation at the barbecue. The conversation with Xavier and Elizabeth. I am scared for Reyne because Elizabeth has taken over. I don't know how she did it, but it felt right at the time when she told me she would help and until you spoke, I thought it was all okay. I didn't remember anything. Now I know I have really screwed up, but I still don't know why or how. I told Lazarus about the conversation, but if she did to him what she did to me...Oh my god. She has been with Reyne for the last four days. She answers and screens all Reyne's calls. She even told Benjamin that Taylor couldn't come over for a while, because he was helping keep Reyne happy and she was afraid if he went away for the weekend, Reyne may relapse. It just doesn't seem right. I am supposed to take over to-night for the weekend. Do you want to come over tonight?"

"I didn't realize how far in she had gotten. I thought she was joking when she said Xavier offered Reyne a job, but it must be true. She's in too close. You heard the conversation, then you know why I need your help. I can offer you a job so that you can stay with Reyne, but I need you to be there as of now, but I know that is impossible. Whatever you do, do not leave her alone or with any-one other than me, Andy, yourself or Brian, whom you will meet shortly. I am sure you told Andy?" Onyx knew he would have to work fast to save her. Xavier and Elizabeth were not wasting any time.

"What job? She can't take it. And actually, no, I haven't told anyone but Lazarus. I will give my boss notice…"

"No notice. Just call in on Monday and tell them you quit. I will ensure you are paid well, but forget about it until I am at Reyne's house. Then we will discuss it more. I will be there on Sunday af-ternoon. But for now, I need you to tell Andy what has transpired. I need the two of you to stay with her and the kids around the clock. Promise me."

"OK I promise." Leigh had relaxed; Onyx could hear it in her voice.

"Call her now and tell her you'll be there with takeout dinner. See what she is doing. I'll call back in two hours to find out what she has said. Please do this. Her life may depend on it." Onyx pleaded with Leigh but was trying to stay calm so that he did not scare her more than necessary. "Just pretend that this conversa-tion didn't happen. Elizabeth will know if you keep thinking about it."

"I understand. I will talk to you in two hours. I'm going to get a cup of coffee and call her as soon as I regain my composure. Talk to you later." Leigh hung up and went into her boss's office to ask if she could clock out a little early. She had decided to leave work as soon as Onyx called her back.

She returned to her desk with a cup of coffee and dialed Reyne's number.

Elizabeth and Reyne had just returned home. Reyne was in her office, straightening up the area so that she could start work on Monday. Elizabeth was in the kitchen preparing lunch when the phone rang. She stopped making the sandwiches and answered the phone, "Hello?"

"Oh, hi Elizabeth. I thought Reyne would be up and moving by today. She sounded a little better yesterday." Leigh could tell she did not sound like herself.

"Oh, she's up and in her office cleaning it up. She had something good happen today. We went out today after I got Taylor off to daycare. She is still depressed, but she feels she has to get back into the swing of things. She has a chance to change things with the offer Xavier gave her. Things are really looking up for her. I have gotten used to helping with Taylor, and I'm going to offer to continue to help her. I quite enjoy it," Elizabeth said innocently.

"That would be nice, but why are you doing all this for her?" Leigh blatantly asked.

"She is the first person who has been my friend in a long time. Plus, this is as much Xavier's fault as Onyx's. I am trying to get forgiveness for his actions. She doesn't deserve this," Elizabeth feigned.

"May I speak with her?" Leigh asked.

"Let me check to see if she is up to taking calls. Hold on." Elizabeth put the phone down and walked into the foyer by the stairway.

Leigh suddenly knew that Elizabeth wasn't going to tell Reyne she was on the phone. Now she was really worried. She heard Elizabeth returning. "She is actually laying on the floor in her office sleeping. I'll tell her you called when she wakes up."

"Actually, just tell her I'll be over this afternoon. I am bringing dinner. You have worked so hard all week with her. I figure it is my turn. You and Xavier need time alone. I'll be over around 4. Bye." Leigh hung up the phone without giving Elizabeth time to respond.

"Damn it," Elizabeth thought as she hung up her receiver. Leigh was going to be a problem. But she would have Xavier take care of her as soon as possible. She would have to let her over for the weekend; otherwise, it would seem suspicious. "Damn," Elizabeth scowled as she said it aloud.

Elizabeth finished the lunches and called upstairs to Reyne. Reyne came down the steps in a rush.

"I'm glad you called. I'm famished. What's for lunch?" Reyne hugged Elizabeth.

"Just turkey sandwiches," Elizabeth placed the plate in front of Reyne.

Reyne ate quickly and returned to her office. She sent the email to her boss telling him that she wouldn't be returning to work and finished preparing her office for her new job on Monday. She would finally be working from home. She was so excited.

Onyx called Leigh back at the appointed time. Leigh told him everything that happened while she was on the phone with Elizabeth. She told him how she knew that Elizabeth had never even told Reyne that she was on the phone. "What should I do, Onyx?"

"It's okay. Just go over tonight with dinner and don't leave. I will have everything brought to you. My number and my lawyer's number are in her address book. His name is Brian Gold. If you call either one of us, we will be there immediately." Onyx was relieved. Leigh would be back with his Reyne shortly.

Leigh cringed and asked, "Could you give them to me yourself? I gave the address book to Elizabeth and she may have crossed them out or something. I don't want to be without them. Also, I told Elizabeth that I would be over around 4. I'm leaving work early. I'm still worried, but I'm going to put my faith in you. Don't let me down," she said emphatically.

"Fine. Here are the numbers," Onyx said, giving Leigh the two numbers. "And Leigh, I won't let anyone down. Just remember that if you need anything, anything at all, call Brian or me. Promise me you won't try to do it on your own or leave her alone. Get Lazarus to stay around the clock, too. He is more important than either he or she realizes. I'll hire him too," Onyx pushed.

"I promise. I'll talk to you later. I'll call with a progress report. Oh, yeah. I almost forgot. Elizabeth mentioned something about Xavier offering Reyne a job or something, and now her stress is a lot less. Is this what you were talking about? Reyne had mentioned it earlier this week. She told me she thought Elizabeth had just told her that to help her get out of her funk. What if he really did offer a job?" Leigh asked her voice trembling.

"Oh, he offered, and she is in more danger than I realized. Stay with her. Go now." Onyx hung up the phone. He could not go to her before Sunday. He had to take care of a problem he knew Xavier had created. Xavier and Elizabeth were definitely doing their best to keep Onyx away from Reyne. Protecting her was going to be hard, but he had the help of her friends now and his father's body-guards, but they would only interfere if her life was in danger. However, finishing this centuries old altercation with Xavier was not going to be easy. Onyx had vowed a long time ago that he would do it on his own. He would not call on his father to help unless he absolutely needed to.

CHAPTER 25

Leigh arrived at Reyne's house promptly at 4 pm. She had already stopped at the daycare and picked up Taylor, and gone to the grocery store to get food to make dinner. She walked into the house with Taylor and placed the grocery bags in the kitchen. Elizabeth was nowhere to be found, and neither was Reyne. "Where are they? I told Elizabeth I would be her now. I've gotta find them."

"Leigh? May I go play my video game?" Taylor asked.

"Yeah for a little bit." Leigh wanted to act normal for Taylor's sake. She had to find Reyne.

Leigh walked upstairs to see if Reyne was in her room, and then went into the office to see if she was in there. Of course, she wasn't in either room, but the office had been cleaned up and organized. *"She decided to accept the job from Xavier."* Leigh thought as she walked back down the stairs and into the kitchen. She put the groceries away before they spoiled and then went to check the deck off the living room. As she walked to the sliding glass door, she saw Elizabeth and Reyne at the table on the deck.

Both women had their backs to the sliding glass door. Leigh slowly and quietly opened the door. "Boo."

Reyne jumped and squealed, and Elizabeth jumped. Leigh giggled. "Leigh, you are incorrigible," Reyne giggled as she scolded Leigh.

"I couldn't help it. It was too easy. I had to do it. How are you both doing?" Leigh said as she sat down.

"I'm fine. I'm getting back to my old self again. What are you doing here?" Reyne looked from Leigh to Elizabeth.

Leigh scowled, "Elizabeth didn't tell you. I called earlier and told her I'd be coming over tonight to make dinner and spend some time with you and the kids."

"Oh, I'm sorry Reyne. I totally forgot to tell you. It must have slipped my mind. I'm sorry Leigh. I got distracted and forgot to tell her," Elizabeth said with false sincerity Leigh could now see and the fog that was trying to take over again was blocked. She knew Onyx had something to do with that.

Elizabeth was good, and she might have Reyne blinded, but Leigh knew better now. Leigh knew her plans; she had heard the conversation. Right now, she had to play it cool. "That's all right." She gave a weak smile. "Thanks for helping her this week. It looks like you worked wonders."

"I just kept making her do things, like getting up and showered. She really came back to life when Xavier offered her the job with his company and she accepted. It was like a ton of weight had been lifted from her shoulders," Elizabeth all but gloated.

"You mentioned it earlier this week. So you accepted?" Leigh turned to Reyne.

"Of course! Who wouldn't? I get to work from home. No more commute," Reyne smiled and glowed with the thought of being able to work from home and be close to Taylor and Tyler. She had always hated the drive to D.C. and now she did not have to do it anymore.

Elizabeth felt the tension and decided to break it, "Well, I have ignored Xavier most of this week. I guess I should go and spend some time with him. Maybe have him take me to dinner. It has been so long since we've fed…dined together. I'll see you two later." Elizabeth got up to leave. "You two have catching up to do. I'll let myself out." She walked over to Reyne and kissed her check and left.

Leigh waited for a few minutes before she lit a cigarette and turned to Reyne. "I am here to make dinner and help you get ready for your new job. I guess we need to get the house in order so that you aren't cleaning instead of working." Leigh hoped she sounded truly excited for Reyne.

"Sounds great." Reyne hugged Leigh. "I've missed you. Thanks for everything. I've gotta go get Taylor still. I'll do that while you start dinner."

"Already home. I picked him up and brought him home. He is downstairs playing video games. Let's go make dinner," Leigh said as she finished her cigarette.

Reyne and Leigh walked into the house and worked on dinner. The whole evening went well. Leigh called Benjamin and told him Reyne was doing much better. She asked if he could take Taylor tonight but not all weekend just, so Reyne could have a night to finally recharge and get back to normal. Lazarus and Tyler went to Lazarus parent's house for the night but promised Leigh they would be back in the morning. Lazarus and Leigh had a few minutes to talk and she filled him in on what Onyx had said. They both agreed that to act normal was best and that for tonight they all would be safe. Tonight he and Tyler would go to his parent's house, but as of tomorrow morning, they would stay there. Once everyone was gone, Leigh and Reyne spent Friday night alone watching movies and catching up.

On Saturday, Reyne, Leigh, and Lazarus cleaned the house. They scrubbed every room until it gleamed. They wiped down all the walls, took the blinds down and washed them, changed all the bed linen, finished all the laundry. When they were done, Lazarus went to Tyler's room, and Reyne and Leigh fell onto the sofa exhausted, just as the phone started ringing. The two women just looked at each other and said in unison, "Fuck it."

After a few minutes, Reyne got up, went to the kitchen, and grabbed some glasses and a bottle of wine. She returned to the living room and was about to sit down on the floor with Leigh when the doorbell rang. "Who could that be?"

"I don't know. You want me to get it?" Leigh asked. She knew it was probably Andy, but wasn't completely sure. She had told him enough that he wasn't going to be leaving there side much unless he had to or it looked suspicious.

"Nope, I'm up; I'll get it." Reyne walked to the door and peeked through the peephole. "It's Andy." She said, calling to Leigh, "Should I let him in?"

"I don't know. Let me think about it." Leigh had run to the door and was talking loud enough that Andy could hear them.

"Come on girls, let me in." Andy shouted through the door.

"That is so pathetic." Reyne said as she opened the door.

"Thanks." Andy said as he walked into the house. "How you doing Reyne?"

"I'm fine. And you?" Reyne answered with a smile.

"Better if Leigh would have called this morning like she said she would. I tried calling a few minutes ago and there was no answer…" he started.

Leigh and Reyne started laughing.

"What is so funny, you two?" Andy was getting upset. He had been worried. What did they expect of him?

"Honey, we had just sat down from cleaning all day. We were exhausted and when the phone rang, we couldn't move to answer it. I'm sorry. Forgive me?" Leigh gave him her best puppy dog pout.

"All right. I'll grab my own glass and meet you in the living room," he said as he headed to the kitchen.

The three of them congregated on the floor in the living room. They sat there most of Saturday night, just talking, enjoying themselves, and getting silly. Eventually, they all fell asleep in the living room from exhaustion and wine.

Reyne had called Benjamin and Taylor and asked if Taylor could stay until Sunday so she could finish cleaning the house and prepare for her new job. Of course they both said yes, so Reyne felt that the free time Saturday was well deserved and earned.

Sunday morning came and went. Not one of the three awoke before 2 pm. Reyne was the first to wake. She went outside and got the Sunday paper. She brewed some coffee, then sat at the kitchen table and began reading the main article on the front page.

"NO!" Reyne shrieked.

Leigh groggily came running to the kitchen. She saw Reyne just sitting at the table oblivious to most everything going on. "What's wrong? Tell me!"

"Onyx is in the paper." She said in a monotone.

"What?" Andy had come around the corner of the kitchen.

Leigh fixed two cups of coffee for Andy and her and sat at the table with Reyne.

"There have been a bunch of murders in the Washington, DC area in the last several weeks. Two more occurred last night. They saw the person who did it. The suspect is 6'2", mid-twenties, brown hair with golden highlights, hazel eyes, strong thin build…"

"Reyne, Sweetie, it can't be him. It sounds like Onyx, but I don't believe that he is a murderer. Call him. Call him now. I don't even think he is in town. Remember, he said he had to take care of some stuff out of town this week? He said he would call you today. Remember? Call him," Leigh pressed. She did not want to believe Onyx was in this mess, but she wanted to be sure.

Reyne picked up the phone and called Onyx. When she hung up, she told Leigh and Andy that Onyx would be over in an hour. She called Benjamin and asked him if Taylor could stay with him one more night. She hated to ask, but she wanted this finished before her son returned home especially if Onyx was a murderer. When that was agreed, she told Lazarus to keep Tyler away from the house. He agreed half-heartedly knowing he was going against what Onyx wanted. He told her they would stay at his parents later than normal but that they would be home tonight.

"OK, I need a shower. Come on Leigh. You gotta help me stay sane through this," Reyne rasped in disbelief.

Leigh followed Reyne to the bedroom. She straightened up the room and made Reyne's bed, while Reyne took her shower. She finished getting ready while Leigh took her shower. The two returned to the kitchen to wait for Onyx. Reyne prepared another pot of coffee and started pacing.

"Stop pacing, you're making me nervous," Leigh grabbed her and sat her down. "It will be okay. Just believe in him if you really love him as much as you say you do."

The doorbell rang as soon as Leigh had finished speaking. Reyne went to answer the door. "Hello, Onyx. Please come in," she said curtly.

"Thank you." He walked into the kitchen with her.

Leigh went to the family room in the basement after saying their hellos to Onyx. Andy shook his hand and gave him a look of good luck before following Leigh to the basement.

"I know why you have asked me to come over. You saw the article in the paper. I saw it on the way over and figured it out. I guess that I have to tell you things that I should have told you before, but I was afraid that it would turn you from me." He hesitated and then continued, "I am not what I appear to be."

"What do you mean, you're not what you appear to be? What should a murderer look like?" she asked suspiciously.

Onyx took a deep breath, "I am not the person who has been murdering in DC the last few weeks. I am a dhampir. I have been living my life as a vampire until I could find my Beloved. Once I found her and introduced myself to her, I would court her. If and when she fell in love with me again, she and I would decide if we live as vampires or as mortals. I still have the choice. But let me stop for a moment, I am getting ahead of myself, and I want you to understand."

Reyne was astonished. She couldn't imagine this being the truth. She decided to call him on it. "May I see where you sleep? Can I watch you suck someone's blood?" asked Reyne in a snide voice. She was having a hard time believing that he was really a vampire.

"It is just a bed. I do not need a coffin, if that is what you think. Moreover, I don't think watching me feed will help the situation currently. I think you should let me explain first," he answered.

"I just want to understand what you are telling me. It doesn't make sense to me. What I have read and heard about vampires doesn't seem to fit you. You seem to have only the vampiric attributes you find necessary to create your public persona. Plus, they are just myths," her voice rising.

"My persona is who I am. I am not a vampire, I told you that. I can exist in daylight as can most vampires, can look upon a crucifix, and can even touch holy water and salt. Again, we are getting ahead of things. Maybe I should explain my heritage and my past for you to better understand what I am. For I am not a vampire, nor am I one of the people in today's society that find living and acting in a vampiric way as fun, interesting or even necessary as some of their cases may be. They are all human in the end. I am not. At least not totally. I have chosen to live this in-between way only until I could be with you again," Onyx stated.

Reyne so wanted to believe him. She knew she had to give him a chance. Leigh had told her to and Leigh wouldn't steer her wrong especially as she did not like Onyx initially. Something had changed. "I still don't understand. Please tell me your past, tell me everything. I want…No. I need and deserve to know."

"Are you sure you are ready for all of it?" Onyx asked.

"No, but I have to be," was all Reyne could say. She wasn't sure she was ready for it, but if she was going to be with him, she needed to know.

He took her hand and led her to the sofa. They sat down, he turned to face her, and started his tale. "Here is my family heritage and history. It is a long story. It is one I feel you need to hear, and obviously one you want to hear. I am sure that I will be leaving things out, but here are the basics. My full name is Adrik Ondrej Dracul. In my native language, it means Dark Strong Dragon. My mother gave me the name the day I was born. My cousins nick-named me Onyx, well, one cousin, and it stuck. I have been going by Onyx since my 5th birthday, 546 years ago."

"You can't be that old! You...." she interrupted.

"Can and am. Now you wanted to hear this, so don't interrupt again or I will not continue," Onyx said as he scowled at Reyne. "Now listen. You want answers? You want to know about me? Then listen. I will answer any questions you have when I am done telling you about me. The story of my life should clarify some questions as it goes on."

"My mother and father did not tell me I was different. The whole village knew, but all agreed to let me be raised normally, as my parents wished, and maybe I would never realize that I was different. And so it went for many years. It was not a stigma in my village to be a dhampir; in fact, it was a place of honor. However, my mother wanted to raise me as normal as possible. I don't know why, but it was ultimately her choice until I was an adult. I was 17 years old when my arranged marriage took place. I never had a problem with it because I had been in love with my future wife for as long as I could remember. Her family agreed to her marriage to me only because of what I am, for it is an honor, even though I still remained oblivious to it. Her name was Sofija. In modern times, her name would have been Sophia. She was 15 at the time of our marriage. She looked very much as you do. I agreed to go and live with her family until I could build a house for us to make a home. Within a year, our home was completed and Sophia and I moved in. We were very happy. However, when she was still not with child after our first year together, people were beginning to get worried. Sophia and I were not, but others were. To put it delicately, she had much pain during intercourse and I agreed to wait until she felt she was ready. Therefore, since our marriage consummation, I had not touched her in a sexual way. We could tell no one; not even our families." He took a breath, as if reliving this memory was painful.

Reyne reached out to touch him softly. He smiled at her touch and continued.

"It was three years before we even tried again. She was 18 years old, and I was 20. I went slowly and gently. All went well. Within 2 months, she was with child. However, it was during the first three years of our marriage before she became pregnant, strange things began to happen to me and I didn't understand why. I would be attracted to her pulsating veins. The veins didn't need to be her neck, as many vampire legends would have the world believe. It could be any vein. I longed to drink her essence. Thoughts occurred to me. I wanted to rip her skin off and drink from her as one would drink from a bottle of wine, the thought of which was extremely arousing and sensual and it scared me to death. I stopped sleeping with her when we moved into our own house. I had not told her of my new urges because I thought something was wrong with me and could not stand the thought of losing her. In addition, I began to prefer the night to the day. I never let on because I had my farming chores, but I would take naps in the middle of the day, and would work long after dark when others couldn't see."

"One night, we got into a fight when I again refused to sleep in the same bed as her. She looked at me in confusion and hurt and asked me why. She asked if I wanted to find a concubine until she was ready. She asked me to tell her what she had done to drive me away. I couldn't stand hurting her. I broke down crying. I fell to my knees, wrapped my arms around her, and explained that she wasn't the problem. I told her it was I that was the problem. That I was afraid of telling her about the strange thoughts and cravings because I couldn't bear losing her. I didn't know why I was having these thoughts and cravings, but I was afraid if I told her, she would leave me. She took me and held me for a long time. She said that it was all right. She knew I would be having these cravings eventually, and she was surprised it took this long for them to appear. I was mortified. She knew, but why had she kept it a secret from me? Why had my mother and father kept this secret from me? I wanted to go confront them. Sophia would not let me. She sat me down and told me everything. She started by telling me that my mother's husband was not my father. My father was Vlad Dracul, the First, and I was the child of a human and vampire. I was a dhampir. She giggled and said I should have noticed the signs in myself, but I hadn't. I had known other dhampirs all my life. My cousin, Xavier, was one. But I never saw it in myself. Maybe I just refused to accept what I saw in myself."

"After that night she would bring me live animals from the forest as tokens of love and to let me know that she would be with me forever or until our deaths, which ever we decided. For we were allowed to decide between immortality and mortality, but once chosen, we could not change our minds. We had many discussions and decided that we would take immortality after we had children, because it is excruciatingly painful for a woman to breed as a vampire, but not impossible. I contacted my father and told him of our decision, and he agreed."

"As I said earlier, she was 18 years old when she became pregnant with our first child. I slept late into each day and stayed up late into the night. It was acceptable, for I was a dhampir and had acknowledged my heritage by that time. I talked with my family about the secret and we made amends. Everyone was so happy when Sophia became pregnant and all went well for many months. When she was a month from her due date, she began hemorrhaging. No one could stop the bleeding or the stillbirth of my son. The blood. Her blood was driving me mad. It smelled so sweet, so exotic. I had never tasted human blood at this point. My mother, my human father, and Sophia's family were all there. They knew I was in agony, but I refused to leave her side."

"Then my true father arrived. He walked into the bedroom like he owned it. All backed away from him except me and my mother.

He saw the small dead child and began to weep. He picked up my son and told me to drink. I was horrified. He said I must before the baby completely died and the blood cooled. I must drink now. My mother came to me and told me to do as my father said, so I did. I almost completely drained my son. I saw the man he would have become, and I wept. Then my father told me to drink of Sophia because even he couldn't save her at that point, but if I truly loved her, we would be together again. But first I would have to drink from her. He emphasized that I will not kill her but take just enough to become one with her. I, again, was mortified, but I did as I was instructed. I became one with her and it was both beautiful and sad. I wept for my losses. I held Sophia for hours until she finally passed on to the next realm. I missed her already. Her and the baby's bodies were taken from the house and given a proper burial within a few days. After their burial, I was summoned to my true father's house. I spent twenty years there, living as a vampire, never returning to my village. My mother would visit me at my true father's house, but I would never go to visit her and she understood that I could never return to the village, where my Beloved and my child were buried."

"After the twenty years with my father, learning the ways of the vampire, he told me that it was time to begin my search for Sophia and over the next five centuries, I ran into her seven times. I have met her in each lifetime. Unfortunately, in each life, she has either already taken a companion for the lifetime or she was not accessible due to other reasons. However, this lifetime, I have located her and to this point do not see her with a permanent companion or find any other reasons she cannot be with me. It is you, Reyne. You are my Sophia. I know you and have known you from the day of your birth in this lifetime. I have not come to you before now, because you were hard to locate. And that is my fault. I do not live as a vampire completely now and therefore, do not have as many of my gifts in their fullness. However, when I discovered that Xavier and Elizabeth had found you, I began living as a vampire again. Taking only what I needed and leaving survivors. Those folders you saw are survivors I take care of, and I will tell you all about them another time."

"Now, it is time to decide if you are willing to be my wife and companion, or if I should leave and wait another lifetime." Onyx stopped. He held out his hand to Reyne, waiting for her to respond. Hoping she would take his hand and commit to him for eternity.

Reyne sat at the table totally stupefied, "How dare you! How dare you tell me all these things, make me feel sympathy, love and caring, and then tell me that it was me! Tell me you have found me and met me in other lifetimes. Yes, I believe in reincarnation, but this is crazy. Vampires and dhampirs are just myths! You are insane! You can't be telling me the truth. GET OUT OF MY HOUSE! GET OUT NOW! And don't come back!"

"Don't you want an explanation of the article, because they are talking of me." Onyx offered the explanation knowing he had nothing to lose.

"NO! GET OUT NOW!" Reyne screamed and started swinging at him.

Onyx conceded, "I will leave, but know that I did not commit those murders. Your supposed friends, Xavier and Elizabeth," he sneered, "they committed the murders and have put it on me. Remember, he is my cousin. That should be clear now."

"Enough of your lies. GET OUT!" Reyne collapsed to the table, crying.

"As you wish. I will leave you now. I will not bother you again, but I will forever protect you. Good-bye my Beloved," Onyx walked out of the house defeated. He had hoped she would be understanding.

"Hey Onyx. Lose something?" Xavier called and started laughing.

"Never. I may not have her but neither will you." Onyx growled.

"She is mine, or should I say, Elizabeth's already," Xavier retreated into his house laughing.

Onyx climbed into the limousine and told the driver to take him back to the hotel. He sat back against the cool leather of the seat, closed the screen between him and the driver, and began to weep for the loss of his Beloved. Each lifetime, it was getting harder to find her. That was a piece of information that he could not admit to anyone. He had truly hoped that she would understand. Of course, the way it was pushed into discussion was not how he had anticipated it either. He had hoped for a little more time before he had to explain. He picked up his cell phone and called his mother.

"Hello?"

"Hello mother. I have lost her. What am I to do?" He sobbed into the phone.

"My son, all will be well…"

"No, it won't," Onyx interrupted, "Xavier and Elizabeth got here first and got to her first. In fact, she is now working for Xavier. How can I compete? Not to mention, Xavier's minions set me up for murder, at least in her eyes. She wouldn't believe a word I say." Onyx sounded heartbroken to his mother.

"Adrik Ondrej Dracul, I have never heard you this distraught over Sophia. You know that you will eventually have her again. You may just have to wait a little longer." She hoped her tough love would snap him out of the depression that was promising to overtake him.

"Mother, I am tired of waiting." He finally was ready to admit it. "It is getting harder to find her with each lifetime. I've decided I will not remain in this form much longer. If I lose her this time, I will begin living as a mortal again and will die of despair. What good is the gift my father offers if I cannot have her at my side?" She could hear the tears he shed.

Onyx's mother knew she had to get the fight back into her son and quickly. "Is she as beautiful now as she was originally?"

"She is almost the exact same image as my Sophia. Moreover, she is just smart too. I can't believe that she cannot see what is going on in front of her." Frustration entered his voice instead of sadness. He thought, "*how can I not see what is going on in front of me?*" He took a deep breath and said, "All right Mom, you win. I will not give up, at least not yet. I will continue to try to win her love in this lifetime. But…"

"Yes?" His mother knew what he was going to say, but she wanted to hear it. She wanted to make sure she knew what she was going to have to fight to save her son.

"…if she doesn't come to me in this lifetime, I will stop living as a dhampir and will live as a human and die. You do understand, don't you?" Onyx hoped his mother really understood how lonely he was for his Beloved.

"Of course." She said it tenderly, hoping that he did not realize that her mind was already working and planning to save him.

"I love you Motina. I'm back at my hotel and I'm going to feed. I will talk to you later. Bye." He said as he wiped the tears from his eyes.

"Bye, my son. I will tell your father you called." She hung up the phone.

Onyx knew he would be getting a phone call from his father very soon. He knew his mother would tell him everything. Maybe that was what he wanted. He got out of the limousine and started to head to his room. He stopped before reaching the door of the hotel and called Brian on his cell phone knowing he would have just woken for the evening.

"Hello?" Brian groggily answered the phone.

"Brian, it is time to dine. Do you want me to have them delivered? My suite or yours?" Onyx thirsted for blood. The emotions of sadness, fear, hatred and anger were merging within him and this was never a good combination in any vampire, dhampir, or human.

Brian could hear the emotion in Onyx's voice and knew he would be in for a gory night. He smiled, "Mine this round. Yours for dessert."

Onyx laughed. "First round is my treat. What flavor?"

"Mixture of gender and ethnicity." Brian countered.

"Be right up." Onyx answered as he opened the door of the limousine and told the driver to go find six to eight whores and to make sure that they were mixed in gender and ethnicity. He told him to bring them back to the hotel and personally escort the guests to Brian Gold's room.

He shut the limousine door and walked into the lobby of the hotel. He stopped by the front desk and informed them that he had subjects arriving with his driver for inspiration and they were to be led to Brian Gold's room immediately upon arrival.

He turned from the desk and made his way to Brian's room to await his feast.

CHAPTER 26

Brian was waiting at the door to his room when Onyx arrived. "Okay Onyx, what's wrong? I could tell from your voice that something is bothering you. So, tell me."

"Xavier and Elizabeth have set me up for murder, and Reyne believes that I murder for fun. I told her everything, and she still doesn't believe me." Onyx took a deep emotional breath, "I have lost her," Onyx said with a sob. Tears started rolling down his face.

Brian had never seen Onyx like this. He had seen him extremely lonely and depressed, but this was a whole new level. He knew he pined for his Beloved and knew Onyx was losing his will. He must feed and soon or his desire to feed would diminish and he would die. "How long ago did you send the driver out for dinner?"

Onyx had calmed down enough to answer, "Right before I came up to your room. He should be back soon."

As soon as Onyx finished his sentence, the phone rang. Brian answered it. "Hello? Yes, please bring them up. He needs them for his inspiration, which is quickly dwindling. He may have to go elsewhere if the inspiration does not return. Thank you." Brian hung up and started laughing. "Your driver must have found some interesting specimens. The front desk stopped him and wouldn't let him come up until we approved their coming to my room. You heard my answer, so I don't think they will bother us again."

"Maybe after tonight we should just leave and go home." Onyx no longer had any emotions. He could smell blood all around him.

Brian smiled and watched the vampire being released. He loved watching Onyx transform. He was beautiful as human and even more beautiful as a vampire. "Let's feed and then talk about our next step. I may have a plan."

The knock on the room's door interrupted Brian. He turned from Onyx and stopped for a moment. "Onyx, go into the other room. You may scare them the way you look. There is too much hunger for blood in your features at the moment."

"No. They have to come in willingly to be mine in any way. They either accept and I dine or they don't and I starve." He retorted.

"All right." Brian shrugged and opened the door as eight beautiful people came into the room in single file.

The last person to enter was a tall tan male. Onyx tried to figure out what ethnicity he was, but it was hard to concentrate. The young man blurted out, "What do you guys want? Why are we being herded into this room? We deserve to be told what is going on."

Onyx stood and walked over to the young man. He put his lips to the boy's neck, right on the carotid artery, and kissed gently. "I need inspiration. I am an artist and I need beautiful specimens to inspire me. I believe that you may be the most beautiful person I have seen a very long time. What is your name?"

The youth whispered a moan when Onyx's lips touched his neck. "My name is Seth."

Onyx stepped back from Seth. He looked at all the whores. "All of you are prostitutes? I need to know."

Slowly, they each bowed their head in shame and said yes, except Seth. There was no shame in his eyes when he nodded his answer.

Onyx had a small smile on his face. "Will you do anything for money?"

Again, they all said yes, except for Seth. He stood up and looked Onyx in the eyes. "I will not do just anything for money. I do have limits."

Onyx smiled. "Would you be my companion for a while? Would that be acceptable?"

"Oh no, Onyx. Not again…" Brian started, but both Onyx and Seth ignored him.

"How much time and how much money?" Seth asked.

"Your life will be changed forever." Onyx smiled sexily.

Brian just shook his head and stepped up after the interaction between Onyx and Seth stopped. "May I ask each of you to please follow me into the other room? There is food and drink. There is also a bathroom with a separate shower and bathtub. Please eat, drink, and clean up. There are new clothes for you as well. We will call you shortly."

Seven of the young men and women went into the other room. Onyx pulled Seth aside. "Go get a shower first and then eat. I have something special for you first." He pushed Seth through the door.

As Brian turned around, he stared hard at Onyx and started in on him. "What the hell are you doing? You want to do it again? Seriously?"

"You want me to die?" He asked Brian pointedly. "I need a companion. I need someone to stay with me. You know that this one will stay with me. The other one didn't and had to be destroyed. I went about it the wrong way, just like you said. If I don't get Reyne, I need a companion if you want me to live. Seth will be my companion."

"And if you get Reyne. Will he remain your companion?" Brian stared into Onyx's eyes, "Why would you make another when you could have me as your companion?" As soon as Brian finished, he wished he could take his last statement back. He had never wanted Onyx to know how he felt.

"What did you say, Brian?" Onyx stared at Brian.

"I would be your companion. I know you better than anyone..." Brian started.

"But you wouldn't share me with or take a back seat to Reyne. I would never expect you too. I would love for you to be my companion, my lover, but I could not keep you as I would want to. My Beloved would always come first. Could you live like that?" Onyx looked at Brian tenderly and wondered how long Brian had wanted to be with him.

"No, I couldn't. I guess I understand. I am sorry, but I would have loved to be your lover again." Brian knew the only reason he was not Onyx's lover still was because of the respect the two men shared for one another.

Onyx broke into Brian's thoughts, "Plus, I don't think you would want to push Lilith away for me, and I would never step aside for her. You know me well enough to know that." Onyx smiled at Brian.

"You're right. Go get your companion. I will work the magic." Brian's answer returned the smile to Onyx.

Onyx turned and went to the door to the rest of the suite, where they had escorted the youths. "Seth. Come with me, please." He held out his hand for Seth to grab it.

Seth cautiously took Onyx's hand and allowed himself to be pulled from the room. As the door closed, Brian locked the door from the outside so the remaining youths couldn't get out. Seth pulled back for a moment.

"Would you like to be my companion? You would live with me, possibly be my lover. You would never want or need for anything ever again." Onyx whispered in his ear, asking him the question again.

Seth answered, barely audibly, "I guess."

Onyx stepped in front of him and faced him, staring into his eyes, "No, I need a yes or no answer. There can be no wiggle room."

Seth held his head high and returned the stare, "Yes."

"Then come along. They are partying in there and you know it. They will never miss you." Onyx turned to Brian to see that he was already on the phone.

Seth looked at Brian and listened to the one-ended conversation

"Yes, we need eight to eleven more whores. Actually, make it eleven more. He needs more inspiration. Please hurry, you only have 20 minutes to have them here in my room. Have them eat and get cleaned up immediately upon arrival. Send them into the room with the other seven. And Hurry!" Brian hung up the phone and left the key to the inner rooms on the table by the phone.

"What is that all about?" Seth looked from Brian to Onyx.

"Come with us. You need to receive your payment for accepting the job of being Onyx's companion. We will explain it in more detail, but first you have to tell me you accept. You do accept, don't you?" Brian asked.

"He never told me how long or how much." Seth stated and suddenly became all business.

"Forever and, like I said, you would never want or need for anything again. I would take care of all your needs and wants. I am very rich and you would just have to be my companion, inspiration, lover." Onyx smiled at Seth, knowing that he would accept.

"Well?" Brian asked.

"I accept. I already said yes to him, but where are we going? Why can't we do it here?" Seth looked at Onyx.

"We are going to my room to give you payment. I want to show you where you will be staying until we leave this place. I also want to give you a special gift that no one else here will be given, even if they asked. I don't want them to be jealous. You understand don't you?" Onyx looked seductively at Brian first, and then Seth.

"Yes. Let's go." Seth headed to the door.

"I love watching you work. I never had or will have your abilities. It's wonderful, and it makes me remember when you had used them on me." Brian stated as he followed Seth through the door of the room.

"I respect you too much now to do that again. That happened long ago, before you became my friend. If it ever happens again, it will be straightforward with no games. I promise." Onyx passed him and caught up to Seth.

The three of them made their way to Onyx's room. Onyx opened the door for the two men and followed them in. He locked the door and quickly turned to Seth. "Are you ready to start your new life?" He seized Seth's arms and held them tightly.

Fear grew in Seth's eyes. Onyx smiled wickedly and dove into Seth's neck. Brian went to Seth's side, slit his wrist and put it over Seth's mouth, saying, "Drink Seth and live. This is your payment for your companionship and loyalty to Onyx. Remember, everything will be yours if you remain loyal to Onyx and stay his companion."

Seth was sure he was dreaming. He had lost sight, but could still feel the pain of Onyx's bite and the blood being pulled from his veins by Onyx's soft lips. As he started losing his balance, he felt someone lay him down gently and hear voices. "Drink. Drink Seth. Drink!" He felt a warm liquid drip onto his lips first. Then he felt an arm by his mouth. He grasped it and pulled it to him. The blood entered his mouth warm, sweet, metallic tasting. After the first few swallows, the pain in his neck was gone and his eyes opened. Onyx was still attached to his neck. He saw Brian's arm over his mouth. Brian's head was thrown back in the ecstasy of orgasm. He realized that this taste of blood was definitely like an orgasm. He wanted more. He began to drink harder and as he did, he saw Brian push Onyx off him.

"You must stop or you will begin to drink my blood. Now stop him and get him real food." Brian was trying to pry his arm from Seth's mouth.

Onyx put his finger in the side of Seth's mouth to release the suction and pulled Brian away. "That is enough of Brian. We all need to feed now. But first, you must be given a brief explanation. You are now a vampire. Brian has made you one for me. You will now be my companion. You will remain loyal to me first and my house second, or die. Do you understand?"

"Yes, but why me?" Seth looked in disbelief. Vampires were myth, but for some reason, he knew now what they said was true, but he did not understand why they chose him.

"Because you spoke to Onyx when you entered the room. He knew at that moment he wanted you as a companion forever. But more will be explained later, now let's find out if our feast has arrived." Brian explained.

"You brought us here to feed from us. You were going to kill us. Now you have brought me over to help you kill them." Seth screamed when he realized what was about to happen.

"Technically yes. Yes, you were among the one's to be fed from. In all honesty, most will probably still live and leave this place. We have to survive. We usually choose those who are homeless, sick, or lost to the world. We cannot get sick, so sometimes this is an act of mercy." Onyx stated flatly. "I will never lie to you."

"I understand." He said as he calmed down and thought about what they were telling him. "*I am now going to be taken care of. I hope this is worth it.*" He turned his attention back to Onyx and Brian, "Yes. I do understand. Is that why you...I guess ordered more would be appropriate to say."

"That's right Seth." Brian all but laughed at Seth's statement, "Now let's dine." Brian stated as he opened the door to leave Onyx's room.

They made their way down the hall in silence. Brian and Seth were thirsting for blood, but Seth felt it the worst.

"I need more now." Seth gasped. "I can't keep going on if I don't have some soon. I feel like I am dying."

Onyx picked him up and carried him the rest of the way to Brian's room. When they got inside, Onyx laid Seth on the sofa and asked, "You are dying, but once you have your first real feeding and rest, you will be fine. Now do you have one in particular from the original group that you would like to feed from to begin your new life?"

"How do I do this? Do I just bite and feed?" Seth asked.

"For right now, that would be best, but we will teach you to feed during sex to make the experience wonderful for each participant. It is not really sex for you, but they believe it is. You will soon understand. I promise. Would you prefer to watch the first one, but that may be painful for you? You are young and must feed more often." Onyx sat on the floor next to the sofa.

"I don't have the energy to hold the person. Will you do it for me?"

"I would do just about anything for you." Onyx said.

"I want Glory. She is the one I want to kill first. She deserves the pain of the inexperienced vampire ripping and tearing to get to her blood." As Seth finished his sentence, he realized that his cock was hard and throbbing.

"You don't have to kill her." Onyx said and then looked at Seth's lower region and smiled. "Smell of blood getting you horny, young man?"

"Seems to be." He smiled at Onyx. "I want to kill her. She deserves it. Bring her in and thank you."

Brian moved to the door and called for Glory. Onyx had taken Seth into the bedroom and undressed him. As he undressed Seth, he told him what was going to happen. Seth agreed and allowed Onyx to tie him to the bed. Onyx gave Brian the signal, and Glory came into the room.

Onyx walked over to Glory and extended his hand, "Welcome. We have a gift for you. I believe you know him. His name is Seth. Do with him as you will, but make sure that you are penetrated by him while doing so."

Glory gave a suspicious look to Onyx. "I can do whatever I want to him as long as I'm riding him? Is that it?"

"Yes." Both Brian and Onyx answered as they sat in chairs beside the bed.

"You just want to watch? That's it?" Glory started smiling. She couldn't stand the fact that Seth got more money for doing less because of his beauty. She would make him pay for all the times he took her tricks and her money, "Not a problem."

Glory moved to the bed and began stroking Seth's shaft. It grew even bigger in her hands. Her eyes grew wide as she realized the size of his shaft; it was huge. She almost forgot that she hated him, but the urge to hurt him grew almost as fast as his cock. She pulled a condom from her pocket.

"No condoms." Onyx and Brian said in unison.

"Then no show." Glory stated and started to walk out of the room.

Brian grabbed her arm and spun her around. "You will perform and you will ride him without a condom. If you don't, you will never leave here. I want to see flesh on flesh, not flesh on latex. And I want you naked." He pushed her roughly toward the bed, "Now do it." He demanded.

She quickly undressed, started climbing on top of him, but stopped short. "Is he secure? I don't want him to hurt me during our show."

Onyx smiled at Glory, "I assure you he is secure, and..."

"Don't let that bitch touch me. I've heard she has diseases that are incurable!" Seth yelled as he writhed on the bed showing, he was constrained.

"Bitch? I'll make you pay for that," Glory scowled as she turned back to the bed and took Seth's cock in her mouth. She sucked it hard and deep until it throbbed. She massaged herself to an orgasm while she sucked him. When she reached her apex, she climbed on top of him and slowly took him deep inside of her.

As she descended completely to the base of his cock, she leaned down toward his face, "Now you will pay. You will no longer be the beautiful boy who gets all the tricks and makes all the money. I will ruin you." Glory giggled, then opened her mouth against his and started to bite down on his lower lip.

Seth let her continue for a moment until he saw Onyx nod from the corner of his eye. He brought both arms down in a flash. One hand twined around Glory's waist to hold her to him and the other grabbed a handful of hair and pulled her mouth away from his. "You hurt me? No, baby, you got that wrong because I am gonna hurt you right before I kill you." Seth said blandly and then gave her a little smile showing his newly acquired fangs. Even as weak as he felt, he realized she couldn't pull away from him.

Glory started trembling and squirming, trying to pull away from him. She screamed in fear as he pulled her head and neck down toward his mouth. "I'll be gentle, of course." He hesitated a moment, yelling "Not!"

Seth buried his fangs deep into her throat, ripping it open, spilling more than he actually drank. The thrill of watching the fear being sculpted on her death face was a beautiful sight to him, one he would never see again and would hold in his memory forever. When she was fully drained, he threw her aside and said, "Now how about the feast?"

Onyx and Brian smiled at him. "You chose well this time, Onyx. Yes, off to the feast."

The three men returned to the room with the prostitutes and whores. Brian entered last and locked the door behind him.

"Seth, since you are new to this, you may take the most. Brian and I don't need as much to survive. We will help you and explain all you will need to know after you have sated yourself." Onyx smiled and bared his own fangs. The three turned on their guests and feasted, teaching Seth techniques and answering questions. When the feast was over, Onyx took Seth to his room and laid him on the bed to sleep while he and Brian disposed of the four bodies in the hotel incinerator. The remaining 12 whore were paid handsomely. Eight of the 12 took Onyx up on his deal of going back to school and having his help getting out of the life. The remaining four would be dead before morning, thanks to Vlad's bodyguards.

Onyx was glad that Seth took to being a vampire so well. However, initially he had not planned on killing any of them, but it served a purpose this time. When he returned to the bed, he now shared with Seth, he thought, "*I have a companion to keep me company until I have you again, my Beloved. And I will have you again, be assured. I will have you.*" Onyx shut his eyes and drifted to sleep for the rest of the day.

CHAPTER 27

Andy and Leigh came up from the basement when they knew Reyne's screaming was done, and they heard the front door close. They slowly walked into the kitchen to find Reyne sitting at the kitchen table crying.

"How could he lie to me?" Reyne looked at her friends and asked.

"Reyne, how did he lie to you? Tell us what he said and let us help you figure this out," Leigh sat at the table and scooted close to Reyne.

Andy began making a fresh pot of coffee after filling three mugs with the last of the first pot's dregs.

"OK. This is what he told me in a nutshell. He is a dhampir. He was in love with me five centuries ago when we were married. He has met me in seven of my lifetimes, but was unable to get me to remember him, to fall in love with him, or whatever." She stopped for a moment and sobbed. "He said Xavier and Elizabeth are trying to hurt me and they had the murders set up to make it look like he did it. He also told me that once he finds me and we fall in love, we can decide if we want to take the gift from his father and become full vampires."

Leigh looked at Reyne and then at Andy. She knew she had to tell them both what had transpired the last few days since the barbecue. Andy knew a little, but not all of it.

"Reyne, there is something you should know. The day of the barbecue, I know the reason that Onyx, Xavier, and Elizabeth stormed out of here. I overheard the three of them in the laundry room. I was supposed to find Andy, who was on an ice run, and meet Onyx in the laundry room with Andy. When I got there, I heard Xavier and Elizabeth in there with him. They want to kill Onyx and want to steal you to play with, and then kill you when Elizabeth grows tired of you." Leigh looked at Reyne to see if she believed her. She couldn't tell, so she continued. "Also, I called here at 11 am on Friday and spoke to Elizabeth. She told me you were sleeping on the floor in the office…"

"I wasn't. Now you're lying," Reyne accused her.

"Reyne, Have I ever lied to you before?" Leigh asked curtly.

"No. I am sorry. You are telling the truth. Onyx really is telling the truth, isn't he?" Reyne began to sob again with the realization that she had cast him out.

"Look Reyne, I know Leigh and she is telling the truth. She has been worried sick about Elizabeth being here with you and wouldn't tell me why. I also know from the way Onyx looks at you that he adores you. You know that couples need to be truthful and always keep the lines of communication open. Onyx was just doing both. He loves you unconditionally. Now you have to decide if you will love him the same. We will leave…"

"No, we won't. I promised Onyx on Friday that I wouldn't leave her alone. I have to stay and protect her from Elizabeth. You have to help me. He wants us to quit our jobs and work for him, at least until this is settled with Xavier and Elizabeth maybe longer. I'm doing it because Reyne is my best friend. And I hope that you will help us, but that is your decision. Lazarus is supposed to do the same. He also says we need Lazarus to be strong enough to fight the evil even with him." Leigh looked at Andy as she spoke to make sure he got the underlying message.

"I will stay on. I love you too much, Leigh, to let you go that easily. Either way, Reyne needs to decide what to do." Andy went to the kitchen to make more coffee and waited to hear what they were going to do.

The front door opened, "Hey everyone. What's going on? A party so early." Tyler and Lazarus came into the kitchen. "Mom, what's wrong? Why are you crying? Did that asshole hurt you again?"

"Calm down Tyler. Your mother has a very big decision to make," Lazarus pulled Tyler from her mother.

"Oh! So you want her with the loser?" Tyler's stare at Lazarus burned into him.

"It is her decision, plus Andy is now with Leigh," Lazarus answered. "Plus, there is more to this than you know. You will learn it all tonight."

"Really? Leigh?" Tyler asked.

"That's right. However, Onyx isn't a loser. He loves your mother more than anyone has ever loved her. She deserves his love and needs his protection. Come on, you two, let's go to the living room. Andy and I will tell you what has been going on. Then we have to get Taylor home." Leigh took Tyler by the hand and led her out of the kitchen. Andy followed.

Lazarus looked at Reyne. "You all right Mom? If you need me, I am here."

"Thank you Lazarus. I will let you know. Go out there and hear what happened. I have to make a phone call," Reyne shooed him out of the kitchen smiling.

Reyne picked up the phone and dialed the number for the hotel. The front desk answered. She asked for Onyx's room. They patched her through. No one answered and as the voice mail picked up, she decided not to leave a message. She hung up the phone and went to her bedroom. She started to cry again, believing that she lost Onyx forever.

Reyne spent the rest of the day preparing for Monday. She was supposed to start working for Xavier tomorrow, but with everything she had learned today, she did not know if she wanted the job or not. She had already quit her other job, so there was really no choice. She would have to work for Xavier.

She heard movement in the kitchen after a while and went down to check it out. "What are you all up to?" She asked as she entered the kitchen.

Leigh and Tyler looked at Reyne, and said in unison, "Dinner."

"Taylor should be home shortly. I called Benjamin and told him to go ahead and bring him home. I hope you don't mind," Leigh smiled.

"Not at all. He needs to be here with his family. Thank you all for everything," Reyne hugged Tyler and Leigh.

"Mom, I'm sorry for calling Onyx a loser and an asshole. Leigh, Andy, and Lazarus explained everything to me, and I am here for you, whatever you have decided."

"I decided earlier today, but when I called his room, no one answered. I guess that means I have lost him for this lifetime. My only consolation is that he will look for me again in my next lifetime." Reyne could feel the tears welling up in her eyes. She smiled and tried to push them down.

The front door opened and in came Lazarus, Andy, and Taylor.

"Look who we found out front wanting his Momma" Andy said as he moved to let Taylor through.

"Momma, I have missed you." Taylor ran to Reyne and jumped into her arms. "I love you, Beautiful."

"I love you too, Handsome," Reyne replied as she squeezed him back.

"Dinner's ready," Tyler called.

The group went into the dining room and sat down to eat dinner. After dinner, Tyler and Lazarus took Taylor upstairs to give him a bath and put him to bed. Andy, Leigh and Reyne each got a cup of coffee and went out onto the deck to have their after-dinner cigarettes and enjoy the evening.

After their cigarettes were done, they went back into the house. "We rented movies on Netflix last night. Anyone want to watch them?" Tyler asked.

"Yeah. Come on, Leigh. Let's go downstairs with the kids." Andy said as he turned to Leigh.

"Sounds good to me. How about you, Reyne?" Leigh looked at Reyne.

"No thanks. I am going to fill up my coffee and go back on the deck. It is a beautiful night. I want to enjoy it. But thanks anyway." Reyne smiled, grabbed her coffee and cigarettes, and returned to the deck.

She had just gotten herself seated and her cigarette lit when something caught her attention out of the corner of her eye. She slowly turned toward the side of the deck and discovered Onyx lying on the railing.

"I wondered how long it was going to take you to see me." Onyx smiled, showing her his fangs.

Reyne gasped. "Why are you here?"

"You called me. I was busy when you called. I had a rough day too." Onyx came down from the railing and sat at the table with Reyne.

"What were you doing? No, never mind." Reyne stared into her coffee, afraid of the answer she would get.

"I was creating and feeding. You must know all of me. I will never hide anything from you again. I promise." Onyx touched her hand.

Reyne looked up from her coffee, "You know why I was calling you, don't you? I wanted to apologize for this morning. I shouldn't have yelled at you, and I should have believed you. I am sorry." Reyne looked down into her coffee again.

Onyx touched her chin and lifted her face. "You do not have to apologize. I love you, and you needed time to adjust."

"I love you too, Onyx." Reyne looked into his eyes and knew that he had spoken the truth now and earlier.

Onyx leaned toward Reyne and brushed her lips with his own. "There is something we need to do to seal our fates, do you accept me as I am?"

"Yes." Reyne stated simply.

Onyx stood up and walked over to Reyne. He helped her stand up and then picked her up and carried her into the house, up the stairs, and into the bedroom. Leigh was in the kitchen and watched Onyx carry Reyne to the stairs. She stopped what she was doing and ran down to the family room to tell them what had just happened.

Onyx laid Reyne on the bed gently. He laid beside her and began kissing her. The kisses made her forget time and space. They were on a cloud. She could hear someone speaking to her, but couldn't hear what the person was saying.

Suddenly, Onyx was standing beside her on the cloud. "I am sorry, Reyne. Old habits die-hard. I want you in the here and now when we make love. Please come back."

The spell was broken. She was again lying on the bed next to Onyx. "What happened?"

"I enchanted you without even thinking about it. I am sorry, it will never happen again. I promise." Onyx looked into her eyes to show his sincerity.

"It's all right, but I, too, would prefer to be in reality when we make love." Reyne leaned into Onyx and kissed him. The kiss took Reyne deeper into ecstasy than she had ever experienced, even with Onyx.

"Please, don't enchant me." She begged him softly.

"Just relax. Making love to me will be different than with any other man. You will experience things that you have only imagined. Let go and come with me." Onyx smiled down at her.

He slowly bent his head to hers, brushing his lips gently against hers. Teasing and exciting Reyne in the same moment. As he allowed his lips to touch hers, he pushed her mouth open with his tongue, delving deep into her mouth, causing her to moan and arch up into him. Her hands grasped at him and pulled him to her. Her body began moving and grinding into his, begging for his touch.

"Take me, please. I can't stand it. I want to feel you inside of me. No! I need to feel you inside of me," Reyne growled as she pulled him to her so that she could kiss him.

"Beloved," Onyx said as he pulled back from her, "you must relax. Everything will come in time. I will not rush this for your mortal appetite. You must slow down and follow my lead. If you rush, it will be painful and not as good as you deserve it to be. Please, Reyne. Slow down and relax. I promise you will feel me soon and for an eternity if you choose."

Onyx pushed her down to the bed and stroked her hair to calm her. She continued to grind her hips and run her hands all over his body, but her breathing slowed and her eyes opened to his face.

"I'm sorry. It's just that being with you is intense. I have never experienced this type of intensity." Reyne said huskily.

"I am going to help you. Just relax." Onyx continued stroking her hair.

"OK." She lifted her head and touched his lips with her own.

Onyx stopped stroking her head and moved to her arm, starting at her shoulder, slowly and lightly running down the outside of her arm. When he reached her hand, he caressed it and started back up the inside of her arm. He could tell from her energy that she was finding this exciting. He leaned over and kissed her gently. He realized he would probably have to enchant her to some extent, if he was to make love to her as he had wanted to for centuries.

As he reached her inner elbow, he stopped to caress the tender skin before lowering his head to her arm and brushing his lips across the tender skin of her inner arm. He could feel her sexual energy spike as she reached her first orgasm. He smiled at her as he lifted his head. His hand moved from her arm and gently caressed her breast through her T-shirt, feeling her nipple become hard and erect under the brush of his fingertips.

He dropped his hand to the bottom of her shirt and slipped his hand underneath it, so he could feel the heat from her skin rise as he made her more excited with his touch. He moved his hand from one breast to the other, skimming over her nipples, feeling her back arch toward him. Her nipples were begging for more of his touch. He pulled her shirt over her head and laid it down on the floor as he took her nipple in his mouth, licking and biting, making it become harder and more sensitive under his tongue. Reyne arched her back to get her breast closer to his mouth. She grabbed his head from the back and tangled her hands in his long hair as she pulled his head toward her.

"Ssshhh…" Onyx whispered. "You must be calm," as he began to stroke her hair again while massaging her breast with his tongue.

Reyne closed her eyes and arched her back even farther into the air, breaking the seal Onyx had placed on her nipple. Onyx crawled quickly to the head of the bed and began stroking both sides of her head to calm her down. He knew that he couldn't keep her in this utopia much longer without losing control of himself. He calmed her and slid off the side of the bed. He walked to the foot of the bed and crept up her body until his face was perfectly in line with her navel. His allowed his tongue to explore her flesh. His tongue eventually led him to the waist of her pants. While his tongue continued to taste her, he brought his hand to her waistband. He stopped tasting her and lifted himself until he was towering over her. He held the waist of her shorts, and slowly and delicately pulled them down, laying them on the floor by his feet. He slid backward off the bed, delicately spreading her legs as his knees reached the floor. His mouth found her ankle with a gentle kiss. He worked his way up her calf to her knee with loving kisses. His mouth sought out her sweetness as he stalked up her inner thigh. He stopped suddenly and let his breath heat her. Moisture began building until he could stand it no longer and began to softly lick her and prepare her for his entry into her.

Reyne couldn't say anything. Her head was full of thoughts and things she wanted to say to Onyx, but her mouth wouldn't function. Her hands grabbed at Onyx's hair as he kissed her inner thighs and began his descent. As his hot breath surrounded her, she moaned with the growing anticipation of his tongue touching her. Her hand untangled itself from his hair and glided up her stomach. It found its target and began to tickle her nipple. When Onyx's tongue finally touched her, she screamed in ecstasy and pulled her nipple. Onyx watched her hand as he continued to devour the juices being created.

Reyne could stand it no longer, "Please…"

"Not yet. Soon. Enjoy my mouth, for you may not shortly." Onyx stopped tantalizing her and moved up to her stomach. He kissed all the way up to her nipples. Slowly, he took one is him mouth, gently sucking on it and stroking the other. Carefully, he nibbled on the ripe, pert nipple in his mouth and pinched the other. He could feel the moisture growing on his leg that lay between hers. He moved to the other side and repeated the process, slowly sucking and then nibbling. Reyne arched her back, her body begging him to take more of her into his mouth, yet he would not comply. Reyne tossed her head, moaning and sighing in anticipation of his entry.

Onyx kissed the rest of Reyne's chest and worked his way up her neck until he found her mouth. "Now my Beloved. Are you sure you are ready?"

"Yes." Reyne said in barely a whisper as she pushed her hips into his.

Onyx gently spread her legs farther apart with his knee. He looked down into her eyes as he positioned himself over her. Reyne licked her lips and caressed his back, trying to wait patiently for her Onyx to enter.

Onyx slowly moved his face toward Reyne's and brushed his lips against hers. As the kiss became more passionate, he lowered himself onto her body, delving his tongue deep into her mouth. His kisses started to slope down her neck. Reyne threw her head back, revealing her beautiful long neck. Onyx was now the one whom could wait no longer.

The head of his shaft touched her entrance.

"Yes." Reyne shrieked.

Before the last part of the word exited her mouth, Onyx drove his shaft deep inside of Reyne and at the exact moment of complete penetration, bit her neck and took a deep draw of her blood. She screamed with exhilaration as the intensity of the combined acts filled her senses. He pulled away from her neck, licking and kissing the area he had bitten.

Reyne grabbed his torso, running her hands up and down his back while he rhythmically continued to penetrate her.

"Reyne, listen to me." Onyx whispered into her ear.

"Y...Y...Y....YES!" Reyne screamed as she grew even wetter.

Onyx slowed his grinding, "Reyne, you must do as I say right now. I want to complete this as both human and vampire. Will you help me?"

"Yes." Reyne answered him, looking into his eyes.

"You must drink of me. Do not worry, I cannot change you, and you don't have to drink much. You just really have to draw from me. Can you do this?" He asked quickly as he continued to ease in and out of her.

"Yes. Where?" she said in a breath.

"My shoulder. I will open it for you when it is time. With this, I promise you one of the most intense and passionate conclusions to making love." Onyx began increasing his hips motions, sending Reyne into her ecstasy delirium.

Their caresses, explorations, and touches lasted for hours, until finally Onyx drew Reyne back to reality. "My Beloved," he said, gasping between each word, "it is time." He drew his hand to his shoulder and slit it open. Reyne quickly thrust it into her mouth. Without hesitating, she pulled his blood from the wound on his shoulder, hard and fierce. His pace quickened and grew harder. She had a hard time keeping his shoulder at her mouth from the intensity of the lovemaking but took another deep pull from it before releasing his shoulder and her passion. As his shoulder pulled from her mouth, he thrust himself deeper inside of her than she believed could be possible. She felt him mix his seed with her juices.

Onyx slowed his pace. He remained inside of her but unmoving, trying to catch his breath. "Well, my Beloved, was it what I promised you?" Smiling, he looked at her mouth, still covered with his blood, and felt himself becoming erect again.

"I feel that and yes, it was as you promised and better. I have never been taken to that point of ecstasy in my life. You are wonderful." She snuggled into his neck, nipping at it in between soft kisses.

"I'd best release you from me. Otherwise, we may never leave this bedroom again." Onyx pulled himself from her and stroked her hair. "It is time to rest, my Beloved. Sleep now. We have the rest of eternity, should you desire, to spend together."

Reyne's eyes closed, and her breathing became steady. Onyx only then closed his eyes, knowing that his Beloved was with him again and was safe.

CHAPTER 28

Reyne woke the next day and found herself alone in the bed. She felt a sudden panic filling her as the bedroom door opened and Onyx walked in with two cups of coffee.

"I thought you might like a cup when you woke up. I am sorry if I worried you. Just to let you know it is after 1pm and everyone is OK. Leigh and Andy took Taylor to the movies, Tyler and Lazarus are at his parents, and you and I are alone in the house." Onyx smiled and handed her a cup.

"How did you know how I liked my coffee?" Reyne asked, surprised.

"Leigh showed me before she left. Reyne, there are a few other things that I need you to know about me. I know I should have told you before last night happened, but it's too late to regret that now…"

"What?" Reyne cut him off, "Your married? I sucked in bed? You really don't love me? What?" Reyne questioned him getting more excited as she asked more questions.

"Nothing like that. I love you and always will. You are incredible in bed, partly because you sucked. And no I have never remarried, yet."

Reyne stared at Onyx. He sat next to her on the bed wearing only a pair of black jeans that fit him snuggly and accentuated his exquisite body. "What then?"

"Please have an open mind when I tell you this." He started.

"OK" was all she could say

"My kind do not necessarily see things as a mortal would. I love you and have since I was a child. My mortal side and my dhampir side acknowledge this. However, my dhampir side does not distinguish between male and female when it comes to attraction. Where my mortal side prefers women, my dhampir side has always preferred the person, not the gender." He explained.

"So…You're telling me you've been with men? Is that all?" Reyne questioned. How could she be upset with him over that when she had been with women in college? Just about everyone explored, and some kept it up. It did not bother her in the slightest.

"You're not upset by that?" Onyx looked at her quizzically.

"Nope. How could I be? I have the same philosophy. The person is what is important, not the gender." Reyne smiled, "Is that all you wanted to tell me?"

"Not really. I wanted to tell you that I currently have a vampiric lover. I am in love with him, in a way. I took him when I thought I would never see you again, but he is not you. He has only been my companion for a very short time. But I wanted you to know, because…"

Reyne giggled, not believing what she was about to say, "…because you would like to keep him as your companion, and possible lover, as well as have me. He would be second to me, but would be part of us. Is that about right?" Reyne started laughing. "He would be our third!"

Onyx was taken aback by Reyne's response. "Yes, that is right, but why are you laughing?"

"Because if I had a lover, I would want to share with you too." Reyne answered.

"Well, I guess we are going to need a bigger place if all of us are going to live together and a bigger bed to accommodate everyone. Especially when you get a vampiric lover. What do you think?" Onyx asked, laughing at the thought of the three of them in the bed.

"I don't think that is problem, right now. Plus, it is only us. Andy and Leigh don't live here, believe it or not…." Reyne started to say.

"But I have asked them to move in already to help me keep you safe. The danger is not over yet. Seth and I will move in immediately, if that is OK with you. Brian will find us a larger house close to here and in the same school district. We should have it before Christmas. Brian is great at getting things like this done."

"You've figured all this out already? When were you gonna tell me about it?" Reyne was trying to sound like she was upset, but she knew her smile was poking through.

"I figured it out lifetimes ago. I was going to let you know as soon as you accepted me for who and what I am. I couldn't chance telling you prior to your understanding everything." He explained solemnly, even though he knew she was accepting everything. He did not want to make this a joke or have her feel that he was not serious.

"I know. I was just teasing." She said realizing that this was important to him. "So, what is the next step?"

Onyx took Reyne in his arms tightly, "Next we go downstairs and I call Brian. While Seth is bringing everything over, Leigh, Andy, you and I will sit down and discuss our next step until we have a new house. Once Seth and Brian are here, Andy and Leigh will leave to put things in order to move in. I hope this is not moving too fast for you?"

"Not at all. I just think that you are hoping to find a house before Christmas, and in this area that isn't very likely. At least not the size we need." Reyne nuzzled into Onyx's neck and felt him stiffen immediately. She quickly withdrew from his embrace, "What's wrong?"

"The neck is a very erogenous zone on mortals. But on vampires, it is more like another sex organ. You must realize that anywhere there are major arteries is very much a part of a vampire's sex life..."

Reyne cut him off, "You mean that you would prefer to share blood than physical intercourse?"

"Not exactly. Do you remember how I made love to you last night?" Onyx drew her back into his arms.

"Yes," she whispered at the memory.

"Drinking each other's blood is as intimate as intercourse, if not more so. You just got my vampiric side aroused by playing with my neck. You will come to understand it more, I promise." He kissed her gently. He let go of her long enough to grab her hand and lead her down the stairs to the kitchen.

Onyx called Brian and left a message to check out of the hotel and find himself a hotel closer to Reyne's house. He hung up the phone and joined Reyne at the kitchen table.

Reyne looked at Onyx for a moment. "Does your attorney know what you are?"

"Yes." Onyx answered, as if it was not a big deal.

"Well, isn't he afraid of you?" Reyne couldn't understand this at all.

Onyx smiled, "He would be if he were mortal. But since he isn't, there is no worry. I called him and left him a message. He and Seth will complete everything and will be here late tonight. Until then, I'll stay and will not leave for any reason. Brian, Seth and I will watch over you until everyone moves into the new house when we can take shifts to watch you and the kids. Once I talk to Brian tonight, he will be house hunting by tomorrow night."

Reyne giggled, "Let's be realistic, at least for me. I am not used to things happening so fast, so let's say within six months. Plus, I want to get rid of some things before I move."

"Let Brian take care of things, Reyne. You just let me know what you want moved or if you want everything new. Either way it is your decision."

Reyne looked at Onyx in astonishment. "You mean I could say trash everything, but the clothes and a few other articles and you would buy all new furnishings, accessories, and stuff?"

Onyx looked deep into Reyne's eyes. "It is what I would prefer. I would prefer you let all of your old life go and start completely fresh with me. That would include clothing, but I know that is asking too much."

"No, it's not. I would actually prefer that as well. Everything here has memories that are no longer important. I will have the kids decide what they want to take with them. As for me, I want to start over with you," she said excitedly.

Onyx smiled and gave Reyne a small, sweet kiss on her lips. "Then we begin shopping tomorrow for you, the kids, and Lazarus. Today, we have other things to take care of. First thing is to buy things for the bedroom so that Seth can use the room with us. How fast can you be ready?"

Reyne smiled, "Hour at most." She got up and ran upstairs to get her shower.

CHAPTER 29

Reyne and Onyx spent the rest of the afternoon shopping for new bedroom furniture and accessories. They scheduled immediate delivery of the new king-size black lacquer bed and matching dresser, wardrobe, and nightstands thanks to Onyx's status in the financial world. Until that moment, Reyne didn't really have any idea of how rich this man was.

They also picked out pictures for the walls, candle holders and candles for soft light, and a lamp. Once everything was in order, they left the store and returned to the house to find Leigh, Andy, Tyler, Lazarus and Taylor waiting for them.

As soon as Reyne and Onyx walked in the door, Tyler started in on Reyne. "Well, I hope you are happy. We have been worried about you for hours. Did you plan on coming home or were you just seeing if we would really worry? You just love to cause drama, don't you Mom?"

Reyne giggled and squeezed Onyx's hand, "Sweetie, Leigh and Andy knew where we were. Did you ask them?"

"No…I figured they would tell me. They started dinner, and I started worrying. Still. You should have left a note for Lazarus and me. We are part of this family," Tyler snapped.

Onyx gave Reyne's hand another squeeze and answered for her. "I wanted to take your mother out and get her some new things. She deserves to be pampered, and I wanted to show her that I am not just here for the present, but for always. They will be delivering our new bedroom set tomorrow. I am sorry if I made you worry. I asked her to hurry when she woke up, so we had plenty of time to find exactly what we wanted."

Tyler frowned at Onyx, "Okay. But don't let it happen again."

Taylor walked up to Reyne and hugged her, "Momma, can I have a new bedroom too?" he asked innocently.

"Of course, my love. We will go out this weekend and get you a whole new bedroom." She looked at Onyx as she answered Taylor.

Onyx smiled, "Of course. We will get you whatever you want. If you want some new clothes or something else, just let me know."

"Dinner's about ready. Tyler, take your brother up and get him cleaned up for dinner," Leigh said while staring at Reyne. Once the kids were out of the room. Leigh turned to Onyx, "What are you doing? Trying to buy her kids? That isn't fair to Reyne or them. How dare…"

"Hold on," Reyne interrupted, "he offered to buy us new things to start a new life with him. He also offered to buy you guys new things for the new house. It is just a way to wipe the past away and begin anew. If he has the money and wants to do it, why would I take my thrift store buys with me? I am keeping some things, but the bedroom I have now is part of my marriage and I want it gone. Plus, if Taylor gets a new bedroom set for here, Benjamin can take the old one and Taylor will still have his own things at his daddy's house. Is that wrong?" Reyne was glaring at Leigh now.

"I'm sorry. I am still not used to all this. It is so strange. It is totally throwing my sense of reality to the wind. I'm sorry Onyx," Leigh said.

"It's all right. We will all sit down and discuss this more after dinner. Hopefully, I will be able to explain everything by then. Others will be coming over around 11 pm or so. There is no need to fear them. They should have fed prior to arriving." Onyx reached over to Leigh and pulled her into a hug to let her know all was forgiven.

The kids returned and the whole group sat at Reyne's big table to eat dinner. Over dinner, Reyne told everyone what the new bedroom set looked like, describing each piece of furniture down to the smallest detail. Taylor told them what he wanted and again Onyx and Reyne promised to take him out the coming weekend to get him a new set. Tyler and Lazarus offered to clear the table and clean the kitchen, while Reyne took Taylor upstairs and got him ready for bed.

"Momma, do I have to pick out my clothes for all week, since I didn't do it yesterday? I really hate doing that." He said sulkily as he went into the bathroom for his shower.

Reyne realized that she was supposed to start working with Xavier today. She had to tell Onyx after she got Taylor to bed. She smiled wickedly at Taylor, "Nope. We will pick your clothes out in the morning. And how would you like Momma to take you to school? You have to go tomorrow, no matter what. No more days off for a while."

Taylor couldn't contain his excitement, as a giant smile grew on his face, "Woo hoo. Momma's taking me to school!" he yelled.

"Get in the tub now and let's get ready for bed so that I can take you to school tomorrow," Reyne said as she started the shower for Taylor.

After his shower, Taylor went into his bedroom, picked out the book for the bedtime story and climbed into bed. Reyne read him the story, kissed his head, and tucked him in for the night. "I'll see you in the morning, my little love."

"I love you Momma. Goodnight."

Reyne walked out of the bedroom and joined the group that congregated in her living room. "Okay, what did I miss?"

"Nothing yet. Onyx has been on the phone. We were waiting for you to have a cigarette and discuss what needs to be done," Leigh answered and patted the sofa beside her.

Reyne walked over and pulled Leigh up. "Coffee ready?"

"Well, duh. Of course it is." Leigh and Reyne went to the kitchen and got coffee for themselves, then returned to the living room. "Come on guys, let's go talk."

Onyx looked at Leigh and Andy, "How much time do you need to give to get out of your leases?"

"Two months' rent and I can leave tomorrow. But I would like to give them the 90 days' notice. How about you Andy?" Leigh snuggled beside Andy on the sofa.

"Same, and if we wait the 90 days, we may be able to move into the big house and not have everyone crammed into spaces in this townhouse. No offense, Reyne, but I don't think there is enough room for the four of you, plus Leigh and I."

Reyne turned to Onyx, "You didn't tell them about the other two, did you?"

"I wanted to tell you first. But you're right; I haven't told them." Onyx looked at Andy, "Actually the list of residents is as follows: Reyne, Taylor, Tyler, Lazarus, if you're willing, Brian, Seth, Leigh, you and me. That makes a total of eight. Brian is my best friend and attorney and will be the one finding the house..."

Leigh giggled, "You mean mini mansion, don't you?"

Onyx laughed, "I guess you are right. I don't see a problem with you both giving your ninety days as long as you're here during the day. Brian is getting a hotel room..." The doorbell rang and interrupted Onyx.

"Keep talking; I'll get it," Reyne says.

"No, I'll get it." Onyx said as he turned Reyne back toward the living room and answered the door. The three men walked into the living room, "This is Brian and Seth. Now, as I was saying, Brian is getting a hotel room down the street, and Seth and I will be here with Lazarus to protect Reyne and the kids until we get a safe house."

"For now, Leigh and Andy can go home and get some rest. Just be back in the morning. You will have a lot of work to do in the next few weeks. Decide what you want and mark the things you don't want. If you need anything, call Brian, leave a message during the day. He will get it for you." Onyx instructed.

"Brian, please get their information and pay the next six months of rent for them. Tell the management company they will be moving out at the end of that time."

"I know, you both said 90 days, but if anything happens, we have two other places to work with. Here is Brian's card and my card. There is one for each of you. Call us anytime. I will be able to be reached directly at any time, Brian, only at night. Do not change your routines more than you have to, other than quitting your jobs. We can continue this talk tomorrow."

"Wow, Reyne, he is a real take charge kind of guy," Leigh told Reyne before turning to Onyx, "Do we ever get told why Reyne is in danger?"

Onyx realized that he has just talked to them as if they were his servants or employees, and not his Beloved's friends. "I'm sorry. I have treated you all like employees. Here's the deal. Xavier is my cousin. He is four months older than I am and has tried to take everything of mine from the earliest of my memories. He has found Reyne. It has only been in the last three centuries or four lifetimes that he has been able to locate her but has always known that I love her beyond all time and existence. So, he has decided to find her in each lifetime and kill her. He has never succeeded in killing her, but he is closer now than he has ever been. He and Elizabeth would turn her and play with her like a toy. When they tire of her, they would kill her. If she dies after being turned, I will never find her again and that is why she is in danger. We have to keep both of them away from her and her children, whom they would have no problem using as leverage to get to Reyne."

"Damn." Leigh and Andy said in unison.

"What am I in all this?" Lazarus spoke up.

"Lazarus, you know you are not what you show yourself to be. We need you to help us. You and your powers are necessary for Reyne, Tyler, and Taylor's protection. Are you willing to help?" Onyx asked Lazarus.

"I would give my life for this family. I am in," he answered.

"What are you not telling us about yourself, Lazarus?" Reyne asked.

"My Beloved" Onyx turned Reyne to him, "it will all become clear in time for even he does not truly know. Let it go for right now."

"Okay." Reyne stood up with Andy and Leigh.

Seth, Brian, Lazarus, and Onyx started talking amongst themselves, while Reyne saw Andy and Leigh out. When she returned, she looked at the group, "Okay, now tell me, before I go ballistic on each of you separately."

"Feisty as ever, Onyx," Brian said with a laugh.

Reyne glared at the man, "You must be Brian." She turned and smiled at Seth, "You must be Seth." Reyne returned to glare at the group of them, "Tell me now."

"Reyne, you will know everything. Sit down. Please." Onyx took her hand and led her to the sofa.

Reyne sat down and stared at him, waiting patiently for him to begin.

"Lazarus is like me. He is one of my kind. He is dhampir. He has only just begun to realize this and now he needs us as much as we need him. His father is a Vampire, his mother is a Witch, such as you are. The love created the immortal you know as Lazarus. Immortal, if he so chooses, as is his right." Onyx turns to Lazarus, as if awaiting an answer.

Without a moment's thought or hesitation, "I choose immortality." Lazarus replied as if the decision isn't out of the ordinary.

"So be it." Onyx turns from Lazarus and looks at Brian. "You may give your son his gift now Brian. It is time and he has chosen."

Reyne's eyes had grown wide with astonishment. "Brian is Lazarus' father? We knew he was adopted, but..."

"He is as I am. I have my true father and my mortal father. Both are dear to me and both loved my mother. He is not adopted. His mother is his mother, but Brian is his true father. He was truly in love with Lazarus' mother, but her mortal husband could not understand and could not accept that she had another lover. He banned her from ever telling Lazarus the truth, although he knew he was different from a very young age. It was to Brian's relief that he was here for you and that he would be able to tell Lazarus everything." Onyx finished.

Brian had moved over to stand in front of Lazarus. Both men were tall and solid. You could see the resemblance in the build and the eyes of the two men, but those were the only similar characteristics. "Are you sure you want this my son?" Brian asked of Lazarus with the formality of a ceremony.

"Yes, Father. I want to live my life as I am entitled to." Lazarus answered formally as if he had known Brian all his life.

"But you will no longer be living. Have you thought of how that will affect your life?" Brian asked.

"Yes, I have thought about it. I want to be as my Father and learn everything I can. Tyler will love me still if she truly loves me." Lazarus answered with all sincerity and finality.

"Then I shall proceed." Brian turned from Lazarus and looked at Onyx. "You may want to take Reyne to another room. She may not want to be part of this."

"She has to learn. She will be given the same choice very soon and I want her to understand what will happen. She will remain in the room." Onyx said calmly, while holding Reyne's hands to keep her from bolting.

"Don't I have any say in this?" Reyne asked quickly

The four men turned to her and said, in unison, "No. You must know."

Brian embraced his son in his arms. As soon as he felt Lazarus' arms surround him, he bit into the side of his neck. Lazarus arched his back as if to pull away, but held Brian tightly against his chest. The move actually lifted Brian off the floor.

Slowly, Lazarus began to drift downward in his father's arms until he was barely breathing and lying on the floor.

"Your turn, my son. Seth, help him, please," Brian said.

Seth knelt beside Lazarus' head and bit into the elbow area of Brian's arm. He immediately picked up Lazarus' head and placed his mouth on the open wound. Lazarus drank gently, gaining his strength, until Seth pulled him from Brian's arm.

Reyne watched all of this in disbelief. Her mind drifted. Was she going to have to do this too if she wanted to be with Onyx? The thought terrified her.

Onyx leaned over and whispered to her, "It will be different for you, my beloved because should you choose to be turned, we will be making love, so do not worry right now. Just watch."

Seth laid Lazarus back down and then offered his arm to Lazarus, who grabbed it greedily and pierced the wrist area hungrily. Seth winced slightly at the pain of Lazarus' inexperience, but knew it was necessary since he was almost as new.

Onyx let go of Reyne, "I'll be right back. I must contribute to his first feeding. I will need nourishment myself afterward. Decide whether I may feed from you by the time I return." Onyx moved from Reyne and went to sit beside Lazarus.

Onyx pulled Seth's arm away and gave his in its place. He knew Seth was too young to be drained much. Lazarus opened his eyes and looked at Onyx. Their eyes met, and an understanding was acknowledged between the four men. Lazarus slowly let go of Onyx's arm and sat up.

"Come, Lazarus, with Seth and me. We need to feed and so do you." Brian offered a hand to Lazarus to help him stand. Lazarus took his hand and the three men left for the night to feed and prepare for rest.

Onyx returned to Reyne, "Have you decided? May I feed from you or do I go out when they return and feed?"

Reyne knew her answer before she even realized it came from her mouth as a whisper, "From me."

CHAPTER 30

Reyne woke the next morning and got Taylor up and ready for school. She left Onyx sleeping in the bed while she walked Taylor to school and promised to pick him up in the afternoon. When she returned, as she opened the door to the townhouse, someone grabbed her arm and yanked her through the door.

"What the hell were you thinking? Leaving without one of us is forbidden. Do you understand?" Onyx started yelling at her.

"What the hell am I thinking? What the hell are you thinking, talking to me like this? It is daylight. Who is going to hurt me? You all can't go in daylight. There is no one out there." Reyne screamed back.

"That is where you are wrong." Lazarus stepped into the room.

"What the…" Reyne stared wide eyed at Lazarus.

"Vampires can and do walk around during the day. They are not affected by sunlight like the movies portray. They are weaker during the day and tired, but that is only because it is much easier to hunt at night. Think about it Reyne. Elizabeth was here during the day. The Labor Day Party occurred during the day. You know they can and do walk in the sunlight." Onyx interrupted her.

"But Brian and Seth…only at night…" Reyne spurted the words out, not understanding what was going on.

"My Beloved. We cannot all be with you during the day and the night. We each must sleep. Lazarus and I have the day shift, and Brian and Seth have the night. Brian is so old that he has just gotten into the habit of sleeping during the day. He is older than I am. Seth is almost as new as Lazarus and can sleep whenever." Onyx explained. "Would you rather have Lazarus asleep all day and up all night so that Tyler can complain about this? He hasn't even told her that he is a vampire yet. What would you have me do?"

"I didn't understand. I'm sorry." Reyne hugged Onyx.

"From now on, you do not leave this house without one of us. Understand?" Onyx gripped her tightly in his embrace.

"I understand. So, who will go with me this afternoon to pick Taylor up?" Reyne smiled at Onyx.

"You know I will. Lazarus will be dealing with Tyler and explaining to her what is going on. I think they will need some time alone. Don't you think?" Onyx smiled back.

Reyne shook her head yes and hugged him again.

Lazarus turned to go back downstairs when Tyler appeared in the basement doorway. "What did you mean about Lazarus sleeping all day?" Tyler asked Onyx. She then turned to Lazarus. "What is going on?"

"Tyler, let's go downstairs; I have to talk to you." Lazarus touched Tyler's arm.

"You're freezing and you haven't been to bed yet. What is going on?" Tyler demanded.

Onyx turned to her, "Tyler, go downstairs with Lazarus. He will explain everything."

"Fine." Tyler stomped off with Lazarus following her back down to the basement.

Onyx turned to Reyne, "Now you need to call Xavier and tell him you not working for him. Or are you still going to put yourself in danger?"

"Nope, I am calling him now." Reyne went into the kitchen and dialed Xavier's number. She explained that she is unable to work for him at this time and thanks him for giving her the opportunity. Onyx stood beside her while she is talking with him. Suddenly, she turned white and dropped the phone. "Oh my God." Reyne screamed.

Onyx picked up the receiver, "Xavier, what have you done?"

"Nothing yet. But she better get to her son before the new volunteer at his school does. Otherwise, she will not have a son." Xavier started laughing and hung up the phone.

Onyx ran to the bedroom and woke up Seth. "I know you haven't slept long, but I need your help. Elizabeth is going after Taylor. We have to go now."

Seth sat up and threw on some clothes quickly, while Onyx ran down the stairs to get Lazarus. "Lazarus," he started to yell from the top of the basement stairs. "Taylor is in trouble. Stay with Tyler. Seth and I are taking Reyne to get Taylor. Be back soon."

"They're after my baby brother? Oh no, I'm going too. Come on Lazarus," Tyler bellowed.

"No, please stay here Tyler. I need someone at the house to keep it safe. This could be a ploy to get us all out of the house. I need you here," Onyx explained.

"Okay. Fine," she answered.

The talking from the basement got softer as the two were working things out.

Seth met Onyx in the kitchen where Reyne sat at the table, unable to talk or move. The two men looked at one another for a moment, and then Onyx picked her up and they ran to the car.

"You'd better hurry, Onyx. Elizabeth has been at the school for hours. It may already be too late for the little morsel!" Xavier yelled before returning to the confines of his house.

"Taylor. Oh My God. What's going on?" Reyne started crying.

Seth got in the driver's seat, while Onyx put Reyne in the back and climbed in with her. Seth took off out of the parking lot just as Reyne became completely hysterical.

"Reyne. Get yourself together. You need to go into the school with us and get Taylor. Tell them that there has been a family emergency and that you all will be away for a while. Do you understand?"

Reyne tried to calm herself. "Yes, I understand." She slowed her breathing and wiped her face.

Seth pulled the car up to the front of the school. Onyx helped Reyne out of the car and the three of them walk into the school to the office.

"Hi, I am Taylor's mom. There has been a family emergency and I need him to come with me right now. We are leaving for a few days." Reyne said to the school secretary.

"Hold on one minute. We will get him for you." The secretary said as she turned away from Reyne and calls "Elizabeth, can you go get Taylor from his classroom? His mother is here to pick him up."

"NO!!!" screamed Reyne.

Onyx grabbed Reyne to keep her from jumping over the desk and attacking the secretary, "Seth, go get Taylor. Now."

Seth took off out the office door to search for Taylor. The secretary yelled after him, "Stop! You are not authorized to go into the classroom area." Seth ignored her and kept moving. He opened his mind in search of Taylor, hoping to locate him before Elizabeth, fearing she would find him first.

"Well, hello Onyx, Reyne." Elizabeth smiled at the two of them.

"This is highly unacceptable. I want you to know that I have called school security and the police for your disregard for school policy. We have volunteers to ensure the safety of the children." The principal stated as she stared in Onyx and Reyne's direction while coming out of her office.

Reyne glared at her with hatred and distrust, "And what about the killer you have standing in this office? Is she going to protect my child or try to kill him? She has already threatened to kill me. You want me to believe that you are protecting the children. You are so full of self-righteous bullshit. You don't do any type of background check on these people. She doesn't even have a child in this school. I can't believe that you are calling security on me and my family. You all need to go to hell…"

Onyx interrupts her by placing his hand over her mouth, "That's enough, Reyne. Seth has returned with Taylor. Let's go." Onyx kept his hand over her mouth and his other arm around Reyne as they walked from the building. Reyne fought the entire way out of the school. She wanted to tell the Principal what she thought of her. Seth took Taylor by the hand and finished what Reyne started, "And as for you and your school. This county will be hearing from our attorney regarding your actions and your choices of volunteers. I will have your job for upsetting Reyne as you have. Do not underestimate my family. You have chosen to mess with the wrong person." Seth turned briskly on his heel and left with Taylor.

The principal turned to Elizabeth, "What was that all about?"

"I don't know, but you had better get the Department of Education to get the best attorney available, because he will destroy you and this school system." Elizabeth giggled and walked to the door. "And by the way, you really should check people who want to volunteer out better. I would have kidnapped her son. No comment on the killing. I guess she pegged you right." Elizabeth laughed again and walked past the school security and out the front door. Security ran after her, but to no avail. She was gone.

Reyne held Taylor tightly in the car as Seth drove them back to the house. "What now, Onyx? What am I going to do? It is no longer safe."

"It will be fine, my Beloved. I have some ideas on how to take care of this. You and Taylor just stay together and with one of us at all times," He said as he held Reyne and Taylor close.

Once back at the house, Taylor and Reyne went to the basement to watch TV. Onyx told Seth to return to bed, which he did gratefully. Onyx went into the kitchen and prepared a pot of coffee, knowing that Reyne would be needing a cup soon. While the coffee was brewing, he called his father and told him the whole story. His father promised to call Xavier back to the homeland for a while to ensure that they have time to regroup and prepare should Xavier try to harm Reyne or her children again.

Onyx hung up the phone, got Reyne a cup of coffee, and took it to her. "My Beloved. All is going to be well, at least for a while. After tonight, you will be able to relax."

"How is that possible?" she asked as she took the cup of coffee from Onyx.

"Xavier is going to be called back to his father's house. He will be kept there until we can get things taken care of." Onyx explained.

"I don't think I will ever feel safe again. And you did say for a while. Not forever, right?" Reyne questioned him.

"No, not forever. I have to take care of the forever part. It is the vampiric way, but the elders will interfere long enough to make sure it will be a fair fight. Trust in me and my family. We will protect you." Onyx hugged Reyne and pulled Taylor to his lap. Onyx wanted them close to know they were safe. He sat there with them the rest of the day, watching movies on the television.

Onyx and Reyne watched Xavier and Elizabeth leave later that night. Reyne immediately felt a weight lift from her shoulders. She knew the feeling wouldn't last long, but it would be enough to prepare for their return and prepare to move into the new house once Brian found one.

Tyler gradually forgave Lazarus for not telling her his secrets before being turned. Throughout the day, it was apparent to all that she really did understand why he did not tell her and all of the things happening in their lives. Taylor was kept from the drama as much as was possible. He was enjoying life, being home-schooled, and spending lots of time with Reyne and Onyx, and his new Mega Man bedroom.

By the end of October, Brian had not only purchased a house for them, but most of the modifications were completed. They all planned to take the first week of November to move and get the house set up. Movers had been hired for Leigh, Andy, and Reyne. Excitement was mounting, and fear had all but disappeared. Everyone was so relaxed and happy. No one even thought of Xavier and Elizabeth returning any longer, except Onyx.

CHAPTER 31

Several days before Halloween, Cindy, one of Reyne's neighbors, stopped by the house and invited all of them to her Annual Halloween Party.

Reyne giggled, "Of course we will come. It will be a great. Our last blow out before the movers arrive the next morning."

"Well, we will make it a good-luck moving party as well." Cindy hugged Reyne.

"We aren't moving that far. We will be in Poolesville on a little farm. Of course, you will have to come visit." Reyne gave a tense smile, knowing that her last statement was a lie. No one would be allowed to know where the estate was located to protect her and the children until Xavier and Elizabeth were no longer a problem.

It struck her as strange that she thought of those two, but quickly put them out of her mind, saw Cindy to the door, and returned to packing.

Leigh stopped by later that day. Reyne told her about the party as they made their way to the living room. "We've got a lot of work to do and costumes to get ready. This will be great." Reyne said as she and Leigh sat down on the sofa.

Eventually Tyler, Lazarus, and Seth joined the two women in the living room. They all decided what costumes they wanted to wear, what foods to take, and who was going to do each part to get it all together in a few short days.

Onyx and Brian were spending time at the new house overseeing the final modifications. They returned the morning of the party and retreated to the slumber room created for daytime sleep.

Reyne went into the room and laid down beside Onyx. "I've missed you." She whispered to him.

Onyx grabbed her and rolled her into him. "Sleep with me for a while?" He asked her wearily.

"Gotta work with Taylor on schoolwork, but I'll be back. We have a party to go to tonight. So you rest now." She continued to lie with him until his breathing became deep and rhythmic. Then she crawled out of the bed and went to find Taylor.

She found him in his room, and they started working on the day's assignment. They were interrupted as Leigh, Andy, Lazarus and Tyler started preparing for the party. Reyne finally gave up and told Taylor to go play while she made grilled cheese sandwiches and vegetable soup for lunch, then she sat to eat with Taylor.

As she and Taylor were cleaning up the lunch dishes, Seth walked through the front door and yelled, "Taylor, come here. I've got a surprise for you."

Taylor left Reyne to finish cleaning the kitchen. He followed Seth into the living room. Reyne followed as well to see what Seth got for Taylor. When she arrived in the living room, she started in on Seth, "You know that he has chores and schoolwork to do. This better be good."

"It is, Reyne," Seth smiled at her and squatted down to look Taylor in the eye. "What do you want to be for Halloween?" he asked.

"I don't know. Maybe a skateboarder," Taylor answered.

"How about Yu-gi-oh?" Seth lifted the bag from the hanger he was holding to produce a handmade Yu-gi-oh costume and wig.

Taylor grabbed it, "Thanks." He took his costume and ran up to his bedroom to put it on.

Reyne stood there and glared at Seth, "Well, I guess chores and school are over for today."

Seth grabbed her around her waist and pulled her into him, "Sorry Reyne. Onyx told me to pick it up today and give it to him," he explained while giving her his best puppy dog eyes.

"I'll let it go this time, but…" Reyne felt the passion in Seth. It was erotic and sensual. Even without Seth trying she knew right then why Onyx loved him.

Seth interrupted her and finished the sentence, "…don't do it again." He started laughing, let go of her and went to help the others finish getting everything ready to move the next morning.

The rest of the day was spent finishing the packing of essentials, that up until this point, had remained unpacked. Leigh and Reyne made dinner for everyone, cleaned up the dishes, and packed them in a box. When Reyne finished in the kitchen, she yelled down the stairs to Taylor, "Sweetie, come on up and let's get on our costumes."

Taylor came running to his mother. "OK." He passed her and ran up to his room.

Everyone else also slowly began to prepare for the evening's festivities. Once Reyne got Taylor ready, she let him go to the basement to play video games and wait for Seth and Lazarus to play with him. She then got ready herself. After the last touches were completed, she went in and woke up Brian and Onyx, telling them to get ready. The two men found their costumes had been laid out, so they were ready in no time. Onyx as a zombie and Brian as a bloody surgeon.

They entered the living room and started laughing when they saw the array of costumes sitting there patiently waiting for their arrival.

Taylor was dressed as Yu-Gi-Oh. He was sitting between Seth, who was dressed as a Polynesian girl and Lazarus, dressed as a Scottish warrior, kilt and all. On the sofa sat Leigh, dressed as Smurfette, Andy, as Gargamel, and Tyler, as a dominatrix. Only Reyne was not in the room. Onyx looked around worriedly.

"She is getting the camera and will be right back up. She wants a picture of this." Leigh said, noticing Onyx's worried face.

"I'm back. Ready for our picture. I'll set the timer and you all get into position." Reyne smiled as she directed the positioning of each person.

Onyx stood in his spot, just staring at her dumbfounded. Reyne smiled mischievously at him. She was wearing a low-cut, form fitting, vinyl cat suit with ears on her head and matching thigh high stiletto boots.

"Onyx. Onyx. Wake up!" Reyne pushed at him.

"You look incredible," Onyx stammered.

"Would you please go stand beside Seth? Make sure there is room for me on the other side of you," Reyne instructed him.

"OK, but we want you between us." Onyx answered as he walked over to his spot, never taking his eyes from his beloved Reyne.

"Do you still want me around?" Seth whispered to Onyx as he took his place.

"Yes, very much so." Onyx said as he took Seth's hand and squeezed it. "I want you both with me and eventually you both to be together as well."

"Here we go," Reyne giggled and ran to her spot.

The camera shutter clicked, and then the group of them left for the short walk to the party.

CHAPTER 32

"Cindy's parties are always incredible." Reyne told them all as they reached their destination. The group walked in, Leigh and Reyne hugged Cindy, who was at the door greeting and directing guests.

"Taylor, Jackie is waiting for you in the playroom." Cindy said.

Taylor looked at Reyne. "Go ahead, baby," Reyne said. Taylor hugged her and ran to the basement.

Cindy smiled, "Okay, now for the adults. Coke upstairs master bedroom, food all over this floor and the basement, alcohol in the basement and backyard, pot in the backyard. Have fun and enjoy."

Brian, Seth, and Lazarus headed straight upstairs. Leigh, Reyne and Andy went in search of the alcohol. Tyler went searching for food, and Onyx headed to the basement and out into the backyard for pot.

Reyne had several shots of moonshine with Leigh and Andy and then went looking for Onyx. She eventually found him in the backyard. As soon as she arrived, he filled a bowl for her and handed it to her. She smoked it with him while sitting on his lap. He still could not believe how incredible she looked. He put his arms around her waist and squeezed. He wanted her to know that she was the most important part of his life.

"I'm going to get a drink; do you want anything?" Reyne said softly.

"No, thank you. If you'll let me, I'll drink of you later though." Onyx said smiling.

"Of course, I wouldn't miss that for anything. I'll be back." Reyne kissed his cheek and went into the basement. She headed to the small bar and started looking around to see what they had. A Dalmatian with a female voice asked her what she was looking for. Reyne replies, "Vodka." The Dalmatian handed her the bottle. Reyne poured herself a shot and slammed it. She did this once more, then proceeded to make herself a drink. She handed the bottle back to the Dalmatian, thanked her, and walked away. Before she even made it halfway across the room, she began to feel really strange and sat down.

Lazarus, Tyler, Seth and Brian made their way downstairs eventually. They saw Reyne sitting in a chair and waved at her on the way out the back door to find Onyx. Reyne waved back at them, but was unable to say anything. She was getting really scared. She wasn't feeling right but couldn't communicate this problem with anyone. Andy and Leigh passed by, and she could only wave again. She hoped someone noticed she wasn't acting right and would tell Onyx or help her themselves. She continued to sit there and wait.

As soon as Leigh and Andy were out the basement door, Leigh headed straight for Onyx. "Onyx, Reyne is looking really bad. I've partied with her many times, and she is just not right. You should go check on her."

Onyx laughed, "She just left my side 10 minutes ago. She is just high and drunk."

"No Onyx. I've been stupid high and unable to walk, talk, think drunk with Reyne. She is different. She isn't right. She is having trouble sitting in the chair and is rubbing her legs and arms. I've never seen her like this. Plus, for Reyne to get really messed up takes a while. Please go check on her. She will be honest with you, but she won't be with me." Leigh pleaded with Onyx.

"Ok, fine. But if she gets mad at me, I'm telling her it was because you asked me to check up on her." Onyx smiled at Leigh and walked into the house.

"I hope Reyne is OK." Leigh said as Lazarus, Seth, Tyler and Brian join her and Andy.

Tyler caught part of what Leigh said, "What's wrong with my mom?" Tyler asked Leigh.

"She is just partying harder than usually. I thought Onyx should check on her." Leigh answered.

"My mom party too hard. That doesn't happen too much. She may not go out, but she can bring the party to her and usually does. We've barely been here an hour, and she is already messed up?" Tyler asked.

"Yes. She is acting really weird. That's why I sent Onyx in to check on her." Leigh answered.

Slowly, the conversation moved from Reyne and the group of them start talking quietly about the move the next day. After a while, Leigh realized that Onyx had not returned. She checked her watch, "Oh my god. Onyx has been gone for over 30 minutes and hasn't checked back with us. I hope she's OK. Maybe I will go check."

Andy touched her arm, "Onyx is with her. She'll be safe. Enjoy yourself."

Leigh smiled and hugged Andy, "OK."

Suddenly Onyx came sprinting over to the group, "She wasn't anywhere in the house. Did she come out here?" Onyx asked.

"No. What do you mean she is not in the house?" Brian asked.

"I looked all over and didn't see her anywhere..."

"Did you ask anyone if they had seen her?" Leigh asks.

"No. I was too busy not finding her. I can usually go right to her. I can feel her energy, but it is nowhere in the house. I am telling you, she is not here any longer."

"It will be OK, Onyx. We will find her." Brian tried to reassure him. "Lazarus, you stay here with Andy and Leigh and keep an eye on Tyler and Taylor. Go on and have a good time. All will be well. Seth, Onyx and I are going to find Reyne. Have you fed tonight?"

"Yes, I fed before we came over here; otherwise, I would not have been able to deal with all the people. I will take care of the family." Lazarus answered.

"We will let you know what is going on, although I figure you will know anyway. I'd better catch up with Onyx. Keep Taylor in the dark about things. Don't let him get excited. Bye." Brian turned and went into the house and straight to the front door.

CHAPTER 33

Onyx found Cindy coming down the stairs to the basement "Have you seen Reyne?"

"Yea, I saw her leave with the Surgeon and the Dalmatian about a half hour ago. It looked like they were taking her back to the house and party some more because they were carrying a bottle of vodka. Why?" Cindy asked and then her eyes went wide as she watched Brian start up the stairs. "Hold on, if you are the surgeon in their group…"

"Onyx, they got her. We have to leave now…" Seth said when he found Onyx and Brian on the stairs.

"What is going on? Who has her?" Cindy asked.

"What was that Seth?" Onyx interrupted Cindy.

"Xavier and Elizabeth have her. She's been drugged with Ecstasy and would have left with anyone. She probably doesn't even know who she is with and doesn't care. You both know about Ecstasy, I am sure." Seth explained.

"Yes, we know about ecstasy, and we also know that she is in danger. More danger than I first anticipated." Onyx said as calmly as he could.

Brian walked up to Cindy and touches her shoulder. "It will be OK. Thanks for the great evening." He told Cindy, knowing she would not remember the conversation. The three of them finish climbing the stairs and heading out the door.

They walk back to the house and changed from their costumes and into their everyday clothes. When Onyx finished changing, he called his father. The phone rang and his mother answered, "Mom, let me talk to my father now," Onyx demanded.

"Now, is that anyway to talk to your mother? Not even a hello, I love you, or anything for your mother." She asked him jokingly.

"Xavier and Elizabeth have Reyne. I need to know the location of Xavier's closest safe house. Get my father, Now!" Onyx screamed at her.

Onyx heard her yelling for his father through the phone. She gave him a rundown of the situation before giving him the phone.

"OK. Your mother and I are flying in tonight. The closest safe house should be in Brunswick, Maryland, but I will check with his father. It is about an hour and half, mortal time, from where you're at. Do not make a move until I get there." He told his son.

"They've drugged her with Ecstasy. She will be very accepting of anything they do. They cannot turn her right now. It could kill..." Onyx broke off.

"Onyx? Is she with child?" he asks.

"Yes, but she doesn't even know. It is too soon. The drug will not hurt the baby, but turning her will and it could kill her too. I cannot deal with the loss of her again. I will die if she does." Onyx voice trembled as he told his father this.

Brian walked into the room when he heard Onyx start yelling. With the last statement, he looked over to see Seth's reaction. Seth turned to leave when Brian stopped him and whispered, "Don't judge him right now. There is more you need to know before you can be upset. Onyx loves you and will always. But he did tell you from the beginning that you are his second. Am I right.?" Brian asked him.

"Yes." Seth answered quietly.

"Then be here for him right now. That is what he needs and will create a strong bond between the two of you that even Reyne won't be able to penetrate. I will tell you everything at another time. I promise." Brian pushed Seth toward Onyx.

"OK" Seth answered.

He walked over to Onyx and grabbed his hand and squeezed it. Feeling Seth's hand in his gave him the strength to continue with his conversation. "For all I know, the baby is already dead and they have already turned her."

"Onyx, the baby is part of her; try to find it and protect it until you can get to her safely. The plane is waiting. We will pick you up as soon as we get there. It will be about four hours, so be ready." His father told him. "Also, make sure anyone coming with us will have fed prior to my arrival. We must be sated before we confront him."

"I will make sure we all feed. Goodbye, father." Onyx hung up the phone.

"Well?" Brian asked of Onyx. "Tell us what he said and why haven't you two told us about the baby?"

"She doesn't know. She is barely pregnant. Maybe two or three weeks. I felt a new energy in her. I was going to tell her first and let her announce it," Onyx whispered.

"When were you going to tell her?" Seth asked calmly.

"Tomorrow, when I show her the nursery at the new house. The room I would not let anyone see. You know which room," Onyx broke down again.

Seth moved around Onyx so he could hold Onyx in his arms to give him strength and support.

"Onyx, stop it. We have things to do. What did your father say?" Brian demanded, trying to get Onyx back on track.

"Find the baby and protect it if I can. Wait here for him. He said he would be here in four hours. I guess we should prepare and feed." Onyx said listlessly.

"Yes, we have to save her and the little one. Come on." Brian said as he grabbed Onyx by the shoulders and shook him. "Seth, he needs to drink to find the baby. May he can drink from you?" Brian asked. "No, he can't. God, we have to find a donor."

Leigh and Andy had come home with Taylor and heard part of the conversation. Leigh walked into the room, "What about me?"

Without a word, Onyx walked over to her. Onyx brushes his lips against Leigh's neck finding the large vein he needs to fill his hunger. He moved past the vein as he took her arm and brought it to his mouth. Once he found the vein in the bend of her arm, he gently pushed his fangs into it. He drank just a few moments, but it was enough to bring a groan of excitement from within Leigh.

Andy watched the whole episode, not knowing what to think or how to take the pleasure she seemed to be receiving from Onyx. Brian walked over to Andy and reassured him he had nothing to worry about. He explained everything they were doing and how they were going to get Reyne back.

Onyx pulled away, slowly kissing the puncture wounds, "I know what they plan for her. I do not know where she is though. They have cloaked that well. She is still drugged, and they plan on feeding her ecstasy to keep her complacent. The baby lives and I have sent protection to the both of them. Unfortunately, it is not enough to protect her from Elizabeth's or Xavier's advances, but it is all I can do. Elizabeth doesn't turn, she just plays. Xavier likes to turn, play and kill. However, Elizabeth likes her, so she should be safe for a while. We must go feed and prepare for the fight."

"Onyx, we will get there in time." Brian said as he led him toward the door.

Onyx turned around and pulled Seth close to him. "Thank you," he mouthed to Seth before kissing him.

CHAPTER 34

Seth drove the three of them to a forested park area not far from Reyne's house. They got out of the car and head down the street before turning toward the train tracks, where a lot of the teenagers, derelicts, and junkies frequented. They could feast and throw the bodies by the railroad tracks with no concern of discovery. They all knew that tonight was not about donors and letting them live; it was all about the blood.

When they arrived, Onyx turned to Seth, "You must feed well tonight. I can tell you have not been feeding as you should for being so young. I could not bear to lose you, either." He kissed him gently on the cheek.

"I have to say that I was beginning to worry you would toss me aside now that Reyne is back in your life." He admitted.

"Never." The two embraced and kissed, only to be interrupted by Brian.

"I'm hungry, and a bunch of teenagers just headed to the tracks. Let's go." Brian said as he followed the teens silently.

Onyx and Seth fell in behind Brian, watching the group, which consisted of six boys and three girls. It became obvious to the three men that the guys were going to get these young women drunk and take advantage of them. They made their plan of attack easily with this knowledge using looks, not words.

They sat and watched while the teens get high and drunk. The young men started breaking off into groups and surrounding the girls, groping, fondling, and kissing the girls. Onyx looked at Seth and knew they would not be able to keep him from feeding much longer. The girls did not realize they were being separated from one another until it was too late and the boys were in a frenzy.

Onyx nodded at Seth and Brian, letting them know it was time. The three of them broke through the trees and into the clearing, startling the boys, who automatically stopped until they realized it wasn't the police.

One of the teens looked at Brian and not knowing what else to do said, "Wanna join our party. The entertainment is just starting."

"Sure." Brian said as he walked over to the young man. He grabbed the girl by the arms and threw her toward Seth. "We'll take her."

"Wait a minute. She is ours, you have to share." Another of the young men interjected.

Seth had thrown the girl over his shoulder and said with a menacing grin, "We are sharing." His vampiric features began to become noticeable.

Onyx realized they had to work faster than he first anticipated. Seth was going to go into a feeding frenzy if he did not start soon. He shot a look at Brian and they rounded up the other six people into a circle. Seth shoved the two guys in the circle with the others and sat the girl down gently.

"Now. We can do this the hard way or the easy way. Which would you prefer?" Brian asked.

One of the young men answered, "Do what?"

"Shut up!" Seth said as he slaps the kid. "He wasn't speaking to you."

Onyx and Brian looked at one another. They knew the smell of blood was tormenting Seth.

Onyx spoke up, "We will do this the easy way. Pick one my lover and show the rest of them what they have to look forward to. You can have five of them total for you are so young. When it gets to only the three girls and three guys slow down so that we may have some fun too." Onyx said, knowing the results of such a statement.

Seth walked over to Onyx and kissed him. "You are so wonderful. Thank you." He returned to the spot he had just left, grabbed the boy he had slapped and stood him up. "I bet you think I'm going to fuck you," He said with a smirk. "Guess what? You're wrong. What I'm going to do is much worse. Do you think you can take me?" He asked.

"You're a fag. I can take you easily," the kid replied.

"Now Seth, you shouldn't play with your food tonight. We are in a bit of a hurry," Brian said in a tone that seemed paternal to the group.

"Food?" One of the girls asked.

"Yes, food." Onyx answered calmly, with no sign of emotion. "Show them, Seth."

"I guess I will never know if you can take me. But I am going to take you. Be prepared to feel pain," Seth said as he smiled widely, showing his long fangs before he bit deep into the teen's throat.

The girls started crying and screaming immediately. All the teens watched in horror as Seth drained the kid. They watch him continue to pull, only stopping when the kid stopped twitching.

"That is enough from that one. Who's next, my love?" Onyx said.

Brian looked at the remaining youths and then at Onyx and smiled. "Yes Seth. Have another. You need your nourishment."

Seth obeyed and took another of the young men. Onyx watched Seth's choices. He noticed that one of the young men had Seth's eye. Onyx knew that Seth would not touch him because of looks and beauty. Onyx thought to himself, *'I will gladly take this little snot to his death.'* Seth followed his instructions and stopped when only three of the young men and the three girls were left.

"Take your pick. I will take the last that you have not chosen." Seth looked at Onyx while he said this.

Onyx and Brian each took a young man from the group, and Seth took the remaining one. Onyx looked at the three girls, "Sit down and be quiet. If you follow my instructions, your death will be the most pleasurable experience you could ever imagine and you won't mind the fact you are dying but will embrace it happily. But. If you make any noise or try to run, it will be more painful and grotesque than anything you have seen tonight. Do you understand?"

The three girls shook their heads in understanding and remained seated.

Brian, Seth, and Onyx each began to feed from their chosen youth. Onyx was enjoying the feeling of the blood of his youth fill his mouth until he heard the sounds of movement. When he looked up, he discovered one of the girls decided to try to run. The other two girls tried to quietly call her back, but it was to no avail. Onyx laid his young man down and was in front of her before she realized that she was being followed.

Onyx grabbed the girl by her hair and drug her back to the clearing. He stood in front of the other two girls, "This is what will happen to you if you try to run." He picked the girl up off the ground by her hair. She started screaming in pain and fear. He proceeded to rip the clothes off of her fiercely. She shrieked even louder from being exposed by Onyx. He jerked her to him, bared his fangs and bit into her left breast, tearing it from her body. The girls watching started crying and hugging one another. Brian and Seth, now finished with their prey, sat down beside the girls and watched Onyx finish his work.

Onyx sucked all the blood from the breast wound while still holding the girl off the ground. He stood her back on the ground while licking the gaping wound in her chest. He looked at Seth and Brian, "If she struggles, you know what to do."

Each of the men smiled and nodded. Onyx pushed the standing girl to the ground, making her fall onto her side. As she tried to scramble away, Onyx grabbed her foot, "Have you learned nothing?"

He drug her back to the circle, making sure he was in front of his audience. He turned her so that her back was to him and laid on top of her. He bit her shoulder, not to feed but to inflict pain. He did this all the way down the right side of her back. When he reached her ass, he bit the right side at the fleshiest part of the cheek, gnawing on it, and ripping it from her body. "Seth?" He offered his lover a drink from the place the ass had been. Seth nodded and went to lick the blood from the girl's leg. Onyx held her down until Seth backed away and thanked Onyx.

Onyx rolled her onto her back and Seth held her shoulders as Onyx went down to her feet, biting the sole of each foot. He proceeded up the inside of the left leg first and then the right. He bit all over her thighs before positioning himself in between her legs. He started to lick the magical spot that would bring her pleasure. He licked until she was moaning from pleasure as well as pain, it was then that he knew it was time. He bit down hard and sucked the blood from her soft mound. He continued to suck fiercely until the last breath passed from her body.

He lifted his head, and turned his bloody face to the remaining two girls, "Yours will be much more pleasurable, if you stay where you are. I promise." Onyx turned to the young man he had left and found him watching intently. "Did you like the show?"

"Yes, I did." He answered.

"Just watch the other two. You've seen the ugly, now watch the beautiful side. Nothing human can be so ugly or so beautiful," Onyx helped him sit up to watch Seth and Brian drain the girls while making love to them. The young man watched the girls give themselves freely to their murderers, reaching orgasms right before death overtook them and dying with smiles on their faces.

Once the girls were discarded, Onyx asked the young man, "What did you think?"

"It was beautiful, as you said. I am just wondering which way you are going to finish me? I would prefer the gentle way. I've never been with a man, but it looked so calm, peaceful, and gentle."

Brian returned to Onyx's side and sighed, "Another one. You really must stop this, Onyx."

"Not for me, but for Seth. What do you think?" Onyx asked Brian before Seth reached them.

"I think you should ask Seth. We could leave him with Lazarus until we return." Brian said as Seth arrived.

Seth looked at the youth and frowned, "Onyx, why haven't you finished him? We have things to do."

Brian spoke up, "Onyx was just discussing something with me. It concerns you."

Seth sat down beside Onyx, "What is it?"

Onyx took a deep breath, "I know you worry about your position in my life because of Reyne. I was just thinking you may like a companion. I would be second to your companion, as you are my second to Reyne." Onyx stroked Seth's arm.

"You would give him to me? You worry about me that much, knowing you would no longer be my world?" Seth asked him softly.

All of this time, the young man had been silently listening. "What are you talking about?" he asked worriedly, looking at the three men surrounding him.

Seth looked down at the youth, "How old are you?"

"Twenty." He replied. "What's that got to do with anything?"

"What is your name?" Seth asked him.

"Do not ask that until you have made your decision." Brian instructed.

Seth shot him a look saying, 'shut up' and asked the young man again, "What is your name?"

"My name is Morgan." He answered.

"How would you like to be immortal?" Seth continued.

"If I would get to experience the beauty you have shown me tonight, I would gladly embrace it. I would gladly embrace death to experience the beauty if that is my only choice."

"What about the ugly part, which you have witnessed, of the immortality I am offering?" Seth asked.

"I have experienced ugly and wrong. It doesn't faze me. But beauty rarely makes itself known in my world," he answered, getting stronger in his emphasis.

Seth looked at Brian and asked, "What do I have to do?"

Onyx smiled as Brian replied, "Drain him to the point of death, then he will drink first from you, then from me.

Onyx may give him some, but you and I are what he needs first. He will have to deal with it completely conscious and of free will. You cannot take him to the beautiful place you took the girl. That you will have to save for another time."

"Let's do it." He turned his attention back to Morgan. "Do you want to be my companion and my lover?"

"Yes," he answered without hesitation.

"You will share me with Onyx, as I share Onyx with Reyne. Would you be able to handle that?" Seth asked.

"I would hope I can. If I can't, you will kill me, right?" he answered.

"Yes." Seth stated with no emotion. "Yes, that is how it would normally go, but I plan on killing you anyway."

Seth took a step toward him, grabbed him up and bit down hard on his neck. It did not take long to drain him, since Onyx had fed from him already, and he fed quickly to limit the amount of pain Morgan would have to endure. When he was done, he looked at Onyx, "Thank you, Onyx, for your offer, but I am not ready for another yet." Seth said as he cast Morgan's body aside.

CHAPTER 35

Seth, Brian, and Onyx arrived back at the house to find everyone awaiting their arrival. Taylor was asleep in his room; Tyler was sleeping on the sofa. Lazarus, Andy, and Leigh were at the kitchen table.

When Leigh saw Seth walking through the door, she asked, "Did you find her?"

"We haven't even gone yet. We had to feed and prepare," Onyx answered her.

"Why haven't you gone after her yet…" Leigh screamed.

"Because they were waiting for me." Said a deep voice from behind the group of them.

"This is my father and my mother, Vlad and Svetlina. No, he is not Vlad the Impaler. He is the actual Vlad Dracul I. The Impaler is my half-brother. We needed to wait for him to get Reyne back without too much bloodshed," Onyx explained.

"I am here to help with the move and with Reyne when they return. Vlad and I are sticking around until all of this is settled for good between Onyx and Xavier," Svetlina said.

"How many bloodsuckers do we have now? Are we trying to create an Army?" Andy asked Onyx angrily.

"Young man. You disrespect my son. Has he not given you things that you would never have had without him? And yet you question him about things that do not concern you." Vlad said directly to Andy. "Or is it you are jealous because you are not as we are?"

Onyx held his hand to his father to show that he would answer Andy's concerns. He looked at Andy, "Do I question you about anything?"

"No," Andy replied.

"Give me the same courtesy. I would do nothing to harm Reyne, her children, or her friends. You were given a choice to help protect her. I did not force you. All will be dealt with in due time, but our first concern should be Reyne," he hesitated a moment, then asked, "and are you jealous?" Onyx finished with the question everyone wanted to have answered.

"No," Andy replied emphatically.

"Good, then we are ready to leave," Onyx stated. "We have to strike before nightfall returns, and we have much planning and driving to do."

"Svetlina, let's go upstairs and leave the testosterone to themselves. You probably want to freshen up." Leigh said to the older woman.

"That would be wonderful. Thank you."

Leigh showed Svetlina to Reyne's bedroom, went back downstairs, and started making breakfast for everyone. Taylor had woken up and groggily walked down to the living room and laid on the love seat. Onyx walked over to him, sat beside him, and rubbed his back like Reyne did most mornings.

Taylor opened his eyes and smiled at Onyx, "Where's Momma?" He asked sleepily.

"Momma is out right now, but she will be home tonight. She will meet you at the new house. Would that be okay?" Onyx asked.

"Yes," Taylor replied sleepily through a yawn.

Onyx reached in his pocket and pulled out some money, "Here. Have Leigh and my mother take you to the store to buy your Momma something special for her return.

"Okay," Taylor smiled, "I'm hungry."

"Good, because breakfast is ready," Leigh said. "Wake up your sister, please. Then come in the kitchen to eat."

Taylor hopped off the love seat and ran over to the sofa to jump on his sister.

"What the …?" Tyler exclaimed groggily. "You little shit. Why did you jump on me?" She yelled at Taylor.

"Breakfast," Taylor said, smiling at his sister.

Tyler sat up and saw everyone in the room. "Who is he?" She asked through a yawn, staring at the older man in the room.

"I am Vlad Dracul. Onyx's father. You must be Reyne's daughter, Tyler. It is so good to meet you," Vlad said.

"Cool, Onyx. Your dad's the Impaler," Tyler blurted without thinking.

"No, sorry, Tyler. The Impaler is my half-brother," Onyx said.

"Oh My God. You're older than I thought then. I hope Lazarus ages as well as you," she said to Onyx before turning to his father and extending her hand, "It is an honor to meet you, sir," she shook his hand and went into the kitchen to eat.

Farewells were made, and good lucks were given as the four men set out to rescue Reyne.

"Let's go kick some ass," Seth called out. "What they have done to Reyne is inexcusable. We have got to get her."

"May I go too?" Lazarus asked.

"Not this time, my young one. You must get stronger. Plus, you must protect the family and help them all get to the new house safely," Brian told him.

Vlad led the group to his limousine and gave instructions to the driver where they were going. Once in the car, he turned to Brian, "your son has grown into a fine young man."

"Yes, he has," Brian answered with a smile.

Then, all the members of the team settled in for the ride while Vlad told them how they were going to handle things once they arrived at Xavier's house.

CHAPTER 36

Xavier and Elizabeth put Reyne in the back of their limousine and climbed in after her. Xavier told the driver to take them home and settled down to enjoy the ride.

The back of the limousine had a nest of blankets and one bench seat. Elizabeth laid next to Reyne on the nest once she had removed the Dalmatian costume.

"Sweetie. It's Elizabeth. Let me get you out of that costume." She said to Reyne.

"It's cold," Reyne replied and started pulling blankets over her.

"The heat is on, and you won't be cold for long. Trust me. I'll keep you warm." Elizabeth soothingly whispered in her ear as she started to remove Reyne's costume. Reyne struggled momentarily but eventually gave in and helped her remove the catsuit. Once it was off, she pulled the blankets around her tighter while Elizabeth received a pill of pure MDMA from Xavier and took it. "Soon, my love, we will both be very hot. Do you think I am pretty?" She asked Reyne.

"Yes, you are beautiful," Reyne replied as she began rubbing the fuzzy blanket she had cocooned herself in and making it rub her entire body.

"Here. Have some water." Elizabeth put a sports bottle to Reyne's mouth.

"I don't want any water." She tried to push the bottle away.

"But you must drink; otherwise, you will get sick. If you take a sip for me, I will rub lotion all over your body. You'll love it; I promise," Elizabeth coaxed her.

"Okay," Reyne replied as she imagined lotion being stroked over her body. She took a sip and moaned, "oh my god, that is great. I want more." She grabbed at the sports bottle.

"Not right now. You must drink only a little at a time. Are you getting warm yet?" Elizabeth asked as she pulled the lotion from the side of the blanket nest.

"Yes, I'm starting to feel much warmer," Reyne replied, but she still refused to come out of the blanket.

Elizabeth took a sip of water and had Reyne take another sip. She started pulling the blanket from Reyne's feet so that she could put lotion on them. The cool lotion gliding over her feet made Reyne moan and writhe. Elizabeth moved up Reyne's leg and stopped at her upper thighs. Xavier gave both women a sip of water to keep them from passing out.

Elizabeth moved to Reyne's left hand and worked her way up to her shoulder. She proceeded to do the same on Reyne's right side. Reyne began moaning louder and begging to be touched. Elizabeth moved to Reyne's neck, sliding lotion slick hands down her neck, slowly making her way toward Reyne's breasts but not touching them.

Reyne shrieked with excitement, "Please! Touch me more. Make me cum. I can't stand it. I need more. Nothing has ever felt like this before. It feels incredible. Please don't stop."

Elizabeth graciously complied with Reyne's request. She put more lotion into the palms of her hands and placed them directly under Reyne's breasts, stroking her smooth abdomen gently and playing with Reyne's hips. Reyne arched her back, begging for more with her movements. She grabbed the lotion, put some in own her hands, and started rubbing Elizabeth's arms, feeling the lotion on her fingers and the flesh under her hands, causing her more intensified excitement. She slowly moved her hands up and down Elizabeth's arms as her eyes roll into the back of her head, and she fell backward.

Xavier reached over and sat Reyne up. He put the sports bottle of water to her lips for her to sip. When she was done, he poured some of the ice water over her body and watched her explode with an intense orgasm from feeling the water dripping on her body.

"Kiss her," Xavier begged of Elizabeth as he sat back on the bench seat and picked up a camera.

Elizabeth smiled and quickly complied with his request. She started with soft kisses on Reyne's lips, slowly making the kisses deeper and more passionate, finally parting Reyne's lips and delving her tongue into Reyne's mouth.

Elizabeth stopped kissing her and said, "Pucker up. This will feel incredible."

Reyne followed Elizabeth's instructions and pursed her lips, thinking another kiss was coming. Instead, Elizabeth took coconut flavored lip gloss and applied it to Reyne's lips first and then to her own. Only after they both had on the lip gloss did Elizabeth start kissing Reyne again. Reyne reciprocated, moaning, wanting Elizabeth to touch and kiss her more. She moved her mouth from Elizabeth's lips and down her neck, touching and caressing softly with her lips. Her hands caressed Elizabeth's thighs as she made her way to Elizabeth's breasts. Elizabeth moaned and arched into Reyne to help her mouth find her nipples. Reyne ventured further down and started sucking Elizabeth's nipples, nibbling and biting as Elizabeth grabbed the back of her head and pulled her into her breasts.

Xavier got the spray bottle and began misting the women with ice water. Both groaned and writhed on the blanket even more. Xavier handed the sports bottle to Elizabeth, "Sip?"

Elizabeth took the bottle and sipped it, then handed it to Reyne. Reyne took a sip and swallowed. She took another sip and held it in her mouth, grabbed Elizabeth, and kissed her. The water running from their mouths and down the front of their bodies brought the women to a new level of excitement and intensity.

Xavier took the spray bottle again and sprayed them before handing Elizabeth a plate of oranges, "Now, girls. Gotta save something for when we get home. Here, have some oranges."

"Yes, Reyne. Try these," Elizabeth handed Reyne a slice of orange.

Reyne sucked and licked the slice before devouring it, "Oh my, this is incredible. I've never had an orange taste so good."

"Do you want more?" Elizabeth asked.

"Yes, please," Reyne held out her hands and pleaded.

Elizabeth handed her the plateful of oranges. "Xavier, I need to feed, too."

"I know you do, my love. Go feed. I will entertain our guest if you don't mind," Xavier said.

"I don't mind. Just no penetration without me present, please. I want to watch her enjoy you," Elizabeth replied.

"No problem, my love. Go. Feed. We will be waiting. I will give her more ecstasy if you are gone too long so that she will be ready for you," Xavier told Elizabeth.

"Okay, lover," Elizabeth dressed quickly, opened the door, and left the sanctuary in the back of their limo, the special area they had created for Reyne, to go into what was left of the night and feed.

Once Elizabeth was out of the car, Xavier asked Reyne, "How are the oranges?" as he took the plate from her.

"Wonderful," She replied groggily.

Xavier crawled into the nest beside her and started stroking her arm, hoping to get farther than just touching before Elizabeth returned.

Reyne leaned into him, "spray me, please."

Xavier smiled and complied with her request. He sprayed her with the ice water, then handed her the water bottle, and she began to drink deeply.

"No honey, just sip, or you'll get sick," he told her.

She handed the sports bottle back to him and asked, "Can I rub lotion on you?"

"Yes, you may. Would you like some more lip gloss too?"

"Yes," she replied. She applied the lip gloss and got the lotion while Xavier undressed. She started applying lotion to his chest; he leaned into her and kissed her.

"Is it different kissing a man than kissing a woman?"

"Girls are softer, but men are more feral, almost a hungry energy. I like both for different reasons," Reyne explained to him as she pushed him down onto the blanket.

She started kissing him but suddenly rolled over onto the blanket and started covering up.

"Are you getting cold?" Xavier asked.

"Yes. I'm getting sleepy too," Reyne stated.

Xavier reached into a little box and pulled out another dose of Ecstasy. "This will warm you up," he said as he handed her the pill.

"What is this?" Reyne asked.

"A pill that will make everything feel and taste good. Try it. Remember the lip gloss, the lotion, the oranges?" Xavier smiled and stroked her arm.

"Yes, I remember," she said with a smile. She put the pill in her mouth and took a big gulp of water.

"No, honey. Remember to sip the water only," Xavier said, as he turned up the heat in the rear of the limousine.

Reyne sat there for a few minutes, "I'm gonna be sick," She leaned over to the door, opened it, and threw up the water and the pill.

Xavier pulled her back into the limousine as soon as she had finished. "Here. Try again." He handed her another dose. "Sip the water this time." As she sipped the water, her eyes rolled up into her head, and she fell back onto the blanket nest again.

Xavier sat there smiling, "I guess she just needed to warm up. Oh well, she will definitely be ready for anything now, and anything is what she will receive," Xavier started laughing.

Reyne started laughing with him, "What's so funny?"

"Nothing really, just your reaction to the water. Can I touch you?" he asked.

"Yes, please. I need someone to touch me," she said. "But I want to touch you too." Reyne smiled at Xavier and grabbed at him.

He moved back, just out of her reach. Reyne giggled and rolled onto her hands and knees. She crawled toward him and grabbed at him again. She caught him this time because he had nowhere to go. She pulled him to her and kissed him.

"Hold on, Sweet One. Take a sip of water while I take care of something." Xavier handed her the sports bottle as he swallowed a triple-stacked hit of ecstasy himself.

He sat back and grabbed the spray bottle, misting Reyne periodically. "Play with yourself. Show me how much you want me to touch you," he commanded her.

Reyne rolled onto her back with her moist, throbbing bud facing him. She licked the fingers on both hands and started playing with her nipples. Slowly, her right hand slid down her body to find her core. She pulled her fingers back to her mouth to lick them again. She started rubbing herself until she found the perfect spot that opened her to an orgasm. Her hips began to move up, and she began to rub more vigorously. "Put your fingers in me, please," she begged him.

The ecstasy took hold of Xavier, "I would love to, but alas, I cannot without Elizabeth here. It was her one request. I do so enjoy watching you, though. Please continue, and when she gets back, I will do as you ask.

"Promise!" Reyne screamed through her next orgasm.

Xavier whispered, "Yes."

"I'm cum..." Before she finished the sentence, she came so hard that she squirted onto the blanket.

The sight almost sent Xavier over the edge; he thought, *"Elizabeth better get back here soon."*

Afterward, the two entwined and began kissing, gentle, chaste kisses. Their hands were moving up and down each other's bodies. Reyne rolled Xavier onto his back, her tongue creating a path down his chest, teasing him by licking close to his manhood but missing it each time. Xavier moaned loudly, and Reyne took the moan as a cue to take his shaft deep into her mouth.

Xavier stopped her. "You cannot until Elizabeth is back," he moaned. "She wants to watch you pleasure me. Can you wait just a while longer?"

The door of the limousine opened, and Elizabeth climbed into the back and into the nest. "You two have been busy, I see," she said, smiling at both of them.

"Well, she was," Xavier said, "Take one side and join us, my love." He held out his hand to Elizabeth. When Reyne saw Elizabeth had returned and Xavier's outstretched hand, she too, reached out for Elizabeth.

"My pleasure," she replied as she took another hit of ecstasy. She grabbed the lip gloss and put some on before crawling next to Reyne. "Come on down here and help me," she said to Reyne as she wrapped her hand around Xavier.

Reyne stopped kissing Xavier's chest and shook her head yes as she slid down Xavier's other side to meet Elizabeth at his shaft.

Xavier tapped the window between the driver and them to signal to continue the drive to Brunswick as the two women start kissing and licking his shaft and each other.

The three remained entwined, touching, tasting, and kissing for the remainder of the ride. Xavier received the majority of the attention. When they arrived at Xavier's safe house, Xavier and

Elizabeth wrapped Reyne up and carried her into the house. They took her straight to the room created just for this night.

They laid Reyne down, keeping her bundled up until the heat in the room was high enough to keep her rolling and enjoying their playtime. Elizabeth crawled to Reyne and started unbundling her. Xavier handed her the water bottle, and she had Reyne sip at it. Elizabeth began to rub Reyne's nipples, causing her to moan and drop the water bottle. Feeling the wetness that has spilled onto the blankets and Elizabeth's fingers on her breasts, she began writhing with pleasure, again begging for more.

Xavier asked Elizabeth, "Do you want the honors of tasting her first, or may I?"

"I would like the honors, but I give you full rights of first penetration for the honors of tasting her first," Elizabeth replied.

Xavier took over, fondling and sucking on Reyne's breasts as Elizabeth kissed down Reyne's abdomen. Xavier watched Elizabeth's descent from the corner of his eye, listening to Reyne moan with excitement and anticipation as Elizabeth teased her. Xavier began pinching Reyne's nipples as Elizabeth got closer to her goal. He watched closely as Elizabeth prepared to plunge into the sweet spot between Reyne's legs. He picked up the spray bottle, and just as Elizabeth plunged her tongue into Reyne, he misted the two women, causing Reyne to squirt into Elizabeth's mouth and scream in ecstasy.

CHAPTER 37

The group of them had been driving for almost 45 minutes when Vlad turned to Onyx, "Reach out to Reyne. Find out what is happening."

Onyx closed his eyes and searched for Reyne. He found her at the height of orgasm and quickly got sucked into her emotions, stemming from the orgasm. He began rubbing everything and writhing to the point that Seth and Brian had to hold him down. Vlad started talking to Onyx, trying to pull him back from Reyne's mind.

"What is wrong with him?" Seth asked Brian.

"He connected with her at a very intense moment. Until we can bring him back, we don't know much more than that. When you connect with the person, you can usually feel what is going on, but I have never seen anyone connect like this before." He answered.

"You mean he could be feeling them torturing her?" Seth asked fearfully.

"Yes. It is important to bring him back quickly." Brian replied.

"You are his lover, yes? Touch him as lovers touch. Bring him back. I cannot. You may have a strong enough connection with him to break his connection with Reyne." Vlad demanded of Seth.

Seth began to awkwardly stroke Onyx's leg, slowly making his way up to Onyx's hard shaft. Before he got any further, he stated, "We've never actually been lovers yet, but I will try." He unbuttoned Onyx's jeans and began stroking his flesh. Onyx moaned and reached over to Seth, grabbed him by the back of his neck, and pulled him toward his mouth. He kissed Seth deeply, "Thank you," he whispered.

"You're welcome," Seth whispered back.

"What did you see and feel?" Vlad asked.

"She is rolling hard. They have drugged her, as we already know, and are taking advantage of her drugged state to fuck her." Onyx said as he began to cry. "They are both fucking her."

"Go to her. Make her cold. Make her really cold from the inside out. It is the only defense against Ecstasy. But do not allow yourself to get sucked into the emotions this time." Vlad told his son.

"I cannot." Onyx sobbed.

"Fine. Get Brian or Seth there. Let them protect her until we get there. But you must take them there." Vlad instructed.

"I'll go," offered Seth. "I'm close to her. I may find her without Onyx."

"No, he must lead you to where you need to be. I do not doubt that you can find her, but you cannot get into her mind without Onyx. You need to be able to control her body and emotions. Only Onyx can take you to that point right now." Vlad explained.

Onyx took Seth's hand, "Thank you again."

They both closed their eyes and go to Reyne. A few minutes later, Onyx opened his eyes and started weeping. "He is there. He is taking care of her. I am a failure and do not deserve her, for I cannot protect her."

"Vlad, why is it that Onyx cannot protect her? I've never seen anyone pulled into another the way he was," asked Brian.

"I believe it is due to several factors. I have seen this before. It is not so unusual. First, they have shared blood. Second, his genetic code is growing inside her, the baby. He almost has too much of a connection with her at this point. They are no longer two separate people; they are one unit with two souls. When two combine as much as they have, this can happen," explained Vlad.

Seth let Reyne know he was with her. He told her what he would do before proceeding to make her cold internally, so even the heat of the room couldn't penetrate. She started to become coherent again and realized what is going on. She pushed Xavier and Elizabeth away from her, crawled off toward the wall, wrapped a blanket around her, and started to cry. Seth kept talking to her, trying to keep her calm by telling her they were on their way to get her and would arrive in just a short time. He told her that when they arrived, he would have to leave her but that Onyx would be in to get her in no time. Reyne asked him to bring Onyx to her now; she just hoped she hadn't said it out loud. He tried to explain why that wasn't possible but did not understand the reason enough to explain it to her thoroughly. Suddenly, he told her he must go because they had arrived and were right outside the door of the house. He promised Onyx would be in the house in a few minutes to get her.

"Seth, Seth. Come on. Come back. We have to finish planning, and we are almost there." Seth heard Onyx's voice saying this to him as he returned to the limousine.

As soon as he opened his eyes, he looked at each person, "They have sexually assaulted her, but at the moment, she is safe. She is humiliated and embarrassed, and thinks Onyx is mad at her. I tried to tell her it wasn't her fault, but she is blaming herself because she willingly cheated on him. I tried to tell her it was the drugs they were feeding her, but she wasn't listening. We must hurry. Since she was refusing the advances of Xavier and Elizabeth while I was with her, they were getting mad. They are not happy with the way things are going; however, with me gone, she will not be sober for long, and the festivities of the room will begin again."

Vlad gathered everyone around him. He told them he had spoken to Xavier's father and received a layout of the house. While showing them the house plans, he told Onyx that his Uncle wished him luck and did not condone Xavier's actions.

By the time Vlad finished giving them instructions, they have arrived at the house. Vlad and Onyx went to the front door and waited for the signal from Brian, who headed to the back door.

"Son, it is imperative you keep your strength until we get Reyne away from here. If they sense any weakness, all is lost." Vlad told his son as they stood at the front door.

"I will be strong," Onyx answered.

They got the signal, and Vlad opened the door for Onyx. "I cannot enter. You must do this yourself. Hurry."

Onyx nodded to his father and entered the house. He went straight to the basement to search for the room. He followed the heat, knowing he would find Reyne in the midst of it all.

He arrived at a door that was emanating heat and thought to himself, '*I am here, my Reyne.*' Onyx crashed through the door and found Reyne naked, arms being held by Xavier and offering her neck to Elizabeth, who was fingering her while preparing her for the bite.

"Stop!" Onyx screamed.

"Why?" asked Xavier laughing at Onyx.

"Reyne, my Beloved, fight. Don't let them take you from me." Onyx said directly to Reyne.

Elizabeth giggled and asked Reyne, "Do you want to be with him or with Xavier and me? Tell me, my love."

"I want to be with my Onyx. I am his Beloved." Reyne answered in barely a whisper.

Elizabeth threw Reyne aside, hissing at her, "After all the pleasure we have shown you. How dare you, you ungrateful whore!" She turned from Reyne and ran full force at Onyx.

"Stay where you are, Elizabeth," Xavier commanded. "He can and will destroy you, and I couldn't bear that." Elizabeth stopped in her tracks, turned, and walked back to stand with Xavier.

"Let her go. She is mine, and you know it. I have consummated the union with her." Onyx stated.

"Yes, we know. We know of the baby too. We had hoped the drugs would have done it in so we could drink that blood." Xavier said before turning to Elizabeth, "But if the baby were to live…" He paused and glanced sideways at Onyx before continuing, "my love, would you like the baby? He can have Reyne; we can get her at any time. But if he wants her back so much, maybe he should give us the son he wants so badly."

"I would like a baby. His will do." Elizabeth replied while watching Onyx's face.

"You cannot have my son or my Beloved. You two will be destroyed by me first." Onyx growled.

"Then you cannot have her. You can go unless you want to fight right now? You are alone. I have many that will be waking very shortly. Your choice." Xavier smiled wickedly.

"Reyne, I cannot fight him and his guards. I will be back." Onyx said aloud, hoping Reyne would understand. He turned and left the room. He made his way back to his father and told him of the situation.

"Onyx, you have maybe 20 minutes to get her out of there. WE have to get her now, or she WILL be lost. They will turn her before the night is out. You know it, and I know it." Vlad turned as Brian returned to them from the other side of the house.

The two men updated Brian on the situation as they moved away from the house. They began building a plan in hopes of saving Reyne. When they had made all the final decisions, Brian ran to get the things they needed. Vlad and Onyx returned to the front door.

"You have approximately seven minutes before his guards are awake and nine minutes before they are alert. You must get in and out in that time. Brian will be back with everything. You know the plan, so do it." Vlad tried to reinforce Onyx's courage and faith.

"I will be right back with my Beloved," Onyx said flatly and entered the house. He returned to the room where he knew they were holding Reyne.

"Hello, again, Onyx. Did Daddy make you come back in and try again? Looks to me like you have six minutes until my guards destroy you and yours," Xavier said.

Onyx looked at Reyne, who was sitting naked with Elizabeth. They were holding one another, talking, kissing, fondling.

"I have come for Reyne and the baby. I will be leaving with them both," Onyx said, never taking his eyes off Reyne.

Reyne slowly turned her head to look at Onyx. "Yes, the cloud. I am coming to meet you at the cloud. Will it be more wonderful than anything before?" Reyne said out loud, like she was talking to someone in the distance. She tried to stand up, but Elizabeth pulled at her hand to keep her from leaving. Reyne turned and frowned at Elizabeth, "You said you wanted me to be happy. Let me go. My happiness is waiting for me, and I must go to him." She grabbed Elizabeth by the shoulders and pushed her hard. Elizabeth fell to the ground with the unexpected strength of Reyne.

"Yes, my Beloved, come with me," Onyx said softly.

"No! She is mine. I want her and her baby." Elizabeth screamed, "get her for me, Xavier."

Xavier stepped between Reyne and Onyx. As Reyne tried to pass Xavier, he grabbed her, "Where do you think you are going? You are Elizabeth's now. You must stay with us."

"My Beloved awaits me. My cloud is waiting," Reyne stated and tried to get away from Xavier.

"Let her go, Xavier," Onyx was growing restless. He knew he was running out of time.

Suddenly Brian appeared in the doorway and came walking up to Onyx. "I have come to help. Seth will be here in a minute, with …" Brian stopped his sentence, knowing that Onyx would understand.

"Well, hello to you, Brian. Long time since I have seen you," Xavier greeted him.

"Not long enough," Brian retorted.

Xavier pulled Reyne into him. "Well, are we ready, my love?" He pulled Reyne's head to one side, bearing her long neck to him. His head started descending, and his mouth opened. Reyne let out a squeal as he bit into her neck and took the first draw of her blood. Xavier moaned with the taste of her hot, sweet blood in his mouth.

"Hold it right there. Stop," Brian and Onyx yelled, as Seth entered the room on a white stallion and charged straight at Xavier.

Xavier looked up from his victim to see the giant beast barreling toward him. He spun away and left Reyne to be trampled. Without Xavier to hold her up, Reyne began falling to the floor. Seth grabbed her, pulled her onto the horse with him, and took off out of the room, up the stairs, and out of the house.

Xavier realizing what had just happened, bared his teeth at Brian and Onyx and growled, "you will both pay for this. I will kill you both." He began running at them but stopped dead.

"You need to stop, for now, Xavier. This battle is done. I have officiated. Until the next time," Vlad stated as he walked into the room. He turned to Brian and Onyx, "Come, you two, it is time to leave, this hellhound and his bitch."

"Onyx, take your slut; we are done with her for the moment. But remember, this is not done!" Xavier screamed.

"You are so right, dear cousin. This is not over. I will kill you both for Reyne. You have destroyed our lives long enough. We deserve peace," Onyx said calmly.

"Beware, cousin. I am wiser than you give me credit. I am only letting you have the bitch, because your father stands in front of me, and my father stands at my front door. They are making me return her. You always were a tattletale," Xavier turned to Elizabeth. "Let's go, my lover." Elizabeth walked over to Xavier, took his arm, and the two left the room.

"We have two minutes to get out of here. Come on, let's go," Brian said.

The three men quickly left the house, climbed into the limousine, and headed off to the meeting place to pick up Reyne and Seth.

CHAPTER 38

The limousine arrived at the new safe house later that evening. Onyx took Reyne into her new home and carried her to their bedroom. Seth followed the two to the bedroom and helped Onyx tuck Reyne into bed, promising to send Leigh to the room.

Onyx went downstairs and found Leigh in the kitchen. "Leigh, please go sit with Reyne. She needs a friend right now."

"Your mother already went up. She felt she could answer any questions Reyne may have. I agreed, so I waited for you to come back down," Leigh replied.

"Well, would you go up, anyway? I think she needs you more than she needs my mother right now. She needs someone she knows, not a stranger or parent," Onyx almost pleaded with her. Leigh smiled and nodded. She turned and went upstairs to sit with Reyne and Svetlina.

Once Leigh had left the room, Onyx collapsed. Tears flowed from his eyes.

"My son. It is over for now. Let the fear, anger, and frustration out. But do not take too long. Your Reyne needs you," Vlad said tenderly to his son.

"I know. But it's not over," Onyx sobbed.

"It is for the moment. Spend time with Reyne. Then you may start your search for Xavier and end this. Your mother and I will stay to protect Reyne and the baby. You can take whomever you want from the house; I will have my people come to stay to help, too. So, do not feel you have to do this alone," Vlad stroked his son's head. "Now go to your Reyne. Your Beloved."

Onyx smiled and walked back to the bedroom. He found Reyne sobbing uncontrollably. His mother and Leigh were both unable to console her. Svetlina noticed Onyx's entrance, "See, Dear. He is here. He has not left you."

Reyne looked at Onyx with shame and guilt in her eyes. Her eyes were begging for forgiveness.

"My Beloved, why do you look at me like that? I have waited to hold you for centuries," Onyx said as he walked to the bed and sat beside her.

Leigh and Svetlina took the cue and left the room to allow Reyne and Onyx to have some time.

"I have cheated on you. I love you so much that I cannot expect you to forgive me, nor can I forgive myself," Reyne sobbed.

"Are you up for taking a little walk?" Onyx asked her.

"I think so," Reyne replied.

Onyx helped her out of bed and through a door on the left side of the room. When Onyx opened the door, Reyne gasped at what she saw.

She started crying harder than before. "How can you want to have children with me? I'm a slut. I all but threw myself at them."

"Reyne, you are not a slut. Do you want your unborn child to hear you talking to his father that way?" Onyx smiled.

"What? You mean? I thought it was part of a dream. What about the drugs?" Reyne stammered as they walked back across the bedroom.

"All will be explained in time. But for now, let's just let everyone know you're okay. Let's spend some time together too because I will be leaving here in a week. This thing with Xavier must end. It cannot continue. Everyone, including my mother and father, will be staying until I return. But forget that for right now. I just want to hold you for the rest of the night," Onyx said as he laid her on the king-size bed and snuggled in with her.

True to his word, Onyx spent the next week focusing all of his attention on Reyne, her children, and Seth. He made love to Reyne every night and spent hours with her talking.

The day before Onyx was scheduled to leave, he sat down with Reyne and Seth, "Let us drink of one another one more time. That way, if anything should happen..."

Reyne cut him off, "We will be able to find each other again."

He nodded to her, but turned to Seth, "I have left vials of my blood for you to drink to help the baby grow. He needs it to grow and be born, so Seth, make sure she drinks it." Seth nodded in understanding.

Onyx turned back to Reyne, "Once the baby is born, are you going to take my father's gift?"

"Yes, I am. I have to if I don't want to be old and ugly when you return." Reyne said, through a false smile. She was trying to hide her sadness, but knew it wasn't working.

"I know I promised you would receive your gift while making love. If you want to wait, I don't plan to be gone long." Onyx promised her.

"I know. I know, but I must prepare for it just in case." She stroked his arm.

"I love you, Seth, and I love you, Reyne. My Beloved."

Seth and Reyne answered in unison, "I love you, too."

That night, Onyx and Reyne made love for hours, sharing each other's souls, lives, blood, and emotion. Onyx was gone when Reyne awoke the next morning. She laid in bed and cried softly, holding onto the pillow where Onyx had lain with her the night before.

She finally got up to start her day. She could hear people moving around the house. She got dressed, put on her strongest face, and set off to face the day, knowing she may never see her Onyx again.

EPILOGUE

Svetlina found Reyne with Seth in the bedroom. It had been two months since Onyx's departure, and the two had become very close, as most partners do. Reyne was sitting in the window seat with Seth at her side, watching the sunset, when Svetlina walked into the room.

"This came in the mail for you today. How are you and the baby feeling?" She said as she handed Reyne the letter.

Reyne took the letter from Svetlina, rubbed her little belly bump and said with a smile, "Thank you. We are fine, I guess." She looked warily at Seth and hoped Svetlina didn't notice.

"Things will be all right. Don't worry, my dear. Do you want some new company, or is Seth enough?" Svetlina giggled.

Reyne laughed gently, "No, thank you, Seth is doing his job. He and I have a deep bond with Onyx, and we are living in despair together. We try to function as a family for the children, but it is tough. All we can do is await his return," Reyne turned back to watch the sunset.

"Okay, sweetheart. But if you want someone to talk to, you know where I am," she said to Reyne. She turned to Seth, "How are you, my son?"

"I am being consoled by the most wonderful and most understanding woman in the world. It could only be better if Onyx were here," he replied.

"My son will return soon; however, you two need companionship." Vlad entered the room. "I am having Seth things moved in this evening. You two need one another right now, and that is normal."

"Sir, I mean no disrespect, but I cannot sleep with Onyx's other lover," Reyne said.

"And why not?" Vlad and Svetlina asked in unison.

"I feel that I would be betraying Onyx again," Reyne replied.

"You only betray Onyx by withholding the parts he loves of both of you. Share the bed platonically if you like, but you need to have someone to hold. It might as well be each other rather than an outsider if Onyx does not soon return," Vlad said. "I also know that Onyx wanted you two to become lovers at some point, and even mentioned this to Seth. Am I correct, Seth?"

"Yes, sir. Onyx was hoping that the three of us would be lovers." Seth admitted as Reyne looked on in surprise. "I understand, sir. I will talk with Reyne about this and make her understand," Seth answered.

"Good. Now Svetlina, my love, let us go feed," Vlad said to his wife, and they left the room.

Seth and Reyne looked at the envelope before Reyne opened the letter that had arrived. The envelope had no return address and no stamp. Both knew that someone had brought it here. Tears welled in Reyne's eyes as she silently read the short note that was in the envelope.

My Beloved,

I am sorry that I have not returned to you yet. I wish I could be there for you and the baby, but it seems that this will be harder than I thought. Xavier has friends, and it is hard to find him. I miss you and love you with all my heart and think about you constantly. I will continue my search now, but I will write again soon. No matter what, you will always be my Beloved.

Make sure that Seth has received his letter from me. I know that this separation is hard for him as well. Please be there for him, as I am sure he is there for you. All of you are deep in my heart and my thoughts daily. The baby and children never wholly leave my mind. I know that what I am doing will make our lives better. Please understand and know that I will return as soon as I can.

I love you and always will.

Your Lover,
Onyx

Reyne read it aloud to Seth, crying while telling him of Onyx's love. The two of them spent the rest of the evening holding one another, talking to one another, and eventually making love to one another for the first time. It wasn't the passion of Onyx, but it was the passion that excited Reyne on Halloween when Seth had taken her into his arms that first time and saved her. She thought back only briefly before pushing the thought from her head. The passion flowed freely, and Reyne couldn't help but think of the white stallion Seth had been riding when he saved her.